Rupert Legge is the s̶ and Comtesse Raine de Chambrun, and the grandson of bestselling novelist Dame Barbara Cartland. He was educated at Eton and Oxford, where he read Chemistry and spent a year researching the Philosophy of Science. He was called to the Bar in 1975 and practised as a barrister before joining a city firm as a maritime lawyer. He now lives with his wife and two children in the West Country.

Rupert Legge's first novel, THE CHILDREN OF LIGHT, was published in 1986. His subsequent novels, FASHIONABLE CIRCLES and PLAYING WITH FIRE, are available from Headline.

A Dangerous Age

Rupert Legge

HEADLINE

First published in 1995 by
HEADLINE BOOK PUBLISHING

First published in paperback in 1996 by
HEADLINE BOOK PUBLISHING

10 9 8 7 6 5 4 3 2 1

ISBN 0 7472 4892 3

Typeset by Avon Dataset Ltd, Bidford-on-Avon, B50 4JH

Printed and bound in Great Britain by
Cox & Wyman Ltd, Reading, Berks

HEADLINE BOOK PUBLISHING
A division of Hodder Headline PLC
338 Euston Road
London NW1 3BH

For my father,
with love

PART I

Katya

One

Sometimes she wished she did not love him so much: the heartache was too great; the pain too intense.

She knew she should feel confident in his love. She could read it in his eyes and in the tender, protective way in which he touched her. Yet he could never say the words enough for her. She needed his reassurance because it was like food to her, it nourished her.

She hated it when he was away from her. Her life seemed to stop, suddenly become devoid of colour. Tasks which would have been fun if he had been around were burdensome. The day was filled with repetitive actions which gave it form but no meaning. She carried out her duties – visiting the supermarket, the dealers, the private clients and the auction rooms – then returned to this room where she sat on this stool.

She was thankful for her work. It made things more tolerable for her. It ate time, made those hours and days pass until he would see her again and her life could recommence.

The room was bright and airy with white matt walls. At the far end it was lit from two windows in the pitched roof, allowing her the luxury of working by natural light. Canvases waiting for restoration leaned against the walls, stood in storage racks and rested on easels.

She sat on the stool beneath the windows, with a

painting – a nineteenth-century seascape – propped on an easel before her. An artist's smock hung over jeans and T-shirt. She was very slim. Her pale, almost translucent skin was unlined and devoid of make-up, her hair cropped and dark auburn. Her eyes were huge and hazel, her bones fine. By her feet, on the kelim rug, a black pug dozed peacefully. On a table by her side stood a mug of real coffee, her artist's tools and a white telephone.

It was Saturday afternoon, about five thirty – an hour he often called. She never made plans for the times when he was likely to ring.

She dreaded the weekends. Then he had to be with Imogen. He had to be down in the country playing the good father, the good husband, living a lie.

She had often thought what a good actor he must be to carry it off without giving himself away. She wondered whether deep down he enjoyed any of his other life, or whether, like her, he was only wading through dead time until they could be together once more. He did it only because of the children, he said, and she believed that was true.

As she reached for the turpentine, she glanced across at the telephone and tried to will it to ring.

She could not fully understand how it had come to this. After all, at the beginning she had been in control of him, not he of her. It is one of life's ironies, she thought, that in the end it is the idol who becomes the captive of the devotee.

But in those days she had not known her true self or of what she was capable. Then, she had thought of love as something out of a fairy story, something benign, not a rapacious force ripping into her soul, leaving her struggling to piece together what was left of her identity.

It had seemed much simpler then.

Two

Katya had already restored two paintings for Raymond Punchard and was working on a third before she met him. It was a small Vandyke portrait of a woman in a red silk and lace dress with a revealing *décolletage*. Initially all that had seemed to be required was a clean, the retouching of a few minor surface scratches and revarnishing. As she began working on the canvas, however, she found an area about the dress which she suspected was by a different hand.

At first she thought it was the work of the artist's studio, but as the paint had aged slightly differently to the rest, she took the painting to be X-rayed and to her amazement, found that underneath the dress was a second figure: a boy in a tunic.

Excited, she had rung Raymond Punchard at his office. He was busy. An hour later, though, his secretary rang back: Mr Punchard wanted to see her with the painting and the X-ray in his office at five o'clock that evening. They would send a car.

She did not live in the mews house then, but in a first-floor flat in Wandsworth. The chauffeur picked her up from the flat and drove her to the City in a huge black Daimler with a beige leather interior and walnut-veneered woodwork.

She had only been in a car as large and sleek as that

once before, and that was when she had been maid of honour at her sister's wedding. She liked the way it glided through the traffic, insulating her from the chaos outside.

It was childish, she knew, but as she sat there with the painting wrapped in a rug on her knees, she tried the buttons on the console. One sent out a blast of air-conditioning, a second closed the glass partition between her and the chauffeur, a third revealed a small drinks cabinet.

The Punchard Building was situated on the north bank of the Thames, close to the Tower of London. It was a monolith of black steel and smoked glass. Opposite the main entrance was a minimalist sculpture consisting of three upright rectangular blocks of rough granite and entitled, enigmatically, 'Achievement'.

The lobby was decked out in various coloured marbles – red, grey and blue. On the left was the reception desk, on the right a blue marble pool from which two single jets danced above a row of tropical plants. The floor was so highly polished she nearly slipped.

Immediately the two security guards saw the package under her arm, they converged on her from either side of the lobby. Then the chauffeur whispered, 'Thirty-fourth floor,' and the guards edged back and nodded deferentially, as if the words had some mystical power.

She signed her name, pinned a badge to her lapel and stepped into the executive lift. She sped up to the thirty-fourth floor in eight seconds. Her stomach followed sometime later.

When the polished steel doors opened, she was greeted by a beige interior and potted plants sweltering under spotlights. A woman in a short black and white checked skirt hurried towards her. Her blonde hair was tied with a velvet bow at the back of her head. 'Miss Cornwale?'

Katya nodded.

'Welcome to the thirty-fourth floor. Mr Punchard is

running a little late so I'm afraid that I'm going to have to cut your meeting from ten to five minutes. I hope that is not going to cause a problem.'

It was not a question.

'That's fine by me,' Katya replied. 'I'm busy too.'

The woman gestured towards a chrome and black leather sofa. 'If you would take a seat in the waiting area, I will show you through just as soon as Mr Punchard is available.'

Katya nodded. She propped the painting against the wall and eased herself into the sofa. She sank down so deep into the soft leather that she felt she was being swallowed. She was glad she was not wearing a short skirt.

In the waiting area there were no windows: the air came from vents; the light from the spots. The copious tropical greenery, she suspected, had to be taken away regularly for intensive care, life support and resuscitation.

Every fifteen seconds or so the telephone rang and was answered by one of four secretaries. All calls were countered by the statement 'I'm afraid Mr Punchard is in a meeting and can't be disturbed.' None was put through.

The lift was busy too. So far she had counted eighteen people arrive while she had been sitting there. They had all been welcomed to the thirty-fourth floor by the woman in the black and white checked skirt, directed to the boardroom to the left, and told that Mr Punchard would be with them shortly.

As there was nothing else to read, she picked a copy of the annual report off the stack on the smoked glass table in front of her. On the cover was a colour photograph of a hydro-electric plant in Brazil. On page two was an announcement that the report was printed on recycled paper in accordance with the company's policy of caring for the environment. On page three was a photograph of Raymond Punchard looking earnest and concerned behind a huge desk. 'Another year of achievement. Dividend up 23%, earnings up 34%. The Punchard Group of Companies now employs over 40,000 people worldwide, has assets in excess of £6 billion and produces everything from potato to computer chips . . .'

Twice she asked whether Mr Punchard had been told that she was waiting. Twice she was told firmly that he had and would see her just as soon as his current meeting was over.

She waited forty minutes, maybe more, then finally the huge double doors in front of her swung open and out walked five men, each in a grey business suit, each clutching a black leather briefcase. None of them was smiling.

She was ushered inside.

The room had glass on three sides. Beneath stretched the roofs of London, the lights, the traffic, the public buildings. From here it looked almost as if the entire city had been miniaturised expressly for the enjoyment of the occupants of the thirty-fourth floor. She could not quite lose the feeling of being up in a crow's nest swaying in the breeze.

He stood on the far side of the desk, one hand buried in his jacket pocket, the clouds and London spread out behind him. He nodded, smiling slightly, gesturing towards her, offering her a chair.

Immediately she was conscious that she was in the presence of someone unlike anyone she had met before.

He was broad-shouldered and fit. He had brown hair, greying at the temples, blue eyes, a strong, prominent nose and a firm jaw. What, however, she found remarkable was the powerful aura she sensed around him, which seemed to fill the entire room with an electric charge.

'I am sorry to keep you waiting.'

'That's quite all right,' she answered, forgetting her annoyance of minutes earlier.

As she carried the half-cleaned painting across the thick beige carpet towards him, she felt as if she were stepping through a force field. It grew more powerful the closer she came.

She propped the painting on the chair in front of the desk, then handed him the X-ray.

He held it up to the light, studying it. 'Extraordinary,' he said. 'What made you suspect that there might be a second figure in the portrait?'

'This area here.' She pointed. 'Do you see where the pigment is slightly darker, and the work a little cruder than the rest?'

Squatting down, he examined the surface of the canvas. 'Of course. It seems so obvious now. Yet I must have looked at it hundreds of times without noticing the difference.'

He glanced up at her as he rose to his feet, and as she watched him, the look in his eyes changed. Suddenly, it lost its impersonal air and became intense and disconcerting.

She broke off the gaze. For all she knew, Raymond Punchard always eyed women in this rather too personal, overtly sexual way. It might, she thought, be just a trick to make a girl feel she had some special quality that fascinated him.

He straightened, and continued as if nothing had happened. 'The painting, as you know, is of Maria, Countess of Dunstable, one of my wife's ancestors. According to family records she died childless. There is no mention of a son dying young, so the extra figure is something of a mystery.

'We haven't met before, have we?' he asked, changing the subject.

She shook her head. 'Not that I know of.'

'Strange,' he answered. 'Right now there are twenty people waiting for me in the boardroom, and I am going to have to go. But there is a project I would like to discuss

9

with you. Could I call you tomorrow?'

She noticed the way he was clenching and unclenching his fist; not the kind of nervous gesture she would expect from someone in charge of a six-billion-pound enterprise. 'A work project?' she queried.

'Sure.'

'Do then.' She smiled at him, wrapped the painting in the rug and headed for the door.

Three

The squash ball bounced off the side wall, touched the end wall an inch above the line, then dropped to the floor.

Catching it just as it was about to die, Raymond slammed the ball hard and low against the end wall. It spun back into the corner, sending his opponent running. He started back to the centre of the court, ready for the ball's return, but it never came.

'Jesus! How could I miss that? And game point too?' The other man scrutinised the strings on his racket as if amazed that there was nothing wrong with them. He was tall and wiry, with wavy pepper and salt hair trimmed close to the scalp, and a Roman nose. His skin was a dark olive against the white of his shorts and shirt.

'Another?'

'No thanks. I've got to be home in half an hour. Jane's having one of her dinner parties. I promise I'll beat you next time.'

Raymond smiled. He swept his arm across his forehead, flicking off the sweat, then followed his opponent out of the court and along the narrow corridor towards the changing rooms, hurrying to catch him up.

'Simon, we're old friends, right?'

'Yes.'

Raymond looked around to make sure that no one was in earshot. 'Do you mind if I ask you a personal question?'

11

Simon turned towards him, surprised. 'No, sure. Fire away. Ask whatever you like – just don't be offended if I don't answer.'

Raymond lowered his voice. 'How often do you meet someone who you have an overwhelming urge to go to bed with?'

Simon pushed open the swing doors and went through into the changing room with its pervading odour of sports socks and medicated soap.

'That some kind of trick question? Who's kidding who? Come on! You walk out the front door and what do you see? A beautiful bimbo. Legs to die for. Body of a movie queen. With nothing better to do than walk along the street outside your house.

'You turn the corner and what do you see? Another, even more sensational than the last. You go to the office. More beautiful girls. You go to a party. More. And some aren't even bimbos. Some are intelligent, sensitive and amusing with interesting careers, and still look amazing. And you ask me how often I've been tempted? I spend my days in acute discomfort in a perpetual state of purgatorial self-denial.

'Don't get me wrong, I love Jane. But this is something else. This is biology.'

Raymond pulled off his left shoe. 'Come on, Simon. I'm not talking about every other woman you see in the street. I mean feeling something – I don't know how quite to describe it – but it's an instinctive thing, something animal, from the gut.'

'All you're talking about is lust at first sight.' Simon gave a dismissive shrug. 'Of course I've experienced it. I wouldn't be human if I hadn't.'

Raymond looked around. There were a couple of men sitting two benches away from them, but they were talking among themselves, and he didn't think they could hear what he was saying. 'And how do you handle it?'

'Do you mean have I ever cheated on Jane? Why do you want to know?' Suddenly he raised his voice. 'I get it. You want me out of the way 'cause you've got the hots for Jane, haven't you? Christ, you're supposed to be my friend!'

The two men on the bench turned around.

'Good God, no. Simon, that's simply not true, and please keep your voice down.'

Simon's jaw hardened. 'No, I won't keep my voice down. What do you mean by "Good God, no"? Are you casting aspersions on my wife? Do you find her unattractive? Does she repel you physically?'

Raymond could not be sure whether Simon was being serious or not. He certainly sounded serious. 'No, I didn't mean that.'

'Well, what did you mean then? I'd have you know that by those with taste, she is considered a very desirable woman.'

'You misinterpreted what I said,' Raymond said firmly. 'I meant that although she is undoubtedly a very attractive woman, as she is your wife, I naturally don't think of her – well – in those terms.'

Simon paused for a moment, letting Raymond's explanation sink in. 'You mean that you might have considered her attractive, but the fact that she married me lowers her somehow in your estimation? You think that makes me feel any better?'

'No, Simon. What I was trying to say was that the fact that she married you makes me think of her as off bounds.'

Suddenly Simon burst out laughing, and, still shaking his head, put his arm around him. 'I'm only winding you up. Now, seriously, why are you asking these very personal questions?'

'I'm interested.'

'What's that meant to mean?'

'It's just that . . .' Raymond shrugged. 'This sounds so

13

silly. I think we should forget the whole thing.'

'No. Come on. Tell me!'

'There's nothing to tell.'

'Don't lie to your old friend.'

'I just met someone, that's all.'

'Slept with her yet?'

'No. As I said, I've only just met her.'

'But you want to sleep with her, right? And you're worried about your wife finding out and having screaming hysterics, the children, damage to your marriage, et cetera, et cetera.'

'This is entirely hypothetical, you understand.'

'Of course. What are we talking here – quick fling or serious relationship? Or a nice bit of mutual confusion – you after a quick fling, she after a serious relationship?'

'As I said, I've only just met her.' Raymond pulled his damp sports shirt over his head. 'I suppose the best thing to do is nothing.'

'The safest, certainly.'

He wrapped his towel about him. 'I mean, it's not like it used to be. I'm no longer a free man, and these days—'

'Quite. I'm sure you're right.' Simon nodded sagely. 'The best thing for you to do is forget all about her . . . and give me her telephone number.'

Raymond laughed. He slapped Simon on the shoulder and headed off towards the showers.

Four

Raymond had long since left the gentrified section of Wandsworth behind and was now driving through a wasteland of failed sixties experiments in cheap community housing and industrial parks.

The address on Cornwale Fine Art Restorers' notepaper was Flat Eight, Fourteen Bridegate Gardens. Bridegate Gardens turned out to be no such thing: such gardens as once there had been had been swept away in a road-widening scheme. All that was left now was a row of soot-black brick buildings bordering a two-lane expressway.

He could not park on the expressway outside the house, so he turned first left. The Aston Martin was conspicuous and out of place in the mean street of tired terraced houses. He'd known it was asking for trouble bringing that kind of car into this part of London, but he had brought it all the same. The car spoke of money and style. He wasn't proud of the fact, but he felt he needed it now, as a prop. The confidence to rely just on himself had deserted him.

He switched on the alarm, locked the car and stalked back through the heavy breathless air to Number Fourteen. The paintwork around the windows was blistered, the mortar between the brickwork crumbling. He walked up to the front door, pressed the flat number on the entryphone and waited.

15

She answered almost at once, but the sound of the traffic on the road outside drowned out the words. 'Hello?' he called, shouting into the metal vent, 'Hello?' He wanted her to repeat whatever it was that she had said. He wanted to hear her voice. But nothing came.

Then he heard footsteps, the lock being pulled back, the squeak of the door, and there she was standing in the doorway in a wedge of light.

Memory plays strange tricks. He had seen her only the day before yesterday, but still she was not as he remembered. He had forgotten the clarity of her eyes and the intensity of their colour. He had forgotten the freshness of her skin.

She smiled. 'Come on in. I hope you didn't have too much difficulty finding the place?'

He cleared the lump that had formed in his throat. 'No, it wasn't bad at all.' He followed her through the beige embossed hallway, up the dimly lit beige embossed stairway until she reached the first floor.

Her door had three different locks. She turned a key and pushed it open.

A black pug jumped out, barking and circling his legs. 'It's all right, Myrtle,' she soothed.

'Do you live here alone?' he asked.

'Yes. Except for Myrtle, that is. If you're worried about the safety of the paintings, they're protected by an alarm, I have no shop front to attract interest, and anyway around here they are much more interested in things like TVs and video recorders.'

'I was thinking more of you.'

'Me?' she asked, quizzically, as if his concern was both misplaced and unexpected. 'I'm fine.'

He stepped inside. Three huge Victorian plate-glass windows dominated the far end of the sparsely decorated room. The walls had been daubed white but the design of the wallpaper underneath still showed through as a faint yellow outline. The carpet was worn to the backing. There was a wooden stool, a sofa and a coffee table.

As he watched her, it struck him how wrong it was that someone of her beauty and energy should live in such a place. He wanted to pluck her out of these dowdy surroundings and give her somewhere warm and well cared for, somewhere more worthy of her.

'This is only temporary,' she explained as if reading his thoughts. 'It's not easy finding somewhere which has the space and the light I need for my work.'

'If you let me know what you are looking for, I'll pass the details on to our property division.'

'That's very kind of you, but I have got a limited budget.'

'No problem. They come across all sorts of deals every day. It's their job. You've got nothing to lose.'

'Thanks,' she answered. 'If you are sure? Would you like a drink?'

'Yes, please. Whisky.'

'I'm afraid all I've got is white wine – would that do?'

'Fine.'

She disappeared through a side door and returned a moment later with a half-empty bottle of New Zealand Sauvignon and two wine glasses.

As she walked towards him, the light from the window caught the side of her face, making the skin glow. With her dark hair cropped close to the face her eyes seemed huge. Outwardly she looked so vulnerable, so in need of protection that Raymond had to remind himself that she ran a successful business. He wanted to take her in his arms. Instead he took the glass of white wine from her and thanked her politely.

'Where did you train to become such a good restorer?' he asked.

'First at the Hamilton Kerr Institute in Cambridge and then with Alex Karzynski in London.'

'The best. It must be so satisfying doing what you do.'

'I only restore. I don't create.'

'Restorers have to be creative artists too.'

'We try to put ourselves into the mind of the artist and imagine what he or she would have done at the time the picture was painted – if that's what you mean.'

'I'd call that highly creative.'

She smiled. 'It takes effort and training, but it's not the same thing as originating something from a blank canvas. Would you like to see some of the other paintings I'm working on at present?'

He nodded. She turned and walked towards the window. The evening light framed her whole body now. He watched her intently, marvelling in the swaying movement of her body, so effortless and full of natural poise.

She swivelled around to face him, and pointed to a painting on an easel – a youth holding a candle, in the style of Caravaggio. She began to explain something of the techniques that she had used and the difficulties that she had encountered, but he found it increasingly difficult to concentrate. He was totally absorbed in the way her body moved and the gestures she made as she spoke.

He moved a little closer to her under the pretence of studying the painting. He could smell the scent she was wearing. It was one that was familiar. He had given a bottle to Imogen last Christmas. Yet Katya had somehow transformed it. Under the florid concoction of oils and musk he could detect something unique to her. He found it intoxicating, felt his head spinning.

The more he breathed in the scent, the more he watched Katya, the more he was hypnotised by her. He loved those huge eyes, and those full lips.

With an effort he made himself think of Imogen and the children and, as he did so, the smell seemed to change too. Now the fluffy cleanliness of Johnson's baby powder and the slightly sharper notes of the scents that Imogen usually wore were there alongside Katya's.

Raymond took a deep breath and stepped back. He tried to sound businesslike again. 'I'm impressed,' he announced as soon as Katya had finished talking. 'I'd like to commission you to restore the paintings at Bradstoke Hall. If you've got time, that is.'

She beamed with a freshness and enthusiasm that sent his pulse racing again. For a second, he thought that she was going to embrace him. 'Thanks. I'd be very happy to take that on. When do you want me to start? I'll come down to Bradstoke later this week if you like.'

'No,' he answered. 'I'll get the paintings sent to you here half a dozen at a time.'

She looked surprised. 'You sure? It would be no trouble for me . . .'

'That's the way I would like to do it,' he said with finality. 'Thanks for the drink. I'll ring you.'

'Yes,' she answered. 'Do.'

Imogen looked up from the velvet sofa by the fireplace as he entered, tilting her head, copy of *Country Life* in hand. 'Good day, dear?'

'Yes, thank you.'

He had slept with Imogen and dined with her most evenings for the last fifteen years, yet he could not remember the last time that he had looked at her objectively: sometimes he would notice that she was wearing a new dress or had a new hair-do and make a suitable comment, but most of the time she was just Imogen, the woman he loved, the mother of his children and a comfortable, reassuring presence.

Tonight he noticed.

He stood on the Savonnerie carpet in the blue drawing room of the Phillimore Gardens house and stared at her.

She was a handsome woman. Her straw-blonde hair, which she used to wear long, was now bobbed. She had a beautiful creamy skin, a fine straight nose and blue eyes. She was slim, trim and fit.

He loved her, he knew he did.

'Darling, please don't look at me like that, it is very disconcerting,' she said, then returned to her magazine.

'I'm sorry. I didn't realise I was.'

'At my age women don't relish being subjected to microscopic examination.'

'But you're the last person who should ever be worried. You haven't changed a bit in fifteen years.'

He strode across to her, bent down and kissed her. By chance she was wearing the same scent as Katya had worn earlier, but on her it no longer seemed exotic.

She lifted her eyes towards him, her lips curving in a little closed smile. 'Thank you, darling. Keep on telling me that, even if it's not true.'

He guessed that she knew from his breath that he had already had a drink this evening, and the thought made him flush with guilt. He wondered why. There was nothing strange about him having a drink before coming home. It helped break the ice before a deal or consolidate a business friendship.

And he had done nothing wrong. Yet still the guilt remained.

It is one of the tenets of the Roman Catholic church that to commit adultery in the mind is a sin even if it is never acted upon in the flesh. But he was not a Roman Catholic and firmly believed it was difficult enough for a man to have to cope with his actions without the added complication of the wilder flights of his imagination as well. Yet he knew that his visit to Katya's studio, innocent though it had been, had in some sense been a breach of trust.

'Archie in bed yet?'

'Yes, darling. If you must see him please be very quiet; you know how difficult he finds it to go back to sleep once

he's awake. I wish you could get away earlier sometimes.'
   'So do I.'
   She rose to her feet and followed Raymond out of the door.
   He climbed to the third floor. Here the rich yellow of the stairwell changed to wallpaper of teddy bears and elephants in bright primary colours. He passed a door on the right where two young girls were slumped, mesmerised, on beanbags, their eyes shining with rainbows from the TV set. He stopped by the third door along. Inside was a boy of five, blond hair splashed on the pillow, arms spread out, sleeping soundly.
   Raymond stood by the jamb looking in, admiring, proud. He listened carefully, then crept forward. A board creaked. The boy turned and for a second Raymond feared that he might have woken him, but then the slow beat of the breathing returned and Raymond went closer. He did not try to kiss the boy but just stood there, staring down at him.
   He was lucky. So lucky. He had a beautiful, loyal wife, three fine children, houses, money and an interesting job. He should be thankful for his blessings, he thought. It would be crazy to put it all at risk, wouldn't it? And for what?

Five

The Prime Minister's Advisory Committee on Trade and Industry met every third Wednesday in Room 152 of the Department of Trade and Industry in Victoria Street, close to the Houses of Parliament.

The fourteen committee members sat around a large mahogany veneered oblong table, at the end of which Lord Lipton, the short, stout head of Midlands Metal, was addressing the meeting on hidden trade barriers within the European Community.

Raymond found it increasingly difficult to concentrate. He glanced up at the track of spotlights in the suspended ceiling, down at the orange carpet squares beneath his polished shoes, but still his thoughts kept returning to Katya.

He could not understand why she affected him so. He was not by nature a Lothario. He had been happily married for fifteen years. He had felt the temptations of other women keenly many times but had never succumbed. While colleagues might have looked upon foreign trips as an opportunity for adventure, he had never gone to bed with anything more risqué than a book.

It had been a point of honour with him. He had thought of Imogen, thought of the children, then asked himself whether it was fair on them, whether it was worth putting all that at risk. The answer had always been no.

What was it then? Was this some kind of breakdown? Was this some middle-age crisis – a yearning for departing youth? Was it weakness, feeble-mindedness? It was true that much as he was fond of Imogen and much as they had both tried, their sex life had lost its spontaneity; but that, he supposed, was almost inevitable after fifteen years.

Was it love then? How could it be when he hardly knew her? Before yesterday he would have scoffed at such foolish talk, but now he wondered whether with certain people it was not just a question of recognition. It was as if you knew them before, as if you had known them always, as if you were destined to be together.

On the other side of the room, Lord Lipton leaned forward and, to emphasise a point, pressed down on the table with two small red fists. 'So in conclusion, I would like to say just this . . .'

Raymond sighed. This was the third time that Lord Lipton had used the term 'in conclusion', and from his demeanour he seemed no closer to reaching one than before.

The industrialist next to Raymond gave him a disapproving look. Raymond had sighed, that was all – sighed as in clearing the tubes. It had not been that loud. At least he had not meant it to be that loud.

When, some twenty minutes later, Lord Lipton finally sat down, Raymond murmured his excuses and left. Outside in the passage, he checked a number in his book, then stabbed it out on his mobile phone.

'Hello. Raymond Punchard here. I'd like to order some roses.'

'Certainly. What did you have in mind? A spray or an arrangement?'

'How many have you got?'

'I'm sorry. I don't quite follow.'

'How many roses have you got in the shop?'

'Any particular colour?'

'No.'

'I'll check, sir.'

Raymond was surprised how unselfconscious he felt. He waited for the assistant's return.

'About three hundred.'

'Good. That'll do fine. I'd like you to deliver them to Katya Cornwale, number 14, Bridegate Gardens.'

'All of them?'

'Yes, all of them. And I'd like that done this afternoon. There's no card.'

'Very well, Mr Punchard. We'll put it in hand right away, sir. Would you like the bill added to your regular monthly account?'

He had nearly forgotten. The monthly account was sent to Imogen. Already he was involved in subterfuge. He should have used a florist where he was not known, where there was no danger of tongues wagging. 'No, send it to my office.

'It's a surprise for a god-daughter of mine,' he improvised. 'She loves roses.'

'Yes, Mr Punchard. A lovely gesture. I'm sure your god-daughter will much appreciate it. And yes, we'll make absolutely certain that the bill is not sent to your home address. Thank you for your order.'

He switched off the telephone and put it back in his briefcase. He doubted whether the assistant had believed a word of his story. But what did he care? What was the harm in sending a few flowers?

The fifteen buckets of roses almost filled the living room, cascading over the sofa, the carpet, the easy chair.

As soon as the delivery boy had left, she stood there staring at the flowers for a long while. Their combined scent was overwhelming, almost suffocating, yet she did not want to open the window, she wanted to bask in it.

She wanted the perfume to seep into the pores of her skin and the strands of her hair. She wanted to draw the scent slowly into her lungs so that it suffused through every part of her.

She was used to the attentions of men. There was something about her that stopped men treating her like a fellow human being, that made them either overfamiliar or unduly reserved and the intelligent start talking gibberish.

She knew that the roses must have come from him. If it had been a less extravagant or more permanent gift there were four or five men who might have sent it to her, but she guessed that nobody else but Raymond Punchard would spend so much on a gesture that would last so short a time. It was a tycoon's gift.

He was a man, she thought, whom she would find it easy to love. No one had ever affected her on first meeting like he had done. If only he had been single, she was sure that they could have had some amazing times, maybe even a life, together. But on a point of principle, she never went out with married men. It was unfair on the wives, on the children, and she did not like subterfuge. She remembered Imogen Punchard from her time at the Convent of the Immaculate Conception and felt sure that she would be an exemplary wife.

Why then when the flowers arrived, did she hope beyond hope that they would be from him? Why was she so excited when he came around to her flat yesterday that she could barely restrain herself from reaching out to him and kissing him?

For all she knew, he always eyed women in that rather too personal, sexual way, he always sent flowers like this. Married men made more effort.

The telephone rang. She was not sure why but she knew it would be him.

'Did you get my flowers?'

'Yes, thank you. They are beautiful.'

'We must meet.' There was urgency in his voice.

'Yes,' she answered.

'Today. In an hour. I'll come round?'

She would see him, but she wanted somewhere safe. Neutral territory. Somewhere from where she could escape, if necessary. 'No. I'll meet you in the bar of the Dorchester Hotel.'

'I'll be there.'

When she replaced the receiver, her hand was shaking. This surprised her. She had the steadiest of hands.

Katya arrived at the Dorchester at seven twenty, forty minutes late. She had taken over twenty-five minutes deciding what to wear. In the end she had settled for a black trouser suit with a white granddad shirt. It was a good choice. It flattered her slim figure.

The bar was crowded, the air heavy and smoky after the cold freshness of the street outside. Visiting businessmen perched on stools before the counter: fingers of grey against the sparkling kaleidoscope of bottles behind.

She felt self-conscious and exposed standing there. She had not expected the room to be such a male preserve. The barman glanced across at her over a jar of plump maraschino cherries, questioning. A grey-suited man swivelled around on his stool towards her, grinning.

She feared for a moment that Raymond might already have left, then she spied him at a table by the window. He too was dressed in a grey suit, but while the other men seemed to wear theirs as a uniform, he wore his as if he belonged in it. He had a better body, she guessed, or, at least, a better tailor.

His eyes remained fixed on her as she walked over. He stood to meet her. Their bodies swayed together, but she pulled herself away before he could kiss her. She did not want him to kiss her now, here, in this public place, and a formal peck on the cheek seemed somehow an irrelevance.

'Thank you for coming,' he said, still staring at her, with, she thought, genuine gratitude.

'Of course, I was going to come,' she answered lightly. 'I love cocktails.'

He signalled to the waiter. She ordered a margarita, he a whisky sour.

His eyes had only left her for an instant. 'I don't know quite how to say this . . .' he began as soon as the waiter had left. The fist on the edge of the table clenched and unclenched.

'Have you ever been completely overwhelmed by a person – someone you hardly know? Unable to get them out of your head? Just desperately wanting to be with them, suddenly prepared to do anything for them, at any risk?'

It was the most extravagant thing anybody had ever said to her. It was what she wanted him to tell her, what she herself knew, but also what she most dreaded. 'What can I say?'

'You needn't say anything if you don't want to.'

'I'm very flattered,' she murmured at last.

'What can I do for you?'

'What do you mean?'

'What I say. Name anything you like. If it's within my power, it's yours.'

A lump formed in her throat. She swallowed to clear it. Why, she wondered, did the bogy of old bourgeois morality come and cramp her style at the most inconvenient moments?

'I don't want anything.'

'Come,' he chided, 'you must want something. What's the point of me running a multinational conglomerate if I can't grant requests?'

'No,' she said firmly. 'I mean it. Thank you very much for the offer but, honestly, I don't want anything.'

He shrugged theatrically and smiled as if he was not surprised by her reply. She wondered whether this had been some kind of test, but then again she honestly believed that he would have granted anything she had wanted, if it had been in his power.

She thought it took guts to make that kind of declaration to someone he hardly knew, especially before either of them had even had a drink. She could do with one now. She wished that the waiter wasn't so goddamn slow.

Usually if a man ever declared himself to her, she lost interest. She believed it to be axiomatic that any man after her would be second rate. She had been told this was a problem of self-esteem. She did not think so. She thought it was just one of the sad facts of life. But not Raymond Punchard.

A waiter came between them and with great ceremony laid two round paper mats on the table. Peanuts followed. When finally he put down the cocktail glass with its salted ring and swizzle stick, she scooped it up and took a long draught, waiting for the alcohol to hit her.

She reckoned she had a pretty enough face, a good enough figure and an agile enough mind, but so did many other girls. She was curious to know what it was about her that Raymond Punchard found so attractive. She was not about to ask him, though. It was the kind of question which could stimulate a man to self-analysis, might make him begin to question his own judgement.

So instead she just looked across at him and gave him a wide smile.

'Like another?' he asked.

'Why not?' She held out the empty glass. 'That's the only trouble with cocktails – too good to sip.'

He took her hand in his and squeezed it. 'Nothing like

this has ever happened to me before.' From the intensity of his gaze and the nervous tension in his body, she believed him.

When she had finished the second margarita, he turned and said, 'Let's go somewhere we can be alone. I hope you don't think it's too presumptuous of me, but I have reserved a suite.'

'Whatever you want.'

He smiled. 'You mean—?'

'Sure.'

'Shall we go up now, or would you like another drink first?'

'I'm fine.'

'We can order dinner or anything else we want through room service.'

'Fine. You go first though. We shouldn't go up together in case you are recognised.'

He let go of her hand only to draw two notes out of his wallet to pay for the drinks.

'It's the Harlequin suite on the eighth floor. You'll find it all right?'

She nodded. 'Of course I'll find it.'

He squeezed her hand one last time, then pushed back his chair and stood. 'See you in a minute,' he whispered, then turned and walked down the passage towards the lift.

She watched him go. He passed four or five other suited men, each with a woman in tow. She wondered how many other assignations were being made this evening, how many other illicit affairs in rented rooms.

She caught the eye of the waiter and ordered a third margarita. While she sipped at it, a man walking past her gave her a questioning look as if to ask whether she was alone and free. A second tried to engage her in conversation.

Despite what she had said, she had no intention of

joining Raymond in the suite. A girl's generosity was so easily misinterpreted. Sex changed things. It made weak men arrogant and boastful, and confident men into savages.

Yet if he had been single, she would not have had the slightest hesitation about following him upstairs. She did not need to sit opposite him evening after evening over expensive dinners to know that they should be together.

Leaving Raymond to kick his heels upstairs before returning home was her present to Imogen, who would probably never know what a sacrifice she had made.

As soon as she had finished the margarita, she rose and walked down the passageway towards the main lobby of the hotel. She stood for a moment, hesitating, between the lift leading to the upstairs bedrooms and the huge revolving door at the entrance to the hotel. Then she swivelled on her heel and made for the street.

Six

She had expected that he would not want to see her again after the way she had abandoned him in the hotel, but he rang the next day to apologise and at the same time asked her out to dinner.

'I'm sorry,' she said, 'but it's a point of principle with me. I don't go out with married men.'

'Please!' he pleaded. 'It's not as you think. After what's happened, you should give me the opportunity to explain. Let's make it lunch, and we can discuss the paintings at Bradstoke at the same time.'

That lunchtime and in the evenings that followed he talked often about his home life. There seemed to be so much that he wanted to unburden. The more she listened to him, the more her heart went out to him.

On their first date he said: 'Do you think I would be here now if I had anything that could be called a proper marriage?'

On their third date he said: 'Often I feel so desperately alone. That's one of the reasons I'm a workaholic. Sometimes I can't face going home.'

On their fifth date, he said: 'The real problems seemed to start after our third child was born. Something seemed to switch off in Imogen. She lost interest in sex, in me. Everything was directed towards the children.'

From their conversations she formed a picture of a man

whose marriage had failed, who was only staying with his wife for the sake of the children, and who for all his business success lived a sterile, empty life.

He was a man with so much love to give, such a generous spirit and such an agile mind she thought it tragic that he had not found happiness.

She resented the way that Imogen Farleigh had failed him, as she was sure that given similar circumstances she would not have failed, and wished again that he had not been married.

Yet the more she thought about him, the more she questioned what rights were conferred with marriage: certainly, she was sure, not the right to force another human being to spend his life without the comfort of love. Love was a law of nature and beyond the legislature of men.

On their seventh date, they were sitting side by side on the sofa in her flat when he leaned towards her and gave her a kiss.

They had just returned from an expensive dinner and Katya was feeling pleasantly intoxicated. His lips were very sensual. She liked the way the sight of her made them swell slightly and turn a deeper shade of red. In the breath of that kiss, she felt the pain in him, the pent-up emotion, the yearning. He seemed to need her more than any other man she had known.

The light from the standard lamp above her was in her eyes when she opened them. She leaned back a little then, and he followed, slipping his arms under her, hugging her to him. His head nuzzled into her, breathing in her scent, planting kisses on the soft white skin above her breasts.

He made to slide down the strap of her dress. Her hand crossed it, denying him, but the message from her lips, her eyes, was different. Raymond first kissed her hand, seeking permission, then slowly lowered the strap, gently pushing her hand away.

The areola of her breast was very dark against the whiteness of her skin. It looked huge too, much larger than would be expected on her small, beautifully formed breasts. His mouth seemed almost to swallow it. She felt the pressure of his tongue on her nipple, teasing her, playing with her, bringing it to life. She felt the nipple stretch and expand and become hard and at the same time the hunger of desire was making every part of her sensitive to the slightest touch.

He tugged at the hem of her dress. She rose up slightly from the sofa, freeing it, and he pulled the dress over her shoulders, over her hair. For a second her face was trapped within the confines of the silk and the smell of her own perfume was intense. Then, with one small tug, she was free.

Why did she trust this man? she asked herself. He was married and she hardly knew him. But she felt the need in him and that somehow it was right.

His hands ran down her body, electrifying the skin wherever they went, making her feel so alive. He stripped off his jacket, his tie, his shirt, and she felt the warmth of his chest against hers, his skin on her skin, the pressure of his body on hers, and their mouths met again.

Still his hands were working. They were stroking her legs, her thighs, tugging at her knickers until they slipped down to her ankles and he could flick them away.

His touch was so gentle and slow there was nothing to disturb the magic of it, nothing to jar with the ever-increasing sensation. Then suddenly she drew in her breath as his finger went deep inside her. She could feel how smoothly it entered her, how wet she was, how excited, and so could he. After a few minutes, crouching beside her, he began unfastening the buckle on his trousers with his free hand.

'No,' she said firmly. She got comfortable in the sofa, spread her legs a little, then took his head in both hands and guided him down.

35

His lips worked on her first, caressing and kissing, drinking of her. Then his tongue went deeper, darting inside.

She lay back, staring at the ceiling, feeling inside her the heat of him, the touch of him, the warm gusts of his breath, the spark of his tongue, while all the time his hands stroked and kneaded her breasts.

Then suddenly her body became rigid. She felt waves of pleasure passing over her, through her. She reached out for something to hold. She grabbed the cushion, the sofa, his hair, tugging and digging in her nails. She cried out again and again until she had no breath left.

She had not expected it to be so good. Not from a captain of industry.

The drive home to Phillimore Gardens seemed to take longer than usual. Raymond did not care. He had lost all sense of time.

He turned right on to the parking area beside the house, drew the Aston Martin to a halt and climbed out. As he locked the car, he glanced up at the double-fronted house with its freshly painted white stucco glistening under the streetlamps like the icing on a wedding cake, its box pyramids in swagged terracotta pots, its welcoming lantern, its gleaming Georgian brass doorknobs, its window boxes overflowing with begonias and ivy. Its very homeliness seemed to be mocking him now.

He hesitated for a moment on the doorstep. He could not but help feel differently towards the house. It was a symbol of all that he had striven for – the security, the style, the status, the visible fruits of success – yet now he felt acutely that they were no longer enough. He had done all of this for the family, to give them the security that he himself had lacked as a child, to give them the best possible start in life. Now he had undermined it all and exposed the hollow core.

What he already had should be enough, he told himself, but he felt numb to the trappings of wealth and success. He was amazed only that he had been able to live for so long within an emotional void, in a world of play-acting, of pretence, dully, mechanically going through the motions of married life, whispering endearments which had long since lost their meaning.

He did not know why he so worshipped that waiflike girl with the brave, vulnerable eyes. All he knew was that, for the first time for as long as he could remember, he felt alive, vibrant. And as he smelled again the heady scent of her which still clung to his lips and nostrils, he had to steady and shake himself to bring himself back to the present.

He wanted to jump into the street and dance. He wanted to yell to the world that he had found his love. But this was a neighbourhood of stolid, respectable citizens enjoying a stolid, respectable night's sleep.

Before him was his home which was, as he had so often been told, one of the nicest houses in London. It should be. It had cost him three million. Why then did he get this sinking sensation, this feeling of fear, of desperation, of gathering black clouds, as he stood on its exquisite Portland stone threshold?

He turned the key in the lock and walked in. The lights were still on. The hall smelled strongly of the citrus-scented candles which Imogen had sent over especially from Paris. He resented the way the citrus made the smell of Katya suddenly faint, as if he had been doused in antiseptic. He stepped quickly across the marble floor, avoiding the children's bikes, then climbed the stairs two at a time to the second floor. He turned sharply right and opened the first door.

Imogen was in bed, reading. He had hoped that she might already be asleep, so that he would not have to go through this charade. He hated lies. But he would have no choice now. This time would only be the first of many. He would have to learn, to adapt, to lie.

She was dressed in a fine cotton nightdress with a pink ribbon around the neckline. Her blonde hair touched her shoulders and splayed out on the pillow behind her. Her skin was creamy. Her lips were a dusky pink, her eyes cobalt blue. She was a handsome woman. Why did the sight inspire in him only feelings of guilt and duty and fear rather than love and lust?

She glanced up from *Vogue*. 'Ah, there you are, darling. Good meeting?'

Already her eyes had returned to the magazine. She asked the same question, in the same tone, evening after evening, out of a sense of politeness, he guessed. She was absorbed in the magazine now and it occurred to him that he could say anything at all and she would not bat an eyelid.

He would not risk it tonight though. What mattered was that she was not suspicious of him. He was sure he was blushing like a schoolboy who has just had a fag behind the squash courts.

'It went fine,' he said.

She nodded without looking up from the magazine.

He felt suddenly swamped by all the clutter that Imogen had accumulated around her, by all this homeliness, by all this good taste.

The room was done out in a shade of dusky pink. But this was not any common-or-garden dusky pink. After the walls had been painted with three coats of white eggshell, the colour had been mixed personally by the fair hands of Julian Sands, London's premier decorator. Then the walls had been rag-rolled by specialists and varnished twice.

The curtains were a work of art, too. The silk that was interlaced with the chintz in the pelmets had come from Paris – or rather, not come from Paris: the consignment had taken over seven months to arrive, then had to be sent back as the colour did not match the sample. The trimmings had been specially dyed to match but had since faded.

The three tables in the room were so crowded with little enamel boxes that it was impossible to put anything down on them. Even the chair which he tried to sit down on while taking off his shoes and socks boasted three needlework cushions: there was only room for him to perch on the very edge of the seat.

He undressed quickly, went through to the bathroom, brushed his teeth vigorously, then padded back across the floor and climbed into bed beside her.

An invisible wall had gone up in the bed since last time he had slept there, and he knew that it was his doing. Imogen did not seem to notice, or maybe, he wondered, in her eyes it had been there for a long time already.

'If you're ready, I'll switch off my light,' she announced.

'Yes, darling. I'm ready.'

He wanted and welcomed the dark. He sighed when it came.

Seven

Sunday should have been the perfect day. Samantha and Willa were both home. Archie was neither overtired nor ill. The sun was shining. The spring flowers were bursting into bloom. Why then, Raymond wondered, was he feeling so on edge?

It wasn't as if he did not love his children and the simple pleasures of the country. It must be possible, he thought, to compartmentalise his emotional life just like he divided up his working time between projects. The Spanish, French and Italians all did it. Why couldn't he?

Sunday morning was one of the times when Imogen and he sometimes made love – or, more accurately, had sex. When he woke up that morning in the huge oak four-poster in the master bedroom of Bradstoke Hall, their country seat in Gloucestershire, he lay there for a few minutes, trying to remember the last time that Imogen had instigated sex. All he could recall were three occasions six years ago, around the time when Archie had been conceived. Since then, her favours had been bestowed with increasing infrequence and her sighs had been more from forbearance and impatience than passion.

He bathed and got dressed, leaving Imogen to read the tabloids over her breakfast tray in bed. He allowed himself a poached egg and bacon, which were cooked by Maria, their Portuguese maid, then settled down to help

Samantha with her homework.

At thirteen she was the elder of the two girls. She had long red hair and freckles, a colouring which mystified him, as neither he nor Imogen had red hair in their families. A year ago she had been painfully thin, angular and gawky. Now, suddenly, she was beginning to look more like a woman than a girl.

She was working on a history paper. As Raymond scanned the questions, he was already beginning to regret his offer of help.

'What's wrong, Daddy?' she asked, twisting around towards him from behind the pyramid her elbows and clasped hands made on the table.

'Which book are you working from?' he asked.

'It's called *The History of England from 1720 to 1860.* Not a very imaginative title, I'm afraid.'

'Fetch it, please.'

'Don't be cross, Daddy, but I left it at school.'

'How do you expect me to help you if you haven't got the book?'

'I don't know, Daddy, but I'm sure you'll think of something. Please don't let me down.'

They did what they could out of an old edition of the *Encyclopaedia Britannica* which was in the library. Then, at about ten thirty, Samantha went off riding.

As soon as she had gone, his second daughter, Willa, came into the room, pushed her spectacles further up her nose, kissed him through her brace and asked for help with her maths. She was just eleven, and had fine blonde hair, like her mother.

He was relieved to be asked to help with something that he reckoned he could do, but halfway down the page the questions turned to sines and exponentials and he was lost.

Raymond enjoyed the business of being a parent, and he wanted to do whatever he could for his children, not least because even in the days before his parents had separated, his own father had always been distant.

To Samantha, Willa and Archie, he was parent. To Imogen, he was husband and provider. To his business colleagues, he was boss. He could define himself with reference to the needs of others. But what was he to himself? He felt that somehow his own identity had got lost among the endless role-playing, among the demands and definitions of others.

Only with Katya did he really feel free. Only with her could he feel himself – though was it himself, he wondered, or just a projection of what he wanted to be – the charmer, the sexual athlete he had failed to be in his youth? It didn't matter. Whatever it was, it was good. And he needed her. Only she made it happen.

Raymond had forgotten that Simon and Jane Beaven and their two sprogs had been asked to lunch. Fortunately no one else had. As soon as they arrived, he made a jug of Bloody Mary while the children played and Imogen took the grown-ups on a tour of the garden.

From his vantage point by the orangery, Raymond looked down on the terrace below and watched the group's stately progress along the beds. Imogen knew every plant in the garden, and could usually give both the common and the Latin names. Jane, a thin blonde who still had the figure of a schoolgirl, seemed genuinely interested in all she had to say, while for all his studied expression and well-timed nods, Simon seemed to be acting only out of politeness.

Raymond admired the love affair with the garden which was the mainstay of so many English women. He wished that it could become a passion for him too or that he could find some other interest within the home which would keep him from straying outside his marriage. But he knew that what he wanted could not be found by digging the soil or from the contemplation of natural beauty. He needed the warmth of Katya's body next to his, her breathless cries in his ears, the sudden tautness of her fingers about him, her heady smell: not the scent of flowers.

After drinks on the lawn, they went through to the oak-panelled dining room for lunch. Raymond had Jane on his right, Samantha on his left and a huge floral arrangement directly in front of him.

'So where are you at school now?' Jane asked Samantha, leaning across Raymond to do so.

'St Paul's.'

'That's a very brainy school. Are you enjoying it?'

'It's all right.'

'Jolly good. What do you enjoy most . . .?'

How comfortable, he thought, Jane seemed with the young. Yet with adults she so often appeared awkward.

He had always been surprised that Simon had married Jane. Even when he had first met her, nearly twelve years ago, she had had a pale, washed-out look and a consumptive air, as if she was not strong enough for the everyday business of living. He knew that he must be wrong about that, though, because she had given birth to two healthy children and brought them up impeccably.

'Do look at that picture,' Imogen told their guests, pointing to the Vandyke of the Countess of Dunstable which now hung in pride of place above the fireplace. 'It's extraordinary. We sent it off to be cleaned and the restorer found that sweet little boy hidden beneath the Countess's skirts.'

She looked beyond Simon, craning round the floral arrangement to see her husband. 'Isn't that right, Raymond?'

'Yes, my dear.' He knew that she was only making conversation, yet still his pulse was racing.

* * *

44

After coffee, Raymond suggested tennis. None of the girls wanted to play so he and Simon set off for a game of singles. No sooner were they out of earshot of the house than Simon turned to him and asked: 'So what did you decide then?'

'About what?'

'About the girl, of course.'

'The jury's still out.'

There must have been something incongruous in his tone because Simon's hand landed hard on his shoulder. 'Don't give me a load of shit. You've either done it or you haven't. My guess is you have and you're smitten.'

Raymond grinned. Was he that transparent? 'What gives you such a crazy idea?'

'The spring in your step, which has got nothing to do with those hideous high-tech plimsolls.' He gripped Raymond's shoulder blade harder. His hazel eyes were curious, perceptive, knowing. 'Look, I understand what you're feeling.'

'How could you possibly understand?'

''Cause I've been there.'

It took Raymond a moment to absorb the import of Simon's words. 'You mean . . .?'

'Yup.' Simon nodded twice. 'I've got someone. We've been together now for five years – longer than most marriages.'

'I had absolutely no idea.'

'Neither has Jane. You see, if you're discreet about it, no one need know.'

They had climbed up the grass bank and reached the green wire cage surrounding the tennis court. Rather than going into the court, Raymond led the way over to the spectators' bench opposite the net and sat down on the damp, mossy wooden slats.

'I always thought that you and Jane were – well – a model couple.'

Simon grinned. 'What do you mean – that endangered species, the perfect nuclear family? Don't get me wrong, I love Jane and the children. Honestly I do. It's just that after some ten years of marriage – well, you know what it's like? Married sex can be about as exciting as a plate of stewed cabbage. Life's moving on, and you're not getting a buzz out of it any more. So what are you meant to do?

'You can grin and bear it – mortifying the flesh and all that – which is fine if you are made that way, but I'm a healthy guy in good working order with a lot of hormones.

'You can go in for divorce and remarriage – serial monogamy – which frankly is messy, very bad for the children, and carries no guarantees that you will be any happier a few years on.

'Or you can do what I do. You keep the family together. You are there to make sure that your wife and children are well looked after. You are there to be a good father, around whenever they need you. It's a very civilised solution to a very old problem, and in many Latin countries considered perfectly acceptable behaviour.'

'But not here. Are you sure Jane suspects nothing?'

'Positive. With lives like yours and mine involving a lot of travel abroad and work in the evenings, how is she to know? And I'm very careful. So careful in fact that when Lucy and I go out we only go to places with such filthy food and so little atmosphere that we are guaranteed not to meet anyone we know.

'Look, why don't the four of us go out to dinner some time – you and your girl, me and Lucy? I'd really like you to meet her. She's a great girl.'

Raymond heard a sound in the grass behind them. He turned and saw Imogen climbing up the grass bank through the daffodils towards them. In the breeze her sunlit yellow hair curled and dipped around the rim of her straw hat, and her thin patterned dress pressed against her body, outlining her breasts and narrow waist.

He only wished he still found the sight as alluring as he used to.

She stood for a moment looking across at them, shielding her eyes against the glare, while Jane caught up with her. From her open, trusting expression he did not think she could have heard their conversation even though the wind was carrying the sound towards her.

'So this is what you call tennis, is it?' she shouted. 'I'd have thought you would have played a set by now.'

'We're just about to start,' Raymond called back.

He walked around the side of the court, pulled back the latch on the gate and went inside. He opened a new tin of balls, and started hitting them one by one down the length of the court.

Eight

'Is this it?'

He nodded.

She arranged her skirt and climbed out of the car. The house was in a cobbled mews. It was pink with a white front door, a picture window where stable doors had once been and two small windows upstairs.

Raymond drew a bunch of keys from his pocket and unlocked the front door.

There was no hallway. They walked straight into the sitting room, which had been extended with a pitched roof and skylights into the garden. It had white walls, a new beige carpet, a carved pine reproduction Victorian mantelpiece, a 'real' gas log fire and some white curtains, which had already turned grey.

'What do you think?' Raymond asked.

'I love it. It's so bright and airy and spacious.' She wandered down to the far end of the room and looked out into the garden. It was minute, but there was a small patch of grass for Myrtle to run in, two squat trees covered in buds and a border full of shrubs. 'And it would be perfect for work. It's got good natural light, which is what I need.'

'That's what I thought.'

She went through to the kitchen, which had been tricked out with a set of antiqued pine cabinets and all the appliances she could possibly need, including a fridge freezer with an ice-making machine.

She climbed the narrow staircase and found a bedroom with wall-to-wall fitted cupboards which would easily accommodate all her clothes. She was amazed how quiet the room was after the continual hubbub of traffic outside Bridegate Gardens.

Across the landing was a bathroom decorated with avocado-coloured tiles stamped with small brown flowers, and with a matching bathroom suite. It was not to her taste, but it could easily be changed.

'It's fabulous,' she called as she climbed back down the stairs. 'Only trouble is, I know what these places cost and I couldn't begin to afford it.'

He smiled. 'There'll be no rent.'

'No rent!' Katya swallowed. She stood at the bottom of the stairs for a moment, trying to consider the implications.

Goose pimples pricked her skin. All that most men had given her was a hot dinner and she would neither have expected nor wanted any more. A gesture like this made a girl feel appreciated, made her feel cared for, made her feel wanted, made her feel special. It could also make her feel trapped.

'What can I say? This is the kindest, nicest thing anybody has ever offered to do for me. But I don't think I can accept.'

'We can look at other houses if you like,' he answered. 'You name it – bigger, smaller, different period, different location.'

'It's not the house,' she said firmly. 'I've been brought up to be self-sufficient, and I don't want to feel obligated. This is simply too generous.'

'I want to help you,' he answered. 'But it's not just that. If we are going to go on seeing one another, for me, Kensington is much more convenient to get to than Wandsworth, so I am not being entirely altruistic. You needn't feel obligated in any way. Think about it.'

She thought about it that evening as she lay in bed in her flat in Bridegate Gardens.

She was sick and tired of being kept awake at night by the noise of the traffic, of the fumes which aggravated her asthma, of the damp and dreariness of the décor, of the uncertainty of knowing that she could be given notice to quit at any time when permission to redevelop the site came through. She had, though, learnt to live with these everyday aggravations.

If she moved into the mews house, it would be only for Raymond, not for the added comforts. In just over a month he had become the most important person in her life. She thought about him incessantly, and waited anxiously for his calls. Yet she still was not sure whether she was ready for the kind of commitment which might come from living in a house rented by him, for she guarded her independence jealously.

The more she thought about it, however, the more she realised she had no choice. She wanted, she needed Raymond, as he needed her, and this was the only way they could spend more time together. The length of the journey to and from Wandsworth made it impractical for him to visit her on the way back from the office, and in the public glare of hotels they were bound to be caught out.

His marriage was something that had to be faced. She would have felt guiltier if Imogen had not squandered his love. Katya believed that she had only nourished what Imogen had discarded. She had let it grow, and made Raymond whole again.

The following morning she rang him at his office and told him she would take him up on his offer. Three weeks later the deal was completed: she was free to move in.

Having spent much of her life in short-term rents or staying with family, this was the first time she had had somewhere she could view as hers, because, even if she did not own it, it had, after all, been rented for her. Despite her aesthetic sense, she had always considered herself to be fairly oblivious to her surroundings, and was surprised how house-proud she felt.

She gave the sitting room a fresh coat of white paint. The removal van followed the next day. The beige carpet she thought too bland so she covered it with three kelim rugs. She placed the kelim-covered sofa from the flat in Bridegate Gardens against the wall opposite the pine mantelpiece, then worried in case the combined effect of so much kelim was too overpowering, but decided to leave it all the same. Her old wooden standard lamp with the tasselled shade she gave away and bought instead a modern one on a black tubular stand. Above the mantelpiece she hung the Japanese wood block of a samurai in armour which had been left to her by her father. At the far end of the room, where the sunlight dappled the floor, she put her canvas rack, her easel, her stereobinocular microscope, her stool and the tools of her trade.

As the light was beginning to fade, a boy from the florist's rang the doorbell. 'Someone must love you,' he said with a cocky smile as he handed her the delivery slip to sign. He brought in two dozen roses. It was as if to say nothing had changed.

At seven, the doorbell rang again. This time it was Raymond himself. He stood in the doorway for a moment, waiting for her to invite him in. He wore a grey bird's eye suit and the light from the evening sun danced in his hair. As he turned his head towards her, the light caught his cheek and she could see the warmth in his smile and in his eyes.

'Thank you for the flowers,' she said. 'Come on in. Have a drink.'

'I'm glad they arrived. A whisky and water, please.'

She left him to go through to the kitchen. She plucked two glasses out of a cupboard, filled one with two fingers of whisky and poured a spritzer for herself.

As she returned to the sitting room, she was suddenly anxious that moving here had not been such a clever idea, that, in doing so, Raymond's expectations of her had changed. There seemed to be something predatory about the way he sat silently waiting for her on the kelim sofa – a man yearning for sex like an alcoholic for a drink. The very predictability of it turned her cold.

Yet when she was seated on the sofa next to him, again she felt his power, again she wanted to feel his arms enclosing her, again it seemed right.

When they had had their fill of kisses and drink, she unzipped him, let him grow strong in her hands, and took him into her mouth.

'When did you last get this at home?' she asked inquisitively, looking up at him.

He grinned. 'You must be joking!'

Nine

The woman in the blue tailored suit walked to the centre of the room, steadied the swinging chain of her shoulder bag and looked about her aghast. 'Katya, it's quite sensational!'

Tamsin was only three years older than her sister but to Katya, at least, she had never been young. From an early age she had worn a lot of make-up, had favoured formal suits and had had her hair chopped to an easy-to-manage length.

She was a woman with definite ideas about life. Upon leaving the Convent of the Immaculate Conception she had announced that she planned to find a man, settle down and have children. Within two years she had found a suitable candidate in the form of Douglas Whittaker, a nice young man with a small private income and a steady job in the City. Almost exactly nine months later, their first child, Jeremy, was born. Eighteen months after that, he was followed by Katherine, who in turn was followed by Martin.

Tamsin walked through into the kitchen. 'Nice cabinets,' she remarked, opening one. 'Carpenter-built. You can always tell.' She ran her hand along the polished granite work surface. 'Very elegant too, but you will have to be careful with wine glasses. A friend of mine broke a dozen stems in a week. We went for one of those new synthetic materials ourselves. Both elegant and practical.'

She hurried out of the room and started climbing the stairs to the first floor. 'I don't understand it. One moment you're pleading poverty in a desolate corner of Wandsworth; the next you're in your own house in one of the smartest parts of Kensington. Your restoration business must be doing well.'

'Yes. I have had a number of new commissions,' Katya answered cautiously.

'Divine bedroom.' Tamsin's laser eyes scrutinised the large brass bed, the fitted cupboards and the framed photographs on the dressing table, which were all old black and white ones of the family.

She went through into the bathroom. 'Pity about those tiles,' she remarked. 'I think it's so important what one sees from one's bath, don't you agree?'

Her eyes lingered questioningly on the two matching sets of towels, then fixed on a bottle of aftershave by the basin. She picked it up and sniffed at it.

'Limes,' she announced. 'Always good on a man.' Suddenly she was all smiles. 'Why didn't you tell us you had someone?'

Katya had checked through the whole house and removed everything personal of Raymond's before her sister had arrived. How, she wondered, had she missed the aftershave?

'It's still early days.'

'What's he like?'

'Tall, good-looking, fortyish.'

'Sounds divine, but quite old to be unmarried.'

'He's been married before,' she said quickly, which was at least partially true.

'Why don't you bring him to dinner next Wednesday?'

'I'm afraid that's not possible.'

'How about the following week?'

56

She shook her head. 'Not possible either. He travels a lot.'

'Some other time, then.' Tamsin was about to climb down the stairs when she turned back towards Katya. 'If he's going to be abroad next Wednesday, why don't you come and have supper anyway?'

'Thanks. I will.'

Katya stood for a moment at the top of the stairs, feeling numb. She had not wanted to lie to her sister; equally, she felt she could not tell her the truth. But if she couldn't tell her own sister about Raymond, who could she tell?

Raymond had taken her to The Gilded Angel twice before. It was a restaurant in the old style: all red plush and obsequious service. She was mystified as to why it was such a favourite of his. Although it was central and discreet, and, with a clientele consisting principally of visiting foreigners, they were unlikely to meet anyone they knew, the food was like a school canteen's.

The head waiter, a bald Italian in a stained tuxedo, greeted them effusively and ushered them to their special table in a dimly lit alcove half-obscured from the other diners.

Another couple were already there. He was tall and wiry with wavy greying hair and was dressed in a dark grey suit. She was a strawberry blonde – a natural, Katya guessed, from her complexion – a well-developed woman in her mid-thirties with a curvaceous figure, dressed in a loose top and short suede skirt.

This was the first time that Raymond had introduced her to any of his friends, and the prospect excited her. 'This is Simon Beaven,' he announced, 'one of my oldest friends, and . . .'

'Lucy,' answered the girl. She did not give a second name. Although she wore a wedding ring, something about the way she looked across at Simon made Katya sure that they were not married to each other.

'I'm so pleased to meet you,' Raymond said, shaking her warmly by the hand.

The girl smiled back at him. 'And I you. Simon has talked about you often.'

'You have been so discreet, I never suspected . . .'

'There's no point in adding to the difficulties.'

As Katya chatted to Lucy during dinner, she could not help noticing a restlessness about her. She seemed so aware of every move that Simon made. At first Katya attributed this to the obsessiveness of love, but later she wondered whether she had been right.

'How long have you been with Simon?' Katya asked her when the men began swapping stories.

'Five years. And you and Raymond?'

'Two months.'

'So still in the first throes of romance.' She gave Katya a slow, knowing smile. 'You know, very little has changed in the years Simon and I have been together. He is still with his wife, and I still see him regular as clockwork three times a week.'

She glanced towards Simon to see if he was listening to her, but he seemed absorbed in the story that Raymond was telling him.

'So, don't expect too much, if you know what I mean. Sometimes I wonder what would have happened if we hadn't met – would he still be married to Jane? Somehow I doubt it. I think she owes me a debt of gratitude.'

She reached in her bag and handed Katya a card. It was inscribed 'Lucy Drew, Interior Designer' in a fine italic script. Below was an address and a telephone number.

'Ring me,' she said. 'We could have lunch.'

Katya turned the card between her fingers, then slipped it into her bag. 'Thank you. I'd like that.'

* * *

It was three o'clock in the afternoon. Opposite Raymond sat Paul Shrieber and Dieter Orin, respectively the chief executive and president of the Orin Corporation. They were discussing the possibilities of mutual cooperation on the Paraguay hydroelectric project when the telephone rang. It was Katya's direct line.

Raymond tensed, galvanised.

The short, bald president of the Orin Corporation was not used to being interrupted. At the sound of the ringing, he paused for a second to register a look of pained annoyance, then continued where he had left off.

'So, as I was saying, we need one another. Our expertise in similar projects combined with your relationship with the Ministry of Public Works makes a joint bid by far the best option . . .'

The telephone had rung twelve times now. Each ring cut through him. Raymond had to steady his hand to stop it grasping the receiver. He tried to calculate how much longer he could keep her holding on. Could he risk waiting until the man had finished his speech? Could he even risk waiting until he had finished the sentence? Dieter Orin never used short sentences where long ones would do.

'I'm sorry.' Raymond smiled apologetically. 'I'd better get that.' Dieter Orin sighed forcibly and loudly; Raymond kept smiling anyway. 'Hello?'

'I want to suck your cock.'

He swallowed, smiled. 'I'm afraid I'm tied up now.'

'Not in the way I would do it.'

'I'm in a meeting.'

'I know. I can tell.'

'I'll call you back later.'

'No. Don't hang up on me. Where are you sitting? On that big leather chair in front of your desk?'

'Yes.'

'Lie back comfortably.'

'I did say I was in a meeting.'

'I know. I heard. I want you to imagine that I am crawling under your desk towards you. You can't see me but you can hear me and now you can feel me. I've touched you lightly on both knees to separate your legs. Do you feel the pressure?'

'I feel it.'

'Good. Then open your legs.'

He did as she said. Paul Shrieber was cleaning his glasses while Dieter Orin stared quizzically at Raymond from the other side of the desk. Raymond covered the mouthpiece with his hand. 'I'm so sorry.' He smiled. 'Something that can't wait. Please, go on talking. I'm listening.'

'Liar.'

Paul replaced and straightened his glasses. Dieter nodded. 'The last two hydroelectric plants we have been involved in,' he continued, 'have both been completed on time and under budget. This was largely due to the new method of off-site construction we have utilised which is particularly beneficial in remote locations lacking a pool of skilled labour . . .'

'Do you feel my hand on your trouser leg? I am stroking it now. I feel the texture of the worsted wool suit you are wearing. I feel the muscle of your thigh. It is hard and firm. I feel your crotch. It is soft just now. I squeeze it very gently. My finger's running down the length of the zipper on your trousers. I've found the toggle now. I'm pulling it down. Do you hear it? Do you feel it? Click . . . click . . . click . . .'

'The prefabricated sections can be lifted in by air if road transportation is impossible, although of course this would add to the expense. In our budget we have only allowed for trucking to the site.'

'My hand's going in now. It is gently separating the flaps of your boxer shorts. You feel very warm. I hope I don't feel cold. I don't, do I?'

'No.'

'I'm sorry?' asked Dieter.

'No, carry on.'

'I'm tickling your balls. How's that feel? Am I doing it right? I think I must be because you are growing. I'm right, aren't I?'

'Yes.' He swallowed. 'You're right.'

'I'm leaning forward now. Can you feel the warmth of my breath on you?'

'Yes.'

'Raymond?' It was Dieter. 'Would you prefer it if we were to come back in a few minutes?'

'Yes. I'm so sorry. I won't be long.'

'No,' said a voice, 'tell them to stay.'

Suddenly the line went dead.

Grinning, Katya replaced the receiver. She loved the games they played. These days every part of her body was an erogenous zone. She seemed to spend her day in a cloud of sensuality. A warm breeze on her cheek, the brush of her clothes against her, almost anything seemed to make her think of his touch, made her want to ring him, if only to hear his voice.

Yet what she found most exciting of all was the power she had over him: he loved her, he adored her, he needed her and would do anything for her.

Raymond Punchard was one of the most successful men of his generation, and she, Katya Cornwale, controlled him. He was her slave.

Ten

Raymond glanced at his watch. Two minutes past six. He slipped his pen into his pocket, pushed back the black leather chair and made for the door.

'I'm on my way now – nothing that can't wait, is there?' he asked as he passed the desk of Pat Simon, his senior PA.

There was a pile of papers on her desk waiting for signature. Still she shook her head. 'No, RP.'

'Good. See you tomorrow.'

For the past ten years, for as long as Pat had worked for him, only rarely had he left the office before eight o'clock. Now, his last meeting was scheduled no later than five fifteen and unless there was an emergency, he left promptly at six.

Before, he had made it his business to ensure that no important decision was taken without his personal involvement. Now he realised the futility of trying to run the company in the same way as he had done when it was a twentieth of its present size. He delegated whenever possible, and so far, at least, no major mistake had been made. The managers of the individual divisions were happier, and so were his PAs: Pat had told him how very nice it was to get home in time to see the children before her husband had tucked them up in bed.

He had not told anyone at the office where he went in

the evenings but he reckoned that Pat and the other PAs must know, and that some of the senior managers might suspect something, if only from the change in his work habits. More recently, he had noticed one of the executive directors looking at him in unguarded moments with the smugness of someone with private knowledge. He was sure he could trust Pat implicitly and, as far as the others went, it was only conjecture.

The lift doors opened. He walked in, alone. No one else on the thirty-fourth floor was leaving yet. He guessed though that once he had gone many of them would be taking the next lift down.

Twenty minutes later he drew up outside Katya's house. When he switched off the ignition he could hear the pounding of his heart. He never knew what to expect. Sometimes she was naked when he arrived. Sometimes she undressed in front of him. Sometimes she stood there naked but would not allow him to touch her. Sometimes she did not undress at all.

He got out and rang the bell. He felt very exposed standing on the threshold where anyone could see him. On occasions she had kept him waiting for anything up to a quarter of an hour. He had suggested to her that he have his own key; she had refused, insisting on her privacy.

He rang the bell again. This time he heard her dog bark.

Moments later she came to the door. 'Sorry, I was upstairs.' She was wearing an artist's smock over jeans and a loose blue shirt. He recognised the shirt as one of his that he had left there last week. She smiled at him, ran the tips of her fingers over the bristles on his cheek, then kissed him lightly on the mouth. 'Come on in,' she said, taking hold of his tie and gently pulling him in after her.

* * *

Later, after their breathing had slowed, they lay in bed together side by side. He held her in his arms and she nestled up to him, slowly running her hands through the hairs on his chest.

'You were a very pretty baby,' he remarked.

She glanced up and saw that he was looking over at the photograph on the dressing table of her as a baby with her mother, father and Tamsin on holiday in Cornwall.

'What's that meant to mean?' she asked, teasing him. 'That I was pretty then, but have gone off now?'

'Not at all,' he said defensively. 'Started off pretty, then just got better and better.'

She knew it wasn't true, but she never argued with compliments, even ones which she had forced out of him.

'And what about your parents?' he asked. 'What do they do?'

This was the first time he had asked her about her family. In a way that did not surprise her. Their relationship was so intense, there did not seem to be room for other people. Sometimes it felt as if they had both stepped out of nowhere and found one another.

She shook her head, trying to keep emotion from her voice. 'They were both killed when I was eight.'

'I'm sorry. I had no idea.'

'It's nothing for you to apologise about.'

'Would you prefer not to talk about it?'

'No, I don't mind. I'd like you to know. It was a pointless, prosaic, avoidable death. It was a Friday evening in February. We were driving from London to Basingstoke to stay with my Aunt Jacintha for the half-term weekend. Daddy was driving, my mother in the seat next to him, and Tamsin and me in the back.

'We were on the M3 just past Farnborough when we went into a patch of fog. The visibility hadn't been bad until then. We couldn't see anything apart from our own headlight beams and the glowing mist beyond.

'Daddy slammed on the brakes. Either he wasn't quick enough or we must have skidded, because suddenly the mist began to take shape before us. All across the road we saw tangled, buckled metal and broken glass. Two cars had crashed and a lorry had jack-knifed. By then there was nothing we could do to stop becoming part of it.

'We just seemed to slide into them as if in slow motion. The juddering impact came first, the windscreen crazed, the front of the car concertinaed, and Mummy and Daddy were flung forward into the wreckage. The car behind hit us then, and I lost consciousness. It was over three hours before we were cut out.'

'I'm sorry. It must have been terrible for you.'

'You just have to try to be brave and keep on going. What else can you do? There is no explanation. When I was in hospital our local vicar came to see me. I asked him why God had let it happen and he began by telling me that accidents of this sort were an inevitable consequence of man's free will. Halfway through his talk, he gave up and just wrapped his arms around me and held me.'

She had her head on his chest, listening to the slow rhythm of his breathing.

'Don't worry.' His fingers ran through her hair. 'You've got me now.'

'I know.'

'What happened to you then?'

'As she was our only close relative, Aunt Jacintha was appointed our guardian. She was a strange woman – small, wiry and self-contained. Up until our arrival, she had lived alone in a grey stone house outside Basingstoke with her six cats.

'Tamsin and I did our best to charm her, but I don't think she ever loved us nearly as much as her furry friends. She seemed to treat our welfare as a necessary duty like scrubbing the floor and cleaning the stove.

'Of course, for half the year we were away at the convent.'

'Which one?'

'The Convent of the Immaculate Conception outside Oxford.'

'That's where Imogen went,' he said apprehensively.

Katya nodded. 'I know. I remember her, although I doubt whether she still remembers me. She was in her last year, when I arrived at eight.

'I'll never forget those long linoleum-floored corridors, the smell of stewed cabbage mingled with the distant odour of incense from the chapel, or the jingle of Mother Superior's keys as she bustled along to take the school for spiritual reading before early morning mass.

'The only man on the staff was Mr Blakely, our biology master. We teased him mercilessly and asked him every week to tell us the facts of life. He never did.

'We were, though, lectured on the moral aspects of sex with great regularity, especially by Father O'Gorman, the visiting Irish priest who led the retreats. I can still remember his words to this day: "Any of you girls who so much as kiss a boy won't be a virgin by the time you're eighteen and you'll burn in hell fire, so God help you."

'I was thirteen at the time and had just had my first kiss at a party the previous holidays. It was nothing worth risking hell and damnation for, and Father O'Gorman's words haunted me.

'A few years later, I vowed I would never sleep with a boy before I got married, and I would save myself for Mr Right. It was so difficult trying to judge which boyfriend might be the one, I probably wrecked some really good relationships in my quest for perfection and purity. A lot of people around at that time thought I might be a lesbian because I was so reserved.

'It was like walking a highly strung emotional tightrope.

One day I knew I would fall and fall hard. I guess that's what's happened now. No other relationship has been anything like this. Here I am in bed with a married man.

'I can't help feeling guilty about it, but – I know this might sound perverse – in a way it's also an enormous relief, a kind of exorcism, breaking through all the cant and emotional blackmail which were being used as much to control me as to guide me. It feels so right being with you, it's difficult to believe that it could be wrong. Love is a force for the good.'

She looked up at him, eyes wide, pleading for reassurance.

'Of course, it is,' he answered and took her in his arms again.

Eleven

The Whittakers' house was in one of the smartest terraces in Clapham. The paintwork was fresh, the brass knocker highly polished, the net curtains devoid of London grime.

Katya pressed the doorbell. Almost at once the latch went back and Tamsin was standing there, smartly dressed in a silk blouse and skirt.

'I'm so pleased you could make it,' she said. As she moved forward to kiss Katya, a sudden burst of laughter came from the room on the right.

'I didn't realise it was a dinner party.'

'More a simple supper,' Tamsin answered. 'I've asked a very nice spare man for you – someone called Patrick Strevens. He's a friend of Douglas's and I thought he was rather you.'

'That's very kind of you. Don't, though, feel obliged to dig up a spare man every time I come to dinner.'

'What are sisters for?' Tamsin asked, smiling. 'Come and meet the others.'

She ushered Katya through into the drawing room, which was decorated in pale peach in some decorator-on-autopilot's idea of good taste. Katya thought it had about as much character as an office filing cabinet.

Tamsin was a perfectionist. Her house was run in a way that seemed to defy the laws of nature: her puppies never left calling cards; her children slept soundly at night; she had a full-time job, yet still managed to cook gourmet meals for her husband every evening.

In the past this had all proved too much for some of her friends. They had left the house with such a deep feeling of inferiority that they had let the friendship wither rather than face persistent comparison.

Katya had always suspected that the military order which Tamsin imposed upon things in her orbit and the ultra-conventionality of her life was her way of coping with the sadness of her childhood. Something of the confidence and courage which she had had before had been knocked out of her by the accident, and now she clung to what she believed was safe.

Heads turned as Katya entered the room. Douglas separated himself from the group by the fireplace and came over to her. He was wearing a destructured blue jacket, cream shirt and jeans. He was medium height, slim and fit, with regular features. Recently he had lost much of his hair and, as if in compensation, had grown what remained until it curled over his collar.

He kissed her on both cheeks. 'Tamsin tells me you have a new boyfriend. I'm sorry he couldn't come tonight. We'll meet him sometime soon, I hope?'

'Yes, I'm sure you will,' she answered vaguely.

He handed her a glass of white wine, then introduced her to the other two couples there; the men were talking share options, the women preparatory schools.

She was about to effect her escape and go and see whether Tamsin needed help in the kitchen when the spare man arrived. Much as she loved her sister, Katya had come to dread her choice in this department. Patrick Strevens, though, seemed to be an exception. He was tall, with dark blond hair and soft blue eyes, his handshake firm, his smile charming.

This was typical of her luck, she thought. The first time

her sister had produced a halfway decent man was when she was not interested.

She had asked Raymond many times to take her to Bradstoke Hall; each time he had made excuses. Nevertheless, she was determined to go. She was intensely curious about where and how Raymond led his life when he was not with her, so when the perfect opportunity to go there arose a couple of days later, she seized it.

The first six paintings which Raymond had sent to her for restoration were now ready; carriers were picking them up from her at eight thirty in the morning to take them to Bradstoke, and delivering a further six to her that evening. What could be more normal than a restorer examining the paintings *in situ* prior to cleaning?

She got up in good time for the carriers' arrival. She bathed, and dressed in jeans, a loose cotton top, and a chunky knit cardigan.

The driver had no objection to her hitching a ride. She sat in the front of the van between the two men chatting idly as they made their way down the M4.

She grew increasingly silent as they approached the turn-off for Bradstoke, and felt a lump in her throat as the van drove through the ornamental gates at the entrance to the estate.

A flock of sheep grazed lazily around ancient oaks. The gnarled limbs of the huge trees saddling the drive reached out at them from either side. Then, after two or three miles, they passed out from under the trees into bright sunshine and the house was before them.

It had a central cupola, rusticated stonework and classical columns in bas-relief. She thought it was a jewel.

The driver drew the van to a halt outside the front portico, jumped down on to the gravel and rang the bell.

Katya waited in the van, looking on. For the first time she had doubts about the wisdom of the expedition. She feared that, if she did happen to meet Imogen, she might unwittingly give herself away.

Even more she worried in case she might feel sympathy for her. At the moment Imogen Farleigh was only a memory from school. But if she was flesh and blood, she might make Katya hate herself, make her feel that she was letting down womankind, rather than breathing life into a man buried in a sterile relationship.

A butler in a black coat stood on the front steps before an open door.

Katya swallowed hard. She had to go inside. Picking up the list of paintings, she climbed out of the cab. She waited until the two removal men were carrying the first of the portraits into the house then followed behind them.

It had all been so easy.

The hall was pale blue with Italianate plasterwork picked out in white. Dark rectangles of unfaded paint showed where the portraits had been hung.

Katya checked her list and strode up to the butler. He had snow-white hair on a puce head. 'We are picking up the second and third Lord Farleigh . . .'

'You should be able to do better than that, love,' joked one of the removal men.

Katya smiled. ' . . . and four Dutch landscapes. Could you show me where they are, please?'

The butler nodded. 'Your shoes clean?'

'Yes.'

'Good. Madam is very particular about dragging dirt through the house.'

She followed him into the room on the left of the hall. It had ochre walls, old faded red silks for curtains and a marble Adam mantelpiece carved with mythological scenes. Photographs in gleaming silver frames lined the top of the grand piano.

'There is the Reynolds of the second Lord Farleigh,' the butler announced, pointing to a distinguished-looking man in a brown velvet coat on the far wall with a face as pale as his powdered wig. 'His son is the one on the wall directly opposite. In life, so Madam told me, they never saw eye to eye. She had the paintings rehung so that now they are forced to stare at one another all day, every day.'

Katya looked up at the paintings. In both, the flesh tones had drained to bloodlessness. It was a common problem with Reynolds' portraits, as he had experimented with unusual pigments, many of which had since proved unstable.

'You'll find the other four you are looking for in the room next door. Now remember, clean hands before you take them down. Madam will be furious if there are grubby marks on the walls.'

'We'll be very careful,' she assured him.

As soon as the butler had left her alone, she hurried over to the grand piano and studied the photographs. The large one in the centre was of Raymond and Imogen on their wedding day, she trying to control sails of white toile in the wind, he clutching her tenderly, all smiles.

There was the christening of Samantha, the elder daughter – Katya guessed that one must have taken some time to get right because though Raymond and Imogen were beaming proudly at the camera, two of the godparents had their mouths set in strained smiles.

There were photographs of Willa's and Archie's christenings too; Imogen in front of the Taj Mahal; both of them in a gondola in Venice; Raymond with the Prime Minister, Raymond with the Prince of Wales, Raymond with Mrs Thatcher, Raymond with President Clinton; and Raymond and Imogen at the opening of the wing of a hospital.

Right at the end was a family group, which she thought must have been taken only a couple of months ago. Raymond was standing next to Imogen, who looked almost beautiful, with her blonde hair, creamy skin and warm smile. They were flanked by Samantha and Willa, while Archie, the baby of the family, stood proudly in front of them between two black labradors.

She knew Raymond must have been acting but she wished that he did not look so in love with Imogen in the photograph. She wished even more that they did not look like such a happy family.

She walked through into the study. It had mellow honey-coloured panelling smelling faintly of beeswax, a huge stone fireplace, a battered Turkish rug covered in dog hairs and comfy armchairs in faded chintz with sagging cushions. An arrangement of slightly tired hydrangeas drooped in a green blown-glass vase. On the desk was a pile of invitations for a charity ball at the Grosvenor House Hotel in aid of the Crisis Call Trust. On the floor by the sofa lay a small toy gun.

From Raymond's description of his life in the house, she had expected something cold and formal. Instead, the atmosphere was warm, cosy and welcoming. It could be just the effect of the room, she thought – anywhere can feel cold if you are with someone you no longer love.

Just then she heard the creak of boards above her, followed by a woman's voice, muffled and indistinct. From its aristocratic tones, she was sure it must be Imogen Punchard's.

Any moment now Katya expected Imogen to come down the stairs, and the thought set her pulse racing; but they rehung the cleaned paintings and loaded the next six into the van and still she did not come.

Then, as they were about to drive away, a black labrador shot out through the door, barking at them.

A moment later, a tall woman followed. She was wearing a green cotton print dress, a scarf and a hat. Her face was hidden by shadow; only the painted lips were distinct. 'Tinker, come back this instant! Heel, Tinker, heel!'

The dog barked one last time, then reluctantly turned and went back to his mistress's side.

'I'm frightfully sorry,' she called. 'He's young, you know, and a little overenthusiastic at times.'

Imogen was looking straight at Katya as she sat in the front of the van with the window down. She gave no sign of recognition.

''S all right,' the driver shouted back, and with that, he engaged gear and pulled away.

All the way back to London, she could not get out of her head that image of Imogen Punchard, waxed lips moving beneath silk scarf and sun hat. She struck Katya as a woman who had come to terms with the passing of the years. The idea shocked her. It seemed so wrong and cruel that a woman like Imogen should wilt and drift into gentrified middle age.

Katya remembered the first time she had seen Imogen: she had been on the netball court, dressed in grey shorts and an Aertex shirt, idly dropping goals into the net. She had slim limbs, long blonde hair in a plait down her back and the easy gait of a natural athlete. To Katya then, a gawky and lonely eight-year-old just arrived at the school, Imogen had personified glamour, privilege and vitality.

The strongest and the sweetest memories Katya held of that difficult first year at the convent were of the times she spent with Imogen. As the sixth form classes did not always end as punctually as the first year's, Katya would scoot down the passage at the beginning of break and wait by the corner closest to the sixth-form class room.

Sometimes Imogen would walk by her with a cheery 'hello', but if she was not in a rush, she would stop and ask Katya how she was settling in. The slightest acknowledgement from Imogen had been enough to make Katya feel special all day.

To Katya then, Imogen could do no wrong. She was

like a goddess dispensing sunlight. She was the girl Katya most wanted to be like, and anything which Imogen had – from a hair band to a tennis racket – she wanted, too.

Katya now felt embarrassed when she recalled how she had hero-worshipped Imogen; but she had been very young at the time, impressionable, lost, and, with her parents no longer there to help her, desperately in need of a role model to feed her dreams.

It was, she thought, only to be expected that she and Imogen would be attracted to the same type of man. She wished, though, that, if Raymond couldn't be single, at least he had been married to somebody other than Imogen.

'Do you ever feel guilty about Simon's wife?' Katya asked Lucy Drew as they walked together in Hyde Park the following day.

'Why? Do you feel guilty about Imogen?'

'I suppose I do.'

'You shouldn't. It's not as if you went out to get Raymond and take him away from her.'

'He came to me.'

'Exactly. It was the same with Simon. He was looking around. Why? Because he was no longer in love with Jane. That was nothing to do with me, in the same way that Raymond falling out of love with Imogen had nothing to do with you. It had already happened before we came on the scene.

'A wife always blames the Other Woman, but that's because she doesn't want to face up to the fact that there is a deep problem with her marriage. We are a symptom of the problem, not the cause.'

'I still can't help feeling sympathy for her.'

'Sure. In the same way that I feel sympathy with anyone who has a problem marriage. But, if it was not for me, I reckon that Simon and Jane would have divorced by now. I've kept a broken-down marriage still workable.

Without me, she wouldn't have him at all.

'I'm the one who has to put up with the constant lonely nights and empty weekends, not her. I'm the one without a family. It's not easy. But I don't resent it because for me the times I spend with Simon make all the sacrifices worthwhile.'

Katya tugged on Myrtle's lead to keep her moving. 'Before I was in this position myself, I assumed the girlfriends of married men must all be heartless homebreakers after the main chance.'

Lucy grinned. 'On the contrary, most of the girls I know dating married men are hopeless romantics. They have to be to live the way they do. Why can't we just fall in love, marry and have babies like normal people?'

'Wouldn't that be great!' Katya exclaimed. She put her arm around Lucy and they went off in search of a sandwich and a cup of coffee.

Twelve

She was seated underneath a huge crystal chandelier in the Great Room of the Grosvenor House Hotel, dressed in the closest thing she had to a ball gown, a low-cut black lace number with a hem approaching the knee. A portion of corn-fed guinea fowl with a selection of seasonal vegetables – three mangetout, a single head of broccoli and two marble-sized potatoes – was on her plate, white wine in her glass. On her right was Patrick Strevens.

Since the dinner party at her sister's, he had asked her out four times. On the first three occasions she had made excuses. He was a kind, considerate, good-looking man, but she did not want to spend an evening fending off the inevitable passes. Above all, she did not want to be under pressure to explain.

Since meeting Raymond, she thought she must have been radiating some kind of sexual energy; she had not been flattered by so much attention from men for a long while. Ironic, as now she did not want it.

The fourth time Patrick rang she invited him as her guest to the Crisis Call ball. He agreed at once, although she knew a charity ball with its mass catering, its crowds and its impersonal formality would hardly have been his choice for a romantic evening.

The more she had thought about the ball since she had seen the pile of invitations on Imogen's desk at Bradstoke

Hall, the more her curiosity had been aroused. Here was an occasion where she could observe how Raymond and Imogen acted in each other's presence. The prospect intrigued her.

Most of the tables had been booked by groups of friends and had a convivial dinner party air. Theirs, at the back of the room, was made up of waifs and strays. There was a German banker and his wife recently arrived in London who had bought tickets in the hope of making social and business contacts; three women from the secretarial offices of the charity who were helping with the tombola and the lucky number draw; and a second couple who spoke only in soft whispers between themselves. Patrick twice gave her a look as if to say 'Remind me why we are here?'

Katya was delighted with the table because from where she sat she had a clear view of the top table on the edge of the dance floor where Imogen Punchard, the chair of the ball committee, sat next to the Duke of royal blood who was patron of the charity and guest of honour.

She watched with a mixture of amusement and awe. Imogen seemed completely unflustered by being in charge of such an event. Three or four times during the evening she had called someone over and issued instructions, and each time had managed to do so without even disrupting her neighbour's conversational flow.

On the other side of the table, his back turned to her, was Raymond. Next to him was the Duchess. As far as she could tell from the movements of their heads, their conversation was polite and convivial rather than animated. Raymond, she knew, thought small talk an inordinate waste of time.

Suddenly all conversation was drowned as the room filled with waiters and waitresses stacking and clearing seven hundred dirty plates. The clank of china encircled the room and echoed off the walls; it was an overwhelming, deafening sound which stopped as suddenly as it had begun as soon as the baked alaska was served.

Later the band struck up, playing Dixieland jazz. As soon as a few couples had braved the floor, Patrick asked Katya to dance.

When they stepped on to the floor, Imogen Punchard was already there, curving slow and perfect arcs with the Duke. The charming smile on her lips never wavered. The nine inches of air separating their bodies neither contracted nor expanded. Katya thought it a very stylish performance.

While circling with Patrick, she looked for Raymond. So far he had not moved from his position on the top table. It amused her to think that they were physically so close and yet he still did not realise she was here.

The dance floor was full now. Body was jostling against body, trying to catch the rhythm of the music. Sequins and tassels and beads were swaying and swinging and snagging. Polished pumps and satin shoes were drumming on the floor. Yet despite the energy, there was a sexlessness about the display due to the worthiness of the gathering, the relentless jollity of the music and the merciless lighting which disarmed all subtlety and artifice.

As she turned slowly in Patrick's arms, she saw Raymond. He was no longer listening to the Duchess. His mouth was set and his eyes were glowering at Katya with a mixture of surprise, annoyance and anger.

She returned a small, coquettish smile, then, following Patrick's lead, slowly swivelled away from him.

By the time she had circled round once more, he was standing at the edge of the dance floor, waiting for her, his fingers drumming against the black barathea of his dinner jacket.

Then suddenly Imogen came up to him and he turned away. Their conversation was brief and ended with Raymond giving a small shrug of the shoulders. For a moment Imogen gazed out towards the dancers as if scanning the crowd for the source of Raymond's interest, then she took him by the hand and led him back towards the table.

Another couple had joined the Punchards at their table now. Katya recognised the man as Raymond's friend, Simon Beaven. He was accompanied by a willowy blonde, who Katya assumed was his wife. Katya was intrigued to see her at last as the conversation invariably turned to her whenever she and Lucy had lunch. When Simon glanced across at the dance floor, Katya was sure he had seen her, but he looked straight through her as if she were a ghost.

Of course, as she knew full well, in his eyes she was not supposed to be there. She was meant to be a creature of the shadows, inhabiting a different world, a place removed from polite society where she could look after her lover's needs without the risk of embarrassment.

But at times even fish break the surface and come up for food, light and air. And she wanted a glimpse of Raymond's other side. So far she had seen only what he wanted to show her: the prisoner trapped in a loveless marriage. Now here on display was the public face: the happily married man, the concerned citizen.

Some forty minutes later the call came. One of the waiters, a balding man with a red-veined face, handed her a note with a nodding bow. The message was in Raymond's hand. 'Meet me in the Park Lane suite on the fourth floor when the raffle starts.' There was no signature.

She turned the note away from Patrick, who, while affecting disinterest, was still doing his best to read it upside down.

'It's nothing important,' she said casually. 'I'll be back shortly.'

The cabaret was nearly over. Kevin Sunshine, a reformed alcoholic, who twenty-five years ago had briefly toppled the Rolling Stones from their number one spot in the charts, had given a eulogy to the work of Crisis Call and was now engaged in a medley of his old hits.

She rose and headed for the exit. The crowd clapped politely as Kevin took his bow. His place in the centre of the dance floor was taken by a portly, grey-haired man.

'Only a few words,' he said. 'First of all I would like to thank you all for coming. Crisis Call's invaluable work in providing a twenty-four-hour help line for anyone in distress is funded entirely by voluntary donations, and without your generous support would not be possible.

'Now I would like to call upon the chair of the ball committee, Imogen Punchard, to draw the raffle prizes.'

A spotlight followed Imogen on to the dance floor. She turned to the tables and gave a broad smile through closed lips, acknowledging the applause.

'Thank you, thank you,' she said, her voice suddenly sharp and rasping through the microphone. 'Now I'm sure you are all dying to know who has won the fifty wonderful prizes which have been so generously donated, so without further ado we will start the draw.

'Which is the first one, Cyril?'

The grey-haired man glanced down at the sheet he held. 'Dinner for two and a cocktail of your choice at the El Sombrero restaurant.'

Katya left the Great Room. She walked along the passageway until she was in the main body of the hotel, then summoned the lift and pressed the button for the fourth floor. A porter in livery joined the lift on the first floor. He kept staring at her. Even when she turned away, there were his eyes, still staring, reflected in the mirror.

She was relieved when the lift stopped at the fourth floor, the door slid open, and she walked into the panelled passageway. She followed the signs, turning down three corridors and passing two maids in uniform. She turned once more and the Park Lane suite was in front of her.

No sound came from within. She rapped once on the door.

It opened immediately. Raymond, face flushed from champagne, stared down at her, beckoning her in.

The room had two double beds, a television, an easy chair, a table and a standard lamp. It was decorated in that particular international hotel style which meant that you could wake up anywhere in the world and not have the faintest idea where you were. The only clue in this room was the pair of reproduction prints of coaches in the snow redolent of Olde Englishe Charme.

'What on earth are you doing at the ball?' he asked. 'You must have known that Imogen was organising the damn thing.'

'I didn't think that was any reason not to go.' She smiled coquettishly. 'In fact, that made it interesting for me.'

'You must understand my position. If we are seen together at something like this, it could be disastrous. There would be nothing to be gained by embarrassing Imogen.'

'I've done nothing to embarrass her. I did not attempt to make any sort of contact with you or even acknowledge that I knew you. Remember, it was you who asked me up here.'

'I know.' He sighed and looked away. 'The man you're with. Who is he?'

The tone of his voice had changed. There was a sharpness she had not heard before. He did not try to disguise his feelings behind a pretence of nonchalance, and she admired his honesty in that.

'He's just a friend,' she answered. 'There's absolutely nothing between us.'

His hands were everywhere then, and she felt her body respond to each touch, to the urgency in him. She did not want to wait to undress. She wanted to reassure him, wanted to feel him inside her.

The strength of her own feeling surprised her. On the

sexual side, at least, she had thought that she was master, she was in control, she could mete out sex to him when and how she pleased. She had not expected to become a victim of her own sexuality, for her to crave after him as she did.

At that moment she did not want tenderness, she wanted to feel owned and possessed. Why, she was not sure – because, after all, she cherished her freedom.

Somehow Raymond picked up on her feelings, or maybe, after what had happened, he too was looking for a physical reaffirmation. He did something he never had before. While usually he was tender and loving, this time he laid her down on the bed, and, without foreplay or undressing, freed himself and penetrated her.

She wanted him so badly, she felt herself sucking him into her, hungry for him, unwilling to let go.

The bed shook and the fine lace of her dress scratched her back, but all she was aware of was the burning below and the hard, rhythmic thrusts which seemed to sever her in two.

'Yes,' she called. 'Yes, yes, yes!'

When finally they left the room, the porter she had seen in the lift was standing in the passage outside the suite. His eyes flicked from Katya to Raymond. 'I trust you are enjoying your evening, Mr Punchard.'

'Yes, thank you,' Raymond answered. He reached into his wallet, drew out a wad of notes and slipped them into the man's hand.

'That is very kind of you, sir.'

'Good night,' Raymond said, then added, under his breath, 'and happy retirement.'

When they returned to the ball, the draw of the raffle had only just finished.

'You missed all the excitement,' said Patrick Strevens as she rejoined him at the table.

'What?'

'I've just won a holiday for two.'

'How thrilling. Where?'

The smile left his face. 'Ostend.'

Thirteen

A uniformed chauffeur was waiting for her at the airport in Rome holding a postcard inscribed 'Punchard' in a surprisingly neat hand. Even inside the building, his bronzed and pitted face was hidden behind cap and sunglasses. She sympathised with the Italian love of secrecy.

She stopped in front of him and nodded.

'Signora Punchard?'

She would answer to that.

He picked up her two bags and led her out of the concourse. As the doors slid back, the wall of heat sucked her breath away. He led her to a waiting Lamborghini, shooed away a group of admiring small boys and ushered her to her seat.

If this was the chauffeur's car, she wondered what Signor Bianchini's was like. Although she had met very few of them so far, Raymond seemed to have interesting friends.

At first they drove through noisy, choked streets and along busy roads. It was a frantic journey. Like a man with something to prove, the chauffeur pumped the accelerator, wove between the other cars and screamed at anyone in his way.

After an hour and a half, they left the main road. They drove on for fifteen miles or so, entered a dense wood, then

87

turned down a bumpy dirt track. Every time the sump hit the ground, the chauffeur winced as if he, rather than the car, was taking the blow. They followed the track until the trees cleared, opening to a horizon of turquoise sea. There it ended in a pair of high wooden gates.

A camera mounted on a stone pillar swivelled towards them. The chauffeur gave a signal and, with a pneumatic sigh, the gates creaked open.

At the end of the drive, on a promontory of rock, stood the villa perched between the wood and the sea. The roof was of terracotta tiles, the walls of terracotta stucco, glowing dully in the fading sun.

As soon as the car stopped, a butler in a white tunic with a mandarin collar and gold buttons stepped out of the house and opened Katya's door.

The gulls were calling. Katya climbed out, turned her head to catch the last of the sun's rays, and filled her lungs with the warm salty air.

While the butler took her suitcases out of the boot, she strolled up the small sweep of steps to the front door. Through her shoes she could feel the heat of the stones, baked in the sun all day.

A maid dressed in grey and white stood on the top step. 'Buon giorno, signora. My name is Anna. If you will follow me, please.'

The maid led her through a yellow hall hung with modern abstract paintings to a long, low room opening on to the terrace outside. In a brown suede armchair sat a strikingly beautiful woman dressed in a silk sarong. She had high cheekbones, a swan neck and long golden hair.

'Welcome.' She rose to her feet, eyeing Katya up and down. 'You must be Katya Cornwale?'

'Yes.' Walking up, Katya stretched out her hand. 'And you are Signora Bianchini?'

The woman smiled indulgently. 'No, I am Carlotta Giobano.'

'I'm sorry,' Katya said, suddenly confused and nervous. 'I thought—'

'No need to apologise. Obviously Raymond neglected to brief you. My relationship with Stefano is much the same as yours with Raymond, so there is no need for you to feel anything other than relaxed here.

'Would you like something to drink? We have stocked up with Lipton's English tea.'

'Yes, please. Tea would be great.'

Carlotta issued instructions to the maid, then signalled to the seat next to her with a languid movement of her hand.

'Wonderful place this,' Katya said as soon as she had sat down. 'Has Signor Bianchini had it long?'

Carlotta grinned. 'In fact it's mine. Stefano gave it to me after we had been together for three years. I adore it. How long have you been with Raymond?'

'Only three months.'

'I think you are very brave being a mistress in England.'

'I've never thought of myself as brave,' Katya answered.

'Maybe not, but only because you must love him so much, you don't notice the sacrifice. I know that I would not like to be a mistress in England. They don't have any respect for you there because it has never been part of the culture.

'Here in Italy, as in many Latin countries, a rich and successful man like my Stefano would be expected to have a mistress – someone he could show off, be proud of. I don't want half the things he gives me – I have money of my own – but still he lavishes them on me. When we go out together, he wants me to be the one with the best clothes, the best jewellery. He wants to make other men jealous.' She smiled. 'I'm glad to say that sometimes he succeeds.'

The maid arrived. She poured weak tea into a glass, suspended a slice of lemon on a cocktail stick across the rim, and laid it down on the table. Katya thanked her. She did not have the heart to ask for milk.

'What about his family – do they have any idea of what's going on?'

Carlotta stretched lazily. 'You think they are that naive? Of course they do! They have known from the beginning. It would not surprise me if Stefano had asked his wife if she approved of me before our relationship began. Certainly if his family did not approve of me, or thought I was bringing dishonour to them, I would have known soon enough. I don't say they would choose the arrangement, but they accept it and understand it. It is common enough.

'You see, here in Italy, we understand the human heart. We know not to ask too much of a man. In England the wives want everything. So what happens? The men leave and they are left with nothing.'

After Katya had finished her tea, the maid led her up a flight of wooden steps and along a whitewashed passageway to the bedroom which she and Raymond were going to share for the next four days while he attended an international symposium in Rome.

It had white walls hung with modern abstract pictures and a huge double bed. Her suitcases had already been unpacked.

The maid strode across the room, heels tapping on the terracotta tiles. She threw open the shutters at the windows, letting in the air and the evening light. Beyond the balcony was only sea and sky.

'I hope the signora likes her room?'

'Yes.' Katya sighed contentedly. 'Very much.'

Later Katya viewed the time she and Raymond had spent in Carlotta's villa on the Mediterranean as a turning point in their relationship.

She had already explored every inch of his body by

then, as he had of hers, but something in the quality of the light, in its bright, unforgiving, searching gaze, seemed to make their nakedness more total. Even with the shutters closed and the blinds drawn against the scorching heat of the afternoon sun, the shadows were not dark enough to hide in.

With their physical nakedness, Katya liked to think that emotional and spiritual nakedness came too. In London, although they had spent much time together, somehow the jostling immediacy of each moment had not allowed time for the refinement of sensation. It had to be taken in raw gasps of pleasure or pain, or the lack of it tolerated in the dull passages in between.

Here it was different. On the afternoon of the second day she was in the room alone with Raymond. She was lying back on the bed, body warmed by the sun, nipples erect. His hair, his cheek was against her thigh. She could feel the slightest movement of his tongue and it made her gasp and shudder until the sensation suffused the whole of her.

As she relaxed, she imagined herself floating up towards the ceiling and looking down at the two of them, and she thought she saw their two auras blur and fuse together.

She had feared that going away with him would reveal a different Raymond, one who might be more distant than the one she knew. Yet away from the pressure he seemed to be gentler, a man of finer sensibilities, a man difficult not to love.

On the evening of the third day, when they retired to their room after dinner, Katya was very conscious of someone else in the room with them, and she knew that Raymond was thinking of Imogen.

He wrapped his arm around her and sighed. 'It's all so unfair.'

She was unsure whether he was referring to her,

Imogen or even himself. She did not ask him to explain. It was equally applicable to all three of them. They were locked together in a situation which could not be resolved without pain.

'I know.' She nodded slowly. 'What can I say?' Then she slipped the strap of her dress from her shoulder. As he stared for a moment at the dark areola of her breast half revealed and half hidden among the folds of bleached linen, she felt the spectre of Imogen leave them, and she smiled.

Fourteen

The first anniversary of the day Katya moved into the mews house fell on a Saturday so Raymond could not be with her; he was with his family at Bradstoke. She bought a cake anyway, a walnut cream, stuck a huge candle through its centre and celebrated alone.

She loved the mews house, was still deliriously happy with Raymond, had a thriving business; nevertheless, as she cut the cake, she felt uneasy.

When she had moved in, she had anticipated that being a married man's mistress would only be a temporary expedient; given time, the delicate equilibrium of the triangle would be disturbed and the position would be resolved one way or the other.

However, nothing much had changed in the last year. Raymond still went back home to Imogen virtually every night. He still emphasised what an impressionable age his three children were, and his duties as a family man – sentiments with which Katya fully sympathised. But as she looked into the future, she wondered how much longer she could live like this, being deprived of the man she loved for so much of the week.

'It's such a pity Raymond couldn't join us,' announced Tamsin when Katya had dinner with her later that week. 'I've never known anyone with so many evening engagements. How long have you been dating him now?'

'Fourteen months.'

'And still we haven't met.'

The kitchen of the Clapham house had rustic pine units, a Provençal tiled floor and a maze of brightly polished copper pans and dried flowers suspended from the ceiling.

Tamsin brought the cast-iron enamelled pot over from the Aga and placed it on a heatproof mat on the kitchen table. 'I should imagine you soon will be – well – thinking about things. You don't want to leave it too late.'

'I'm only twenty-nine,' Katya replied curtly.

'I know, but it's nice to have a few years of married life together before you start a family, and you don't want to leave *that* too long.'

She ladled the contents of the pot into three decorated Provençal bowls and handed one each to Katya and Douglas.

Douglas sniffed at his suspiciously. 'What's this?'

'It's Basque fish stew. I found the recipe in a magazine at the hairdresser.'

He returned it to her. 'Only a little for me, please.'

'Why only a little? You know how you like fish.'

'We're a long way from the Bay of Biscay for Basque fish stew.'

'It's only an interpretation of the dish. I got the fish from the supermarket. It's all chilled as soon as it's caught, so I'm told.'

'Even that?'

He pointed to a length of eel, complete with bone, swimming in the thick red sauce.

She smiled and, ignoring his request, put the bowl back on his mat. 'Yes, even that.'

'It's delicious,' said Katya, surreptitiously extracting a bone that had lodged itself in the roof of her mouth.

'I'm glad someone appreciates *haute cuisine*,' said Tamsin pointedly. 'Is Raymond a tricky eater, too?'

'He likes most things.'

'So have you . . .?'

'Have I what?'

'Discussed marriage yet?'

'No,' Katya answered, with a note of disapproval in her voice, trying to infer this was none of Tamsin's business.

Her sister continued regardless. 'Maybe it's time you did. There's a dynamic in any relationship. You don't want to risk it going off the boil.' She turned to Douglas. 'How long was it, dear, before you proposed to me?'

'Can't remember exactly.'

'It was ten months and five days,' she reminded him with a complacent smile. 'I'm sure Douglas would have got around to it himself in time, but men are sometimes rather slow about these things. Take a tip from me – there's no harm in letting a man know it's time he made some tactful enquiries about the size of your third finger. After fourteen months he ought to know his mind. If he's not ready to go to the jewellers then, maybe he's not going to go at all.'

'I'm quite happy with the way things are at the moment,' Katya said firmly.

Tamsin laid down her knife and fork. 'But, dearest, you must think about the future. When you're eighteen it doesn't matter if you are in a relationship which is going nowhere. At twenty-nine it does. You can't afford to just let things drift. If he really loves you, if he cares about you—'

'He does really love me,' she interrupted.

'Then he should do the decent thing and marry you.'

Katya shuddered and sipped her wine, though suddenly it tasted like vinegar. 'Let's change the subject.'

'No,' Tamsin insisted. 'I know it's not easy, but these questions have to be faced. If he's not prepared to marry you after dating you for this long, I think that tells you that you should be looking very closely at the relationship.

We're your nearest family and you've told us next to nothing about him. The first thing that must happen is that Douglas and I must meet him. You give us a date – any date – and we'll be there. When's it to be?'

Katya had dreaded this moment. She had known from the beginning that at some time she would have to tell her sister the truth. She did not think she could put it off any longer. 'There's no point in a meeting,' she said finally. 'He can't marry me.'

'What do you mean?'

'I'm sorry, I haven't been strictly honest with you. Raymond can't marry me because he's married already. There are children, complications. So now you know.'

The only sound was the whirr of the extractor fan. Tamsin stared at her sister with stony eyes, then looked away. 'The thought had crossed my mind but, naturally, I dismissed it.'

Katya shuffled some coley on to her fork. 'Other people's lives can't all be as neat and tidy as yours. You were lucky. You found Douglas. I'm just doing what you did. Following my heart.'

'Katya, there is no comparison. Douglas was single. Raymond, you now tell us, is married with children. For God's sake, you don't want to end up as someone's long-term mistress, do you?'

'All I know is that I've got to be with him. I have no choice in the matter.'

'Don't talk nonsense,' Tamsin replied. 'Everyone has a choice. Now eat up your stew while I think about it.'

The taxi turned another corner and entered a street of red-brick terraced houses identical to the one which they had just passed through.

'I'm perfectly happy,' Katya protested. 'Help is the last thing I need.'

Tamsin put away her lipstick and snapped her bag shut.

'It'll do no harm for you to talk to some people. You're so close to it all, you can't see it.'

'I'm sorry if my private life embarrasses you. I shouldn't have told you.'

'It's not that, Katya – though I admit it's not something I would want everyone to know, and I dread to think what Mother would have made of it. I just can't bear the thought of you throwing yourself away on someone who's using you.'

'I'm sure he would marry me if he could.'

'But, as you said yourself, he can't.'

'Someone not marrying you because he can't is very different from someone who won't.'

'Either way, you're still on the same shelf.'

The taxi slowed down, and the driver tugged at the glass partition separating him from his passengers. 'Do you know where this place is?' he asked.

'I'm afraid not. We haven't been there before.'

'Maybe this is an omen,' ventured Katya. 'We should forget the whole idea. I don't share this obsession of yours with marriage.'

'It's a very sensible institution.'

'Raymond really loves me – that can't be said about every married couple. And I have my freedom – having a man coming home asking "What's for dinner?" every evening would be so claustrophobic. I need time for myself. In fact, for a girl running her own business, I have the ideal arrangement.'

Tamsin shuddered. 'Stop trying to convince yourself, Katya! It's no good. How many men are out there? Twenty million? Fifty? And you, an attractive girl with a good brain and a sense of humour, have to choose one who's married.'

'It's not a question of numbers,' Katya protested.

'What? Are you telling me the choice isn't big enough?'

'No. What I'm saying is that if you fall in love, that's

that. Raymond is a very exceptional man – one in many millions.'

'But why out of everyone did you choose a married man, Katya?'

'As I told you, it just happened.'

'Nothing, but nothing, just happens,' Tamsin said firmly. 'It happens because you make it happen, because you chose him. And why did you choose him, Katya? I'll tell you why – I'm your sister so I should know. You chose a married man because deep down you are lacking the confidence to enter into a proper adult relationship. That's why you ought to talk to someone.'

She put her hand over Katya's and squeezed it. 'I know it hasn't been easy for you. It hasn't been easy for me either. I get dreams even now. Just when I think I am OK, suddenly I am back in that car again. Mother is calling out, the windscreen is like crackleware and I'm trying to brace myself, ready for the impact.'

Katya shuddered. 'You think our parents' death has something to do with it?'

'I don't think; I know.'

The taxi stopped outside a house in a terrace of Victorian red brick. Only the garden and the doorknocker placed it apart from its neighbours.

'I'm only doing this to prove how wrong you are,' Katya protested as she got out. 'I can't guarantee that I'll stay more than ten minutes.'

Tamsin nodded. 'Just see how it goes. Good luck.'

Katya watched her sister depart, then flicked the latch on the wooden gate. The small neat bed of lavender and roses was splattered with London grime.

She walked up the path and rapped on the door. It was opened almost immediately by a tall blonde woman in a long brown woollen skirt and matching cardigan. 'Hi, I'm Jackie.'

Katya held out her hand. 'I'm Katya Cornwale.'

'Katya,' the woman corrected. 'We don't use surnames here.' She shook Katya's hand with limp fingers as if frightened to crush it. 'Come on in. I'll introduce you to the others.'

She led Katya through to the lounge where the oatmeal sofa had been pushed back against the mauve wall. A group of women sat in a circle on the brown carpet. A cloud of cigarette smoke hovered above them.

'This is Katya,' Jackie announced. 'It's her first time here so I'm sure you'll all want to make her feel welcome.'

Eight pairs of eyes looked up at her. Eight smiles followed, from the sincere to the merely polite.

The group shuffled around to make room for her. Feeling awkward and self-conscious she squatted down on the floor in the space which had opened up for her. The woman next to her offered her a mug of coffee; she accepted gratefully.

'We don't believe in setting a formal structure for these meetings,' Jackie explained as soon as she had returned to her place, three along from Katya. 'We all have one thing in common. For better or worse, we all are or have been in relationships with married men, so no one is going to be judgemental. We are here so that you can voice your fears, and if anyone wants to break free from this dependency, we'll offer such support as we can.'

She glanced along the group. 'Who's going to start the meeting off today?'

Katya stared rigidly ahead like a schoolgirl trying to avoid the teacher's eye.

'Yup, I'll start,' said a woman with cropped grey hair. 'In my experience, men suck.'

'You're lucky,' the woman next to her countered. 'In my experience they only want it done to them.'

A ripple of laughter ran through the group and Katya could feel the tension lifting.

'Yes, I'd like to speak,' a third woman interjected. She

had a pointed chin and long blonde hair with mousy roots.

'I did what I said I was going to do last week. I rang him up. Though immediately I heard his voice, I thought I was sunk. It sounds even better on the phone than in real life – it's got a kind of deep resonance that gets you inside.'

She took a quick drag on the cigarette parked between her fingers before she went on.

'Anyway, I got the words out. I don't think I would have managed it if I hadn't rehearsed them first. Made it easier, like reciting a poem. "I don't need this, and I'm not going to put up with it any longer."

'He went very quiet for a while, then he said, "Look, I'll be around later." And I said, "No. Don't you understand what I'm saying. It's over."

'I thought I was going to crack up then, so while I was still sounding all right, I hung up.'

A murmur of congratulations came from the group.

'Well done, Liz,' said Jackie. 'Keep it up. We're all behind you. Just try not to see him one day at a time until you don't miss him any more. OK?'

Four or five of the other members of the group each had their say. Then again Jackie's eyes swept the circle. This time they settled on Katya.

'As this is your first time, Katya, would you like to tell us something about why you've come here? You needn't, of course, if you're not ready yet, and we don't want any names. It's entirely up to you.'

Katya shrugged. 'I'm not exactly sure why I'm here myself.'

'You are someone's mistress?'

'I'm my own woman first. But, yes, I do have a relationship with a married man.'

'You're happy about this?'

'I'm ecstatically happy to be with him. Of course it would be much easier for both of us if he happened not to be married, but there we are – you can't dictate who you're going to fall in love with, can you?'

Jackie nodded slowly. 'One of the things that has come up regularly at these meetings might surprise you – the very fact that the man is married is often one of the main reasons why the relationship starts in the first place. If the same men were single very few of these relationships would have ever got off the ground.

'I know that is hard to believe – I find it hard myself – especially if you are so deep into a relationship you can't look outside. But I know it to be true. We've got to accept that for one reason or another we are people who consciously or subconsciously believe that married men are better suited to fulfil our needs than single men. We should all look at ourselves and ask why that might be so. Any suggestions?'

'Married men have an emotional maturity that single men lack,' said someone.

Two of the women shook their heads in disagreement.

'If a man's already married, you don't have to make a commitment to a full-time relationship with all that entails,' answered another.

'And why don't you want to make that commitment, Susan?' Jackie asked.

'Because I enjoy my freedom, and don't want the responsibility.'

Jackie nodded. 'We don't want to take on the responsibility because at the moment we are lacking the self-confidence to see it through. And why don't we have that confidence?'

'Low self-esteem,' said the woman to Katya's right. Two others nodded.

'Exactly,' said Jackie. She sipped at her coffee. 'How many people here reckon they are in dead-end relationships?'

Eight hands went up. Katya kept hers in her lap.

'So why are you still there, then? Ellen, you tell me.'

'Habit, I suppose. That and lack of confidence.'

'Low self-esteem again,' said Jackie. 'If we had the confidence I think most of us would walk away from the relationships we're in. It's just a question of having the courage to do it.'

'I don't agree,' Katya interrupted. 'Obviously I can only speak for myself, but I'm with my man only because I love him.'

'And you don't resent the fact that you have to share him?'

'Obviously, I would prefer to have his undivided attention, but that's not a choice I have. I much prefer to share him rather than have a lesser man to myself. He is the one I want.'

'That's the way you see it now,' Jackie answered. 'Most of the women here believed that was why they were staying in their relationships. Then, as they thought about it, they found there were other subtler reasons, too. Some are terrified of a full-time relationship because of a fear of being hurt, being abandoned or being controlled. Others are there because they are still trying to resolve their unsatisfactory relationship with their parents and subconsciously seek a triangular relationship to do this. Others because they have been used to emotional chaos ever since childhood and need the excitement.

'All we are trying to do here is help you to break the pattern. You get a raw deal being a mistress. And most of the time it's leading nowhere. Why on earth are we prepared to accept it? Only because we don't ask for more from a relationship. We settle for second best because we lack the confidence to demand more. And if we can't get it from the man we're with at the moment, we should seriously consider leaving him and getting it from someone else.

'So we should ask ourselves why we are the way we

are. Why do we have low self-esteem? For each of us the answer is probably different. In my case I think it was because my mother and father desperately wanted a boy and did nothing to disguise their disappointment when I was born. I felt rejected from the beginning. I can understand the process intellectually, but dealing with it emotionally is something quite different.'

Her body rocked to and fro as she talked. 'I think I am getting there now. But it was only after I'd dealt with my parents' rejection that I felt strong enough to give Jonathan the heave-ho.

'OK, so I want you all to think back and ask yourselves whether there is something in your past which might be the cause of your low self-esteem.' She turned to Katya. 'Well . . .?'

Katya was silent for a moment as she thought back to her parents, back to the crash, back to her school days. She shuddered. 'I'm sorry. I think I made a mistake coming here. I've got many problems but I don't think low self-esteem is one of them. If you will excuse me?'

She rose then and, ignoring Jackie's protestations, made for the door.

Fifteen

That night, as Katya lay alone in bed, she could not help thinking of Jackie's words. She, Katya Cornwale, a victim of low self-esteem? It seemed impossible.

She refused to be a victim – she did not have the victim mentality – and had done everything she could so that she maintained control of her life. She had dealt with the loss of her parents without cracking up; almost anything would be easy after that.

Apart from the crash which had caused her parents' death, there was, however, another memory which defied her best attempts to put it to rest.

The incident had happened seven months after she had arrived in London. She had been dating at the time Clive Petri, a well-built blond boy who was studying to be a doctor.

She was a virgin then. Some of her contemporaries, she knew, ridiculed her prim ways with men, and thought she was impossibly out of date. But she kept her own counsel. She was sure her mother would have been a virgin when she married, and Katya was determined to be one too.

If her school friends had all been so deeply in love they could not bear to wait for the wedding night, Katya would have understood. But Miranda and Donatella had done it entirely out of curiosity, Robina and Jenny out of fear of losing their boyfriends, and Emma to keep up with the others. Only Lisa had protested undying love, and that love had wilted in a week when her boyfriend had gone off with her best friend.

If things were getting serious with a date, Katya thought it only fair to explain her views on premarital sex so that he was not under any illusions. Sometimes the man would listen in stony silence with a look on his face as if to say, 'I've shelled out for three hot dinners, and now you tell me.' One actually said as much to her out loud. Another suggested she become a nun. A third asked her where she had been living for the last twenty years. A fourth, a lawyer, asked for further and better particulars of what exactly was off limits.

Some of the men never rang her again. In those days, she did not care. She knew that the right man would be prepared to wait.

Clive Petri had taken her lecture on premarital sex very well. He had said that it was a point of view and later, warming to the theme, added that he respected her for it. He had not been put off. In fact, he had rung her almost every day.

After a month, Katya made a small relaxation to her strict rule. Already he had felt her breasts through her dress as he kissed her. Now, on the deeper kisses, she allowed him to slip his hands under her dress.

One Wednesday he had been working in the casualty department all day and seemed very tense when he came to pick her up. They went out to dinner in a cheap bistro, talked about going around to some friends of his, but in the end hired a video – a Merchant-Ivory film they had both missed the first time round – and went back to her flat to watch it.

They began by sitting on the sofa side by side, his arm around her. By the end of the trailers, he was leaning over, cuddling and kissing her.

Something must have been unsettling him, though, because she remembered that he got up then, went to the bathroom and, when he returned, switched off all the lights except for the old standard lamp by the television. The flat was in darkness apart from a funnel of dusty light above and below the dull-glowing fringed shade and the small screen with its images of a sun-drenched Italian town.

The springs in the sofa rocked as he sat down. Moving closer, his arm gripped her shoulder. She could smell the scent of his skin now. Whatever expensive aftershave Clive might wear, among the limes and oranges and musk the acrid smell of antiseptic hospital soap was always there somewhere. Katya did not mind, for she admired him for what he did.

He moved closer still, caressed her cheek, then guided her head towards his. She liked the way Clive kissed. She thought it must be odd being a doctor, though, dealing with bodies all day. She had asked him once whether he ever had erotic fantasies about his patients. He had denied it. There was nothing erotic, he said, about illness and pain. But she only half believed him. His reply had been so pat, so deadpan, it was as if it had been taught at medical school.

He unfastened the middle button of her blouse and his hand slipped inside and cupped her left breast. He teased the nipple until she felt it hard against the cotton.

She felt her blood race, her body bloom. She had had the feeling many times, and she knew what was happening to her and how to control it.

He undid two more buttons. His mouth followed his hand, sucking, flicking with his tongue. Then his hand went down further, freeing the button on her jeans.

She stiffened. She gripped his hand, pulling it away. 'We're missing the film.'

'So what?'

'It's a film I've always wanted to see.'

'Watch it then.'

'That's not what I meant. I want you to stop doing that.'

'What?' he asked.

'You know. What you're doing.'

'You don't like it then?'

'I didn't say that. I just want you to stop doing it, that's all.'

'What's the big deal? It's not as if this is our first date.' He tugged playfully at the legs of her jeans.

'No, Clive. Don't be a bore.'

He tugged again, more forcefully this time.

'No, Clive. I said no and I mean no.'

Suddenly his eyes were like marbles. He swivelled around and was tugging so hard her weight was thrown on to her shoulders. Her whole body was lifted into the air.

She kicked out at him, still holding the waistband of her jeans. Then a nail broke. The band slipped from her fingers. She fell, landing on her shoulder blades, hitting the side of the sofa, sliding on to the floor.

Then suddenly he was on top of her, pulling at her knickers, fumbling at his fly.

She slapped him with her free hand, she pulled his ear. But he seemed to shake her off, and then it was too late. Already he had slid inside her. Already his breathing was clogged. Then he clenched his teeth and shuddered and she felt him shrivel.

It was all over before it had begun.

He lay there for a moment on top of her, catching his breath, his weight on his elbows, his head lowered. 'I'm sorry,' he whispered, 'I'm sorry,' as if somehow words were enough.

'Get off me,' she said quietly. The control in her voice surprised her. She was beyond anger. Her body was so cold and empty, it felt as if she had disowned it, retreated to some other place.

In that moment she wondered why she had not

struggled more when he was on top of her. Maybe if she had struck out more forcibly she could have stopped him.

Was it fear that had immobilised her? Or had there been a part of her that had wanted to feel him inside her, wanted to be like other girls?

Now she was. She felt the tacky wetness between her legs and the weight and scent of Clive's body on hers.

He pushed himself up and stood. 'I'm sorry. I really am. It'll be better next time. I promise. Now we've . . . well, broken the ice.'

Was he just pretending? she wondered. Or did he really not understand?

Katya had never told anyone about that night, not even Tamsin. If she had, she felt sure Tamsin would now be making some connection between it and her present situation in the same way as she had with the loss of their parents.

It was true that even after the feelings of humiliation and disgust had lessened, her distrust of men had remained, and at the same time she had lost that sense of pride in her own body.

But Katya did not want to think like that. As far as she was concerned, she had chosen Raymond only because she loved him, because they had to be together. She did not want Tamsin or Jackie demeaning powerful and noble emotions by telling her that she only felt the way she did because she was trying to replicate the emotional chaos of her childhood, was searching for a father figure or was terrified of a full-time relationship.

Twice now the stuff of nightmares had swooped down and touched her, and both times she had tried to continue as before. Often in her life she had felt alone and isolated and empty, but from somewhere deep inside she had tried to find an inner strength to steady her and pull her through.

It was that same resolve, she was sure, which had given her the strength not to conform to society's laws and risk social exorcism to become Raymond's mistress. She knew it to be right because the still small voice inside her told her so.

To Tamsin, her love might be a knee-jerk reaction to the experiences of her youth, but, to Katya, it was about the meeting of two souls.

Sixteen

'I've got to talk to you.'

Lucy Drew lived on her nerves so Katya was not surprised when she lit up as soon as she sat down. She drew on the cigarette once, then stubbed it out in the ashtray with such force she broke it in two.

'Can I get you a drink?' Katya asked.

'Yes, please. Sparkling mineral water would be nice.'

Katya knew immediately that something was wrong. On the many occasions she had seen her over the last year, Lucy had never drunk mineral water.

By the time Katya had brought a glass of water through from the kitchen, a second cigarette lay broken in the ashtray. She put the glass on the table.

Lucy thanked her, but left it untouched. 'I really don't know what I'm going to do. Simon's been no help at all.'

'You still haven't told me what's happened.'

Lucy looked her straight in the eye for a moment, then her face creased as if she were about to burst into tears. 'I'm pregnant.'

Katya's initial reaction was to congratulate her, but she checked herself. 'How does Simon feel about it?' she asked.

'He's not keen. When we've talked about children in the past, he's said he'd really like to have a baby with me. But now the moment's come, he seems to have changed his mind. He says it's not the time, that I should wait.'

'Until when?'

'Until he's left Jane and we can be together. But – Christ – it's been six years now and I'm still waiting!'

'What do you want to do?'

Lucy picked her cigarette packet up from the table, twitched it open, snapped it shut. 'You know, I never thought I would be the maternal type. I thought it might be nice to have a baby one day, but I wasn't really bothered either way. My reaction has taken me totally by surprise. Ever since the doctor confirmed it, I have felt so painfully conscious of it growing inside me and so protective towards it I can think of nothing else. I'd rather cut off one of my own limbs than hurt it.

'There are practical considerations, too. I'm thirty-four now, and have always thought that if I was going to have a baby I should have it before I was thirty-five. Medically it makes a lot of sense and you don't want to be too old to share things with them as they grow up. You don't conceive so easily as you get older either, so this might be my last chance. It's almost as if it's meant.'

'Keep it then,' Katya said firmly.

'I can't.'

'Why on earth not?'

'I've told you already. Simon's against it.'

'So what? It's your body, your baby. If you want it, you have it.'

'It wouldn't be fair on Simon.'

'He can't dictate to you what you can or cannot do. He doesn't have that right.'

Lucy looked at Katya mournfully. 'Do you think he'll still love me when I'm plump? I couldn't bear it if he stopped loving me.'

'I don't see why not. You'll only be like that because you're bearing his baby, and afterwards—'

'Afterwards I'll be all stretch marks and sagging tits

and varicose veins . . .' Lucy's eyes suddenly filled with tears. 'I want it so badly,' she wailed. 'And this could be my last chance.'

Katya moved to her side and wrapped her arm around her to comfort her. Lucy's head fell against hers and her hair, touched with tears, was wet against Katya's cheek.

'Tell me that Simon won't leave me if I have the baby?' Lucy pleaded.

'He won't leave you if he loves you,' Katya answered. 'He should be flattered. Wanting his baby is the greatest compliment a woman can pay to a man.'

'If he really loved me, why hasn't he left Jane by now?' she said quietly. 'I wish I could be certain of him.'

'If you still can't be sure of him after all these years,' Katya ventured, 'maybe you ought to think about finding someone else – someone who is free to marry you.'

'But it's him that I want.'

'If he really loves you, he'll want to make you happy. And if having a baby is what you want, I don't see why he shouldn't go along with that too. Few men can resist children once they are there – so friends tell me.'

The smile returned to Lucy's face. 'Maybe you're right,' she said, her lips so close to Katya's ear that a whisper was enough. 'Maybe I will have it after all.

'I'll try to be a perfect mother – and it's not as if the child wouldn't have a father either. Simon's around three times a week and later, when we're married, he'll be there all the time. He's bound to come round to the idea in the end.'

'That's right.' Katya nodded. 'You can't live for him alone. This is your decision. You must do what you think is right.'

'Thanks, you don't know what a difference talking to you has meant.' Lucy beamed at her. 'I can't wait for the place to be full of fluffy toys and smelling of baby powder. Promise me now you'll be a godmother.'

Seventeen

The telephone call came four days later in mid-afternoon. Katya ripped off her smock and raced around to the hospital.

Although it was only a day procedure, Simon had booked a private room for her – as if that made any difference.

The air was hot and stale and the radiators full on; still Lucy lay there shivering in the bed.

'Come in,' she called weakly. She tried a smile but it was a feeble little thing that died as soon as it began.

A huge bunch of bold, bright flowers stood on the table by the window. Katya assumed that they must have come from Simon. She did not read the card, but wondered what he could possibly have said. What words were there? How could he even say he loved her after this?

Katya carried the spare chair to the side of the bed and sat down. She took hold of Lucy's hand and squeezed it, hoping somehow that she could feed her with strength.

'I feel I've let you down,' said Lucy finally.

'Not me.'

'All those brave words.' Her voice was distant and detached, like a sleepwalker's. 'When you said them, they seemed so right – and I did want it so. But the more I thought about the situation, the more I realised how impossible it was.

'Simon is used to me perfect – not fat or with stretch marks. What was I going to do when he came around? What if it yelled while we were making love? Don't you see? He comes to me to escape from home life, from domesticity. I can't give him the same.

'But I never expected to feel so empty inside.' She looked at Katya with naked, pleading eyes. 'Nothing's worth this feeling.'

That evening when Raymond came round to her flat, Katya did her best to smile and be cheerful but she could not get out of her head the image of Lucy in that lonely hospital bed, empty, scraped clean.

As she looked across at Raymond lying back on the sofa, tie loosened, top button undone, sipping the whisky and water she had just brought him, she wondered how he would behave if the same thing happened to her.

Raymond might be a family man when at home, but here he was a young man again – a stud proud of his conquest. She hoped that his conventional side, which had been dominant for all those years before she had met him, would not reassert itself. However, the more she thought about it, the less sure she became that he would not become awkward and embarrassed and treat the child as a tiresome inconvenience or, worse, an embarrassment: a permanent reminder of lascivious indiscretion.

Of course he would not be able to stop her having it, but she wanted the best for her child and, to her, that meant having a mother and a father who both played a full role in the child's life. She had known what it was like not to have parents to turn to when she desperately needed love or when there was a problem at school. She did not want any child of hers to have to learn how to cope with that numb feeling inside.

She moved over to the sofa, stroked Raymond's cheek, and, as he turned towards her, kissed him on the lips.

'Tell me,' she said lightly, 'what would you say if I told you I was expecting?'

He stared at her for a moment, silent. His jaw made a small downward movement before he regained his composure and held it in check.

'Expecting what?'

'A baby, of course.'

'You're talking hypothetically, aren't you?' he asked, a tinge of hope in his voice.

'Yes.'

He exhaled slowly. 'For a second I thought . . .' He grinned. 'You shouldn't have done that. You got me quite worried for a moment, joking like that.'

She grinned back at him and forced a smile into her eyes. It was not a joke and she didn't think it was funny. He had said so little, but it was enough to confirm her fears. In his voice there had not been the warmth she had prayed for, the excitement at the prospect of a new life of their own devising, or the tone of paternal concern for the unborn: there had been panic and fear.

No child of hers would be spending evenings upstairs with strict instructions not to make a sound when Uncle Raymond came to visit.

'How do you see our future together?' she asked him as lightly as she could, while running her finger down his ear.

His head twisted to one side as he thought for a moment before replying. 'One day I hope we'll be able to get married.'

'What do you mean by "one day"?'

'Obviously, it can't be for a while – the children are at a very vulnerable age at the moment and Imogen has never done anything I could blame her for – it wouldn't be fair on them. But it's you I love, and we are very happy as we are, aren't we?'

'Yes. It's just that I want to spend more time with you.

We are never together for long enough.'

A shudder went down her spine. As she looked into the future, she could see the bloom leave her cheeks, her skin wrinkle, her body sag and still she would be sitting on the kelim sofa in the mews house waiting for Raymond to call.

If he truly loved her, she felt sure he would want to express that love in other ways than physical passion. He would want them to be able to have a life together. She was not interested in the kind of love which could be compartmentalised into neat little boxes, or trivialised into sex; love needed space in which to grow, or else it would wither and die.

They had nurtured their love in secret for fifteen months and now it was strong and true. The time had come for it to break out of the dark. There would have to be changes.

'Where's Imogen tonight?' she asked. Raymond had already told her that he could spend the whole night with her, so she knew Imogen must be away.

'Down at Bradstoke.'

'Are the children with her?'

'Yes, it's half-term.'

'Good,' she said, excited. 'Then if everyone's away, this is the perfect opportunity for you to show me Phillimore Gardens.'

'Why do you want to see it so much?' he asked.

'Curiosity. I want to see where the man I love lives. Is that so strange?'

'It's not a good idea,' he answered. 'Maria, our maid, will still be there, and if she finds out, it'll get back to Imogen.'

'You could ring her and give her the evening off. Even if she was around, there would be no reason for her to suspect anything – I'm your picture restorer, after all.

'We can just drop in for a drink on the way to dinner.

118

I'll even wash up the glasses and plump up the cushions.
No one will be any the wiser. Then I'll never ask again.
Please.'

'OK,' he agreed reluctantly. 'Just a quick drink.'

It was still light when Raymond's car drew to a halt
outside the huge white stucco confection off Phillimore
Gardens. Although she had not told him, she already knew
what it looked like from the outside because, not long
after they had met, curious, she had taken a taxi ride
along the road.

As Raymond walked towards the front door with its
box pyramids and bright brass knobs, she noticed the swell-
ing and relaxation of the muscles on either side of his
jaw; he was grinding his teeth – something she had never
seen him do before. His shoulders were tense, too, and
his eyes had the quicksilver look of a fox sensing danger.

He was nervous, she thought, because here, for the
first time, the two different parts of his life were uniting.
He was bringing her into the place that represented the
heart of the family. Instinctively she reached out to slip
her hand in his to reassure him. Then, realising her
mistake, she checked herself.

Just before he reached the raised steps, he looked down
at the basement windows. None of the lights were on.

'We're in luck,' he said, relieved. 'Maria must have gone
with her friend to the cinema.' He turned the key in the
lock and ushered her inside.

Katya stood for a moment in the half-light of the
hallway while he switched the lights on and the burglar
alarm off. Then she followed him through the marble-
floored hall with Chinese yellow walls and up a flight of
stairs to the drawing room.

She eyed the dragged blue walls, the blue silk curtains,
the patterned carpet, the velvet sofas, and suppressed a
yawn.

This was decorating by numbers – big numbers with lots of noughts on them, it was true – but to her way of thinking there was no pzazz, no imagination.

She had expected better of Imogen Farleigh. If the decoration was anything to go by, the dashing captain of the school netball team, whose casual glance of acknowledgement had been enough to send a girl on to cloud nine, had grown up to be a very conventional woman.

'What would you like to drink?' he asked.

'What have you got?'

'Anything you like.'

'Champagne, then.'

She was not worried what she drank herself, but she wanted him to drink champagne.

He opened a cupboard door beneath a bookcase concealing a refrigerator. He drew out a bottle.

'So what do you think of the house?' he asked as he handed her a glass.

She wanted him to relax, not to feel threatened nor to be forced on to the defensive. 'Very grand and very suitable,' she answered. She walked over to the huge windows and lifted one of the silk curtains. Below was a beautifully tended garden leading to an elaborate lattice-work temple.

'This place must be great for parties,' she said. She imagined the kind of parties she would hold here, and felt sure they would be a lot more fun than Imogen's. 'Will you show me around?'

'Sure.' He led her back down the stairs, across the hall and into the library with its green walls, portraits of Imogen's relatives and fine Chippendale desk. She glanced only briefly at the photographs on the desk of the three smiling children before walking on.

Her heart went out to the children. Inevitably, there would be a difficult period of readjustment ahead for them.

Surely, though, it was less damaging for their parents to separate cleanly now rather than after years of bitter wrangling?

He showed her the dining room, with its mahogany table and black and gilt Regency chairs. He showed her the breakfast room, with its custom-made stippled units and circular table overlooking the garden.

Then, reclimbing the stairs, Raymond headed back towards the drawing room.

'What about the next floor?' she asked.

'There's nothing to see up there. Only bedrooms.'

She could tell that he did not want to take her up there.

'Please,' she insisted. 'I would love to see it.'

Without waiting for a reply, she headed up the broad carpeted stairs to the second floor. Reluctantly, he followed.

On the landing she turned left. The first door along was ajar. She pushed it open and walked inside.

It was his dressing room. On the red-striped walls were five framed engraved plaques with the cipher of the Queen's Award for Industry, which she thought of as the businessman's equivalent of gold discs. Beneath them were photographs and engravings of steam engines. There was even a stationmaster's hat and green and red flags.

She started to laugh.

'What's so funny?' he asked, coming up behind her.

'I'm sorry. I didn't expect one of England's most powerful tycoons to be a closet train-spotter.'

He picked up the hat and ran a finger lovingly around the rim. 'This was my grandfather's. It took him twenty-five years to earn it, and all the family were so proud of him when he did.'

'Was he the father of your father – the oil company executive?'

'Yes.'

She glanced down at the small single bed; the chintz headboard and matching quilted cover were in pristine condition.

'And this is where you sleep?' she asked.

'Some of the time. Usually I sleep with Imogen. I have for sixteen years. If suddenly I were to stop now, she would be bound to be suspicious.'

He led her along the corridor and into the neighbouring room. 'This is the guest room,' he said.

It was done out in yellow, with two single beds, a needlework rug over the fitted carpet, and prints on the walls. Katya only had time to glance inside before Raymond strode back along the landing.

'What's in here?' she asked, pointing to the door opposite the stairs.

His anxious eyes turned towards her as she pushed it open.

The walls were ragged dusky pink, the curtains cream silk interlaced with chintz. In the centre of the room stood a bed with a huge canopy of silk and chintz. From the number of cupboards alone, she knew this must be the master bedroom.

Her pulse raced. This was where Raymond returned after he left her, curling up in the sheets, banishing her from his memory, safe, closeted in the bosom of the family. This was where Imogen's reign resumed. Here, especially here, he must not be allowed to forget her.

Raymond hovered by the door. He watched her as she walked around the room, looking at the tapestry chairs and the three occasional tables cluttered with enamel boxes.

'Don't you think we ought to go downstairs?' he asked.

'In a minute.'

What he meant, she knew, was that her being in Imogen's bedroom made him feel uncomfortable. It was a lapse in good taste, a breach of the unwritten rule that it was all right to have affairs provided no one knew and the sanctity of the home was preserved. It was a point of view, she granted.

She picked up one of the enamel boxes. On the lid were two lovers sitting side by side in a leafy glade. Inside was an inscription in calligraphy so florid that at first she could not decipher the words. She called to him: 'Raymond, can you read this for me, please?'

She did not care what the inscription said, but she was determined to get him to follow her into the room.

He came up behind her and took it from her. He studied it, squinting under the light of the lamp.

'Forever true,' he said finally, triumphantly.

Already her hands were on him. She ran one finger along the back of his right ear, lightly stroking the lobe.

He brushed it away. 'Not here.'

'Why not here?' she asked mischievously.

'Because it's not the place.'

'It's just that I'm suddenly in the mood. When I'm like this, it would be a crime to waste it.'

'The answer is no.'

Her eyes flashed at him. 'I'm not asking you to do anything,' she said. 'But there's no harm in me just kissing you, is there?'

She stood on tiptoe, straining until she was in range of his mouth, and while he stared rigidly ahead, ignoring the whole thing, she planted a kiss on his lips.

She could tell that it was only with effort that he did not respond, and that the effort was greater the second time around. She found his mouth open a fraction, then, and she let the tip of her tongue roam over his teeth.

He offered only token resistance as she loosened his tie and undid the buttons of his shirt and let her fingers scramble over his chest.

She could tell he was struggling for control. But she knew she was the stronger of the two. He could not walk away from the thrill of her fingers and her lips.

When he was firmly in her power, she laid him down on the floor by the tapestry rug, stripped off his clothing and mounted him.

Although the pleasure of the moment was writ large over his face and in the taut muscles of his neck, he said not a word. It was as if he believed that passivity muted the betrayal. But there was nothing passive about the way his body responded to her, about his suppressed sighs, about the fire in him, and about the way that once it was over, forgetting himself and where he was, he hugged her and buried his face in her breasts and told her there was nobody but her. Prophetically, she hoped.

All his earlier inhibitions about making love in this room, in this holy of holies of the family, had been stripped away. The logic of ecstasy had taken over and it had only one rule: it was supreme and nothing must stand in its way.

She thought it extraordinary that there were still so many women of Imogen's class who never bothered to learn how to please men, who took more trouble with the flowers than with their sex lives. What hope, she wondered, had a marriage where ecstasy had died, where there was only the husk of friendship left, when she was there, a force of renewal, offering everything that had been lost?

Raymond had been living a blissfully cosy life of deceit for too long. It was time to bring it out into the open, for him to prove his love.

She rose off him, lifting herself up slowly. Then, picking up her clothes on the way, she headed towards the small door beside the bed.

She had guessed right. It was the en suite bathroom. There were black and white tiles on the walls and prints of horses in black and gold Hogarth frames.

She studied the room. She wanted to leave some sign

124

so that Imogen would realise that another woman had been there, something unintentional which Raymond would not notice. The question was, what?

She walked over to the mirrored medicine cabinet above the basin and flicked it open. She eyed the shelves. Neatly set out in rows were aspirin, Alka Seltzer, cough mixture, moisturiser, night cream, cleanser, toner and an anti-wrinkle gel.

Imogen would need stronger ammunition than that, Katya thought, if she hoped to keep her husband.

Quickly she swapped the bottles and jars around on the shelves until none of them were in the places they had been in before. Then she shut the cabinet. She washed and dressed.

'How are you doing?' Raymond called from next door.

'Nearly ready, darling,' Katya replied.

She was about to leave when she noticed the pair of silver hairbrushes on the table opposite the mirror. She picked them up, brushed her hair vigorously, then studied the bristles. She had left behind two dark brown hairs. She continued brushing until she could see a web of dark brown on top of Imogen's blonde.

Standing here in the en suite bathroom, having just made love to Raymond in the master bedroom, already she was beginning to feel more like a wife than a mistress.

She checked her make-up one last time, then returned triumphant to the bedroom.

PART II

Imogen

Eighteen

On Monday evening, after she had climbed out of the bath and dried herself with a huge white towel, Imogen Punchard flicked open the mirrored medicine cabinet and reached for her moisturising cream.

She picked up the jar from its usual place, twisted the lid and scooped a little on to her finger. Only then did she notice the consistency was wrong and she was about to apply night cream.

She searched in the cabinet for her moisturiser and found it to be in the place where she normally kept the cough mixture. And then she realised that all her creams and gels and ointments had changed places on the shelves.

Her first thought was that Maria, her maid, must have put the jars back in the wrong order after giving the cabinet a clean. But it did not look as if it had been cleaned: in fact the shelves were ringed with sticky, dusty marks.

Next, after brushing her hair, she noticed the dark hairs woven between the bristles on top of her blonde ones. There was no doubt about it: someone had been using her brushes.

She assumed it must be Raymond, despite the fact that she had specifically asked him on a number of occasions not to use them – not because she minded sharing things, but because his hair was on the greasy side, which played havoc with her styling.

Lip curled in distaste, she reached down in between the bristles and extracted one, straightened it between her fingers and held it up to the light. It was dark auburn and about two inches in length.

Imogen tried to recall the colour of her maid's hair. It was definitely a brown of one type or another, but the exact shade changed after almost every trip to the hairdresser. Anyway, Maria, she was sure, would never, ever use her silver brushes.

The only person she could remember using her bathroom in the last week was Robina Slaughter; she had gone there during the Thursday afternoon bridge session as a workman was adjusting the ballcock in the downstairs cloakroom – and she had blonde hair.

Imogen had a sudden, agonising, sinking feeling. Could Raymond have brought some woman back here while she had been down at Bradstoke with the children?

She dismissed the idea. He would never do such a thing. They did, after all, have a good marriage. Her friends often told her how lucky she was.

She was, she was sure, being paranoid. But just because you're paranoid doesn't mean you're wrong. There was bound to be some perfectly commonplace explanation; the trouble was, the only one she could think of right now was that her husband was a cheat.

The door swung open. 'Hello, darling.'

It was Raymond.

He was standing there in a grey business suit, smiling at her warmly, confidently, as if nothing had happened. Maybe nothing had.

She smiled back at him, even managing some warmth. 'Good day at the office?'

'Fine.'

'Who are we taking to the opera tonight?'

'The president of our American tools division and his wife – Patrick and Elizabeth Stein.'

'Not Patrick Stein!'

'What's wrong with him?'

'He snores when he falls asleep. Last time I had to wake him up on three occasions.'

'I wish you hadn't. It embarrassed him.'

'Nonsense. Patrick Stein wouldn't be embarrassed if he farted at a funeral.'

As they were on the subject of hospitality, she wanted to ask him then and there whether he had brought a woman to the house while she had been at Bradstoke. But something held her back.

He put the plug in the bath, turned on the taps and started to undress.

She studied him as he stripped. Every part of him was so familiar. To her, he had hardly changed in sixteen years of marriage. Of course, physically there had been alterations – or, if she were going to be ruthlessly honest, deteriorations – but she did not see it like that. For her, it was the essence of the man that was important, and he was still the same Raymond whom she had fallen in love with and battled for against her family's objections.

Although now she thought about it, over the last year or so he had been acting strangely in certain respects.

He had always been clean and well groomed, but about eighteen months ago he had begun hogging the bathroom, taking meticulous care of his nails, even occasionally borrowing one of her files – although in typical male fashion his assiduousness had not extended to picking the clippings off the bathroom carpet.

She had thought nothing of it at the time. She had not been worried either when a few weeks later she had found a bottle of hair restorer in the bathroom cabinet. His hair was still grey at the temples, exactly as before, so she was not sure what the tonic was for until one evening she noticed the uncommon luxuriance of his chest hairs.

She would not mind if his chest hairs were purple if it made him feel better. Then she had thought it a harmless vanity of middle age: now she was not so sure.

She went back into the bedroom. With a heavy heart she put on a black velvet evening dress and a pair of large gold earrings.

'I don't want to rush you, darling, but we ought to leave now,' Raymond called a few minutes later. He had already changed into a dark blue suit. Around his neck was the Hermes tie she had given him for Christmas.

All she felt like doing was going to bed and crying, but she knew self-pity was never the answer. She sensed that it was important to put on a brave face, at least for now. After all, it could be just her imagination and her nerves playing tricks on her.

Rising from the dressing table stool, she smiled back at him. She wished it was not such an effort to make the muscles of her face work. 'Right,' she said. 'Let's go.'

She sat on a plush seat in a plush box listening to a soprano with a plush voice. She had hoped the experience would make her relax, make her think of other things, but Raymond and this woman obsessed her thoughts.

She wanted desperately to believe she was wrong, that the rearrangement of the bottles and the hairs on the brush meant nothing – after all, if she were the one having the affair, would she make a stupid mistake like that?

But in her heart she knew it was not just these specific incidents which led her to believe that Raymond was having an affair. There were many other subtle changes in his mannerisms, gestures and habits.

When he looked at her these days, sometimes his eyes would slide away from hers as if fearful of enquiry. He was always eager to answer the telephone. He spent longer at the office. His changes of mood were less predictable. His gifts were more lavish.

She only wished she could explain it away as a crisis at work or the male menopause.

The plush curtain lowered. Suddenly the sound of clapping came from everywhere around her, enclosing her, smothering her.

Imogen tried to stop the drumming in her ears. She feared it might send her mad.

Nineteen

She did not go to the lunch party at Pamela Ravenscroft's
the following day. Instead she lay in bed in a darkened
room, an ice pack over her eyes, sipping warm water with
lemon juice. Already she had taken the maximum dose of
painkillers: they made her feel very strange, yet seemed
to do nothing to alleviate the blinding pain.

The cause, she knew, was Raymond. Since last night,
she had been trying to decide what to do and had got nowhere. She had considered cross-examining him, but
suspected he would deny everything, protest his love and
declare that he was bitterly hurt by the allegation, leaving
her none the wiser. She might even find herself apologising.

She needed proof. She could rummage through his
pockets and the drawers of his desk, but since he kept
most of his papers in the office, she would be unlikely to
find anything incriminating.

Anyway, the idea was anathema to her. One did not go
through other people's private things – a message she
had reiterated to Archie only the previous week when
some chocolates had gone missing from the drawer in her
bedside table.

She took another sip of warm water, lay back in bed
and dismissed the thought.

It returned a couple of minutes later. This time the
logic seemed inescapable.

What had Raymond to hide? she reasoned. In fact, once he had rung her from the office and asked her to find some paper or other in his desk and fax it over to him. He would not have done that unless he didn't mind her going through his things, now would he?

As for his suits, she or the maid always checked the pockets before the clothes were sent off to his tailor or the dry cleaner. It was only good housekeeping, after all. Some of the suits, she remembered, were looking distinctly grubby.

The strange thing was that just thinking of these small wifely chores had lessened the pain of the migraine so that now it was almost bearable.

She thought she had better get up before it got worse again. She took one last sip of warm water, slipped on her dressing gown and padded through into Raymond's dressing room.

Passing the engraved plaques and the railway memorabilia, she went straight to the long mahogany hanging cupboard. As she opened it, the smell of cedar filled the room. There were thirty or forty suits hanging from two parallel brass rails, mostly in varying weights and shades of grey and blue cloth.

She started at one end. She found a key fob he had lost months ago, three dirty handkerchiefs, two theatre stubs, four restaurant receipts, a five-hundred dollar bill and a pair of gold cuff links.

Next she examined his ties. She flicked through the two dozen or so staid ones with minute geometric designs which he had bought himself, and the seven or eight wild ones she had given him and he wore only to please her.

Suddenly her heartbeat quickened. She saw one she did not recognise. It was in heavy pale green silk, had an Italian label and looked as if it had never been worn. Then she remembered. A gift from her mother-in-law.

Clearly, this girl, whoever she was, was not into ties.

Ties, Imogen thought ruefully, were a wife's or a mother's present. A mistress who gave a tie was unlikely to be a threat.

Next she went through his shirts. He had shelves of bespoke Jermyn Street poplin shirts, mostly for work, with some in brighter colours for weekends, some cream silk ones, some dress ones, then next to them she spotted three American-cut linen ones. These she was sure were new, although he could, she supposed, have bought them himself.

She had hoped to feel relieved that she had not found anything incriminating, but the search had done nothing to allay her suspicions.

Closing the cupboards carefully, she glanced at the clock on the dressing room table. It was now two fifteen. As she did not have to pick Archie up from school until three thirty, she still had time.

She tightened the cord of the dressing gown about her and climbed down the carved wooden staircase to the ground floor. At the bottom of the stairs, she turned left and opened the door to Raymond's study.

Crossing the room, she scanned the bookshelves on either side of the window. The top three shelves were filled with eighteenth- and nineteenth-century volumes purchased by the yard for the decorative quality of their gilt-tooled leather spines rather than the inspiration of their contents. Further down, the shelves disintegrated into an assortment of much-thumbed paperbacks, business manuals and reference works in lurid colours. On the bottom shelf was a box file. Imogen took it out and shuffled through the dockets. All she could find were VAT receipts.

Next she turned to Raymond's desk. It had been sold to them as a work by Chippendale, but subsequently they had found out that it was a clever fake made about the turn of the century: not that there was anything they could do about it, as the dealer in question had long since gone out of business.

Sitting down in the chair, she tugged at the handle of the top left-hand drawer. She pulled on it three times. To her annoyance, it would not give. She tried all the other drawers one by one. Each and every one of them was locked.

She searched for the key under the blotter, inside the writing paper holder and along the shelves of the bookcase, but could not find it anywhere.

Her jaw set. No matter. She would get into those drawers. If need be, she would break the desk open with her bare hands.

That evening Raymond came home about nine fifteen.

'I'm sorry, darling, I'm late,' he said as he hurried into the drawing room. He came forward to kiss her.

She was not listening to his words, only to the chime and jangle of the keys in his pocket.

His kiss felt mechanical, cold. It was all over quickly. His mouth withdrew, his eyes fell away from hers, he turned his back and walked over to the drinks tray and poured himself some whisky.

Samantha and Willa came to join them. By the time he had kissed both girls and walked downstairs to the dining room, Imogen was sure his keys were in his right-hand jacket pocket.

In bed she did not initiate anything and neither did he. He read a few pages of his book, then turned off his light.

She switched her light off at the same time although her head was racing too fast for sleep. She lay there in the silence, listening to the slow rhythm of his breathing. She waited an hour, maybe more, for his sleep to deepen, then softly called out his name.

When he did not respond, she carefully pulled back

the sheets and swung her feet over the side of the bed. She stood up slowly, trying not to rock the mattress as she did so.

The room was in darkness except for a narrow crack in the curtains where the light from the streetlamps filtered through. She felt her way, searching the floor with her feet for her slippers and groping around for her dressing gown.

She slipped them both on, then padded silently across the thick carpet and along the passage to Raymond's dressing room. Still no sound.

Once there, she switched on the lamps, which were controlled by a master switch by the door. The room smelt faintly of his aftershave, faintly of male sweat. She blinked a few times to clear her vision, then crossed the Turkey rug to the chest of drawers by the far wall. She looked in the small china dish on top of the chest, into which he usually emptied his pockets. There were coins, a pen and a business card. No keys.

She looked around for the suit he had worn that evening. Usually it would be hanging over the back of one of the chairs. Tonight, though, he had been uncharacteristically tidy: the chairs were bare; the clothes put away.

She opened the cupboard and stared bemused at the rows of grey and blue business suits. Whether due to nerves or the lateness of the hour, they all looked indistinguishable to her. Try as she might, she couldn't remember whether the suit he had been wearing only a few hours before was a herringbone, a bird's eye, a pinstripe, a Prince of Wales check or a flannel. All she could remember was that it was grey.

Starting at the beginning of the row, she worked her way along, feeling the pockets of the jackets and the trousers one by one. Ten suits on, she felt a fist of keys and pulled them out. Three of the keys on the ring were narrow and fine, the size of the desk key. They chimed at her, and she smiled.

She walked back into the passage and turned off the burglar alarm, wincing at the bleeping sound it made each time she stabbed a number. Then, taking out of her pocket the small torch she had armed herself with earlier, she crept down the stairs.

The only sounds were the rumble of the occasional car in the street outside, the creak of the banisters and her own muffled footsteps on the stair carpet. The streetlamps cast an eerie light in the hall, sending a cold, dull glow over the black and white marble squares.

She made for Raymond's study. She flashed the torch inside before closing the door quietly behind her, then she walked across to the desk, sat down and switched on the desk light.

She tried the small keys one by one. Her hands were shaking so much the keys kept slipping away from the lock. The first two didn't fit. The third, though, clicked and turned. The sound was like music to her.

She moved the desk lamp closer and pulled out the drawer. It was full of papers: some loose; some in folders. She burrowed among them, pulling out a batch of bank and credit card statements, and studied each in turn.

Most of them did not mean much to her. They confirmed that Raymond spent a lot of time in restaurants: he often had to entertain on business and she usually tried to avoid those dinners. There were hotel receipts too: he frequently travelled abroad. Then she saw on a credit card statement the word 'Cartier'.

Suddenly she felt a twisting in her stomach. He had never bought her anything from Cartier.

She tried to make a note of the date and the amount, but in her haste the point of the pencil snapped. She grabbed a biro and tried again.

'Hello!' a voice called from outside the study. Raymond. 'Who's there?'

In the silence she could hear his footsteps, the creak of the staircase. She would not have time to put the papers away before he came in, so she left everything where it was and raced for the door.

He was standing at the bottom of the stairs. The lights were blazing.

'Raymond, did you hear it too?' she asked.

'Did I hear what?'

'The door banging downstairs. I was worried in case it might set off the burglar alarm, so I came down to close it.'

Why lie? she thought. Why be frightened of him? Why not confront him now with what she had found and ask him to explain himself?

But her instinct told her to hold back. She wanted to have time to think before deciding how to act, and she was ashamed of burrowing about in his desk at night.

'That all?' he asked. 'Are you sure everything's all right?' He stepped towards her, towards the study.

'Absolutely sure,' she answered firmly. 'I've already checked.'

He stood there for a moment only a couple of feet away from the study door, then his eyes lost their look of enquiry and tiredness returned. 'Coming back to bed?' he asked.

'I'll be with you in a moment,' she answered. 'Now I'm up, I might as well make some tea. Would you like some?'

He shook his head. 'No, thanks. It'll only keep me awake. But I'll make some for you if you like?'

'It's sweet of you to offer but it wouldn't be fair. You go back to bed.'

'Very well.'

When he was safely upstairs, she went back to the study, replaced all the statements except for the one with the Cartier entry and relocked the drawer.

She did not want to go back to bed and lie beside him now. She was so angry, she did not trust herself as to what she might do.

Instead, she went upstairs to the drawing room and sat in the armchair by the fireplace, wrapping her arms about herself against the cold.

The skin around her eyes and nose swelled and reddened, but she was determined she was not going to cry. Crying showed weakness and would be a victory for him. And she was not going to allow him any victories from now on. Whatever happened, she was going to stay in control.

Twenty

It was meant to be a relaxing weekend in the country, but Imogen was so tense she was sure her anxiety must be obvious to everyone. She felt as if she had lost control of the muscles in her body. Those in her face seemed frozen permanently in a hangdog expression and only by constant effort could she keep the corners of her mouth pointing upwards.

Where had she gone wrong?

As she lay next to him in the carved four-poster amid the splendour of the oak-panelled bedroom at Bradstoke Hall, a wave of self-loathing shook her body. She had tried so hard. The marriage seemed to work, yet somehow she must have failed him, or else she would not be in this position now. She felt so lost and alone.

It had been love, she was sure of it, at the beginning. She had been a popular girl, fun and lively and something of an heiress in her own right. She had had the pick of the men.

Her father had been appalled by her choice. 'Charming though Raymond Punchard no doubt is,' Lord Farleigh had said grandly, 'he's not quite what we had in mind for you,' which was his coded way of saying he considered Raymond both too poor and thoroughly middle class.

Looking back on it now, she wondered how far her decision to marry Raymond had been a deliberate act of rebellion and defiance to spite her parents.

She had not had a happy childhood at Bradstoke Hall.
She was an only child and a girl, not the son and heir her
father craved. In those days it was not understood that
the sperm determined the sex of the child. She was sure
her mother suffered unfairly for producing a daughter
and no other children. Lord Farleigh was a stubborn and
proud man, convinced he was always in the right.

Imogen was consigned to the nursery and the care of
nannies and nursery maids. What she remembered most
about her childhood was the chill of starched sobriety, a
feeling of physical and emotional coldness, the correctness
of form over substance, the hesitant gestures and
utterings of a father whose code of behaviour did not allow
for the expression of feelings, and the embarrassed look
of her mother who tried to be kind but never failed to see
in her daughter the physical manifestation of her shame
in her inability to bear her husband sons.

Imogen had, in consequence, been a diffident and
awkward child when she had been sent off to the Convent
of the Immaculate Conception for what passed as a girl's
education in those days. She had sought her parents'
approbation by trying hard both in the classroom and on
the sports field, and when they met her efforts and small
triumphs with indifference, had settled for that of the
nuns and her fellow pupils. Above all, she desperately
wanted to be liked.

Emerging from the convent at eighteen, she was thrust
into Society at one of the most spectacular coming-out
dances of the season. With only one daughter to launch
her father could afford to be generous, especially since
most of the guests were his own friends.

During those first years in London she had been un-
demanding in what she looked for in a man. If he were
civil and flattered her a little she was satisfied – she dreaded
being left alone without a partner – but then Raymond came

along and by comparison the others seemed like gangling schoolboys. Already he had the aura of authority about him. He had charm. He was curious about everything. And clearly he was crazy about her. She fell hard.

When it became clear that her parents remained stubbornly opposed to the match, Imogen decided there was nothing for it but to go ahead without their blessing. She married Raymond quietly, without telling her parents, in a small church in the Borders. Her father refused to talk to her for over a year.

After they had married, she discovered that underneath the confident exterior Raymond was a troubled man. He too had had a difficult childhood, spending most of his time in British public schools while his father was posted by his company in North Africa, Arabia or wherever oil could be found.

This geographical distance had been compounded by an emotional one, as from early in the marriage, so Raymond had told her, his father had been persistently unfaithful to his mother with local girls and the wives of the other expatriates. He was a loud, forceful and selfish man who finally left his wife when Raymond was fourteen and, once he remarried, took very little further interest in his son.

Imogen and Raymond had both had sad and lonely childhoods and, during the early years of their marriage, they did their best to heal each other's wounds.

Now she glanced across at the man in the bed beside her and felt only revulsion. All that feeling, all that striving and shared sacrifice seemed incomprehensible and futile now.

Whatever Imogen did, she seemed to have this pressure pushing down on her from above, like a riding helmet two sizes too small, enclosing and slowing the brain.

She tried to stop herself harping on Raymond's betrayal

145

or wallowing in self-pity by keeping herself busy. There was always so much to do. The guests at Sunday lunch announced that they had never seen the flower arrangements in the house look prettier. Samantha and Willa were both in need of help on their school projects, while on Monday afternoon Archie returned proudly brandishing his star for excellent homework. On Tuesday and Wednesday Imogen sent out eight hundred personally topped and tailed begging letters for the Crisis Call Trust's tenth anniversary appeal.

To her, every action was a small but definite triumph. Each had to be accomplished despite the dense grey fog in her brain which stripped everything of its colour and sucked out the joy and the life force. She seemed powerless to shake it off.

'One no trump.'

'Two hearts.'

Imogen stared at the cards blankly. She had added up the points three times and on each occasion had reached a different total.

'Are we playing a strong or a weak no trump – I can't remember?' she asked her partner, a dark-haired woman with a long neck, pale skin and an elaborate, stiff coiffure.

The woman twisted her bright red lips into a grimace. 'Is this some kind of joke of yours? We've been playing together for over a year and now you tell me you don't even know which conventions we've been using all this time.'

'Pamela, it has momentarily slipped my mind. OK?'

'Girls, no quibbling,' interjected Robina Slaughter, the blonde woman in yellow on her right. 'A snappy game is a happy game.'

'We are playing, or at least I've been playing, a strong no trump.'

'Thank you. That's what I wanted to know. Three spades.'

'That's a jump bid,' said Pamela immediately. 'Did you mean to make a jump bid?'

'No conferring,' ordered Robina.

Imogen had not meant to make a jump bid, but it had been made now, so she smiled lamely and let it ride.

The bridge four met every Thursday lunchtime at Phillimore Gardens. Imogen had begun it in order to improve her game and thus prevent hefty losses and social embarrassment when forced to play during country-house weekends. Now she played for pleasure.

The woman in blue on her left, Julia Stafford, said, 'No bid.' Pamela muttered that she considered Imogen's double jump somewhat speculative and bid three no trump.

No one bid again. Robina led with a small heart. Relieved, Imogen laid down her hand and left Pamela to it.

So far she had not breathed a word of her suspicions about Raymond to anyone. She had not planned to either. She did not want to risk the gossip or the scandal, or be thought of as the kind of woman who couldn't keep her man.

She had hoped that the answer to her problems would become clear. Instead, she felt even more muddled than before, immobilised by doubt, uncertainty and fear.

She desperately wanted to ask advice from someone. But even here, among trusted friends, it required courage.

Pamela squeaked home with two lucky finesses. While Robina was dealing the next hand, Imogen casually dropped the subject into the conversation.

'A friend of mine has asked me for advice,' she began, trying not to sound too earnest. 'She thinks her husband is having an affair and doesn't know what to do.'

Three pairs of eyes rose from the table.

'Some people have all the luck,' announced Robina. 'I only wish Philip would have an affair. After all these years it would allow me a decent night's sleep.'

'How did she find out?' Pamela asked quizzically.

Imogen explained, trying to keep the emotion from her voice.

'Doesn't something about this strike you as very odd?' Pamela remarked as soon as she had finished. 'Of course none of us here would even dream of sleeping with somebody else's husband, except in the most extenuating circumstances, but if we did, would we be so careless as to leave hairs on the wife's brushes and the bathroom cupboard in disarray?'

'She might have done it in a state of mindless oblivion brought on by the throes of passion,' said Robina.

'Drink, more likely,' suggested Julia.

'Possible,' answered Pamela thoughtfully, 'but unlikely. I think she did it deliberately to make the wife aware of what was going on. Your friend should be careful. To do what she's done, the mistress must be feeling either very desperate or very confident.

'If I were the wife, I'd pretend I didn't suspect a thing and meanwhile try to find out whatever I could about this minx – she probably knows everything there is to know about your friend down to her choice of breakfast cereal and how she squeezes the toothpaste tube.'

The two other women had already picked up their cards and were anxious to get on with the game. Imogen nodded, trying to act casually. 'Thanks, I'll tell her.'

'Right, that's settled then,' announced Robina. 'I bid one heart . . .'

It would have been too risky to take one of their own cars, so she had rented a Vauxhall Astra for the afternoon. She wished now that she had ordered the next model up, because in the economy range, which she had chosen as the least conspicuous, there was a piece of moulded plastic where the radio should have been. She had been sitting in the car on the single yellow line on the east side of the

Punchard Building for nearly two hours now with nothing to listen to but the sound of the traffic.

That morning she had made a point of seeing Raymond off to work. He had kissed her, told her that he had a meeting this evening and would not be back until nine, then climbed into his company car, a blue Ford.

She suspected the Punchard Group must get a good deal on blue Fords, because already over twenty had climbed the steep ramp leading from the underground car park ahead of her.

As she watched, two more edged up the ramp. A bald man sat at the wheel of the first. She could not be sure about the second, for a reflection caught the windscreen, obscuring the driver from view and the number plate was covered in mud. By the time the windscreen had cleared, the car was almost past her. The man was Raymond's height and had a full head of hair, but something about the angle at which he tilted his head told her it was not him.

A few minutes later there was a knock on the side window. A traffic warden peered in through the glass, his clipped moustache and the tip of his red nose inches from her. 'You can't stay here, madam.'

'I'm waiting for someone.'

'Then I'm afraid you'll have to wait somewhere else.'

She could not drive on now. Two cars had come out of the car park while the warden had been standing there, and more were crawling up the ramp behind them.

'It's vitally important. Just another few minutes, please.'

The corner of the warden's mouth twitched, lifting the bristles above his lip so that they were pointing horizontally towards her. 'I don't make these rules, you know.'

'I'm frightfully sorry, but I simply can't move now.'

She stared ahead at the ramp while the warden took a

ballpoint pen out of the top pocket of his uniform, laboriously filled in each section of the form, bagged it in a plastic pouch and stuck it on the windscreen.

Still Raymond had not come.

By the time she had collected three parking tickets, she wondered whether Raymond had not been telling the truth and she had chosen an evening when he genuinely did have a business meeting.

Then, soon after six thirty, another blue Ford left the car park. This one was larger than the others, had smoked glass and sped up the ramp. When it turned into the road, her heart leapt. It was him.

She quickly started the engine, put the car in gear and raced after him. He was already fifty yards ahead of her. She only just managed to follow him across the junction before the lights changed.

Although it increased the chances of being spotted, she stayed close behind him to be sure not to lose him. From the determined way he was driving, she guessed that he was oblivious to the other road users; he was thinking only of his destination.

He cruised along the Embankment, passed the Houses of Parliament, then went through Pimlico into Sloane Square. Halfway along the Fulham Road, he turned right, then, after a couple of hundred yards, left into a mews.

She slowed the car and stopped opposite the entrance to the mews. She watched as he parked, as he preened himself on the doorstep, as a door opened and he reached forward to kiss someone inside.

She remembered that expression on his face – a sort of nervous happiness – from when he had come to take her out to dinner during their courtship. The vivid memory of those happy times made the pain of betrayal even more intense.

She steadied herself, opened the window and breathed in three lungfuls of air. She felt a sinking sensation deep in her stomach, as if she were going to be sick if she stayed there a moment longer. She turned the key in the ignition and drove on.

She would go back home. She would give Archie his supper, read him a story, and help Samantha and Willa with their homework. Then she would change into a pretty dress, greet Raymond with a kiss when he arrived, ask him whether he'd had a good day, get him a drink and try to be witty and amusing.

She was determined that everything must be exactly as before. At least, for now.

Twenty-One

After dropping the children off at school the next day, Imogen returned to Craythorne Mews. She felt faintly ridiculous in the loose-fitting coat, scarf, wide-rimmed hat and sunglasses, especially since it was such a dull day that the glasses made everything very grey, but she wanted to make sure that she was not recognised. She was certain that the woman, whoever she was, knew exactly what Imogen Punchard looked like.

She passed through the stone archway at the top of the mews and strode over the cobbles. The houses, which once had been stables, were of painted brick – pink and white were the most popular colours – and many of them sported window boxes filled with ivy and brightly coloured bedding plants.

The house on the right-hand side where she had seen Raymond enter was pink, too. It had a brightly polished brass nine on a white door and a huge brass letterbox. Such a desirable piece of property would not come cheap. Imogen guessed that Raymond would be footing the bill.

Blinds obscured the view through the front window, except for a small gap on the left-hand side. She was just about to press her face to it when she heard the yapping of a small dog, and an owner's reprimand.

She quickly withdrew. She did not want to linger outside in case she attracted attention. She walked on until she was nearly at the end of the mews, still trying to think how she could observe the woman without giving herself away.

Then she saw a youth with long dyed hair sauntering down the street towards her, and it gave her an idea.

'Excuse me,' she said, blocking his way. 'Could you help me, please? I've found a key outside number nine,' she improvised. 'I wonder whether you could ring their doorbell and ask whether it's theirs?'

The youth, pelvic bone cocked, pushed his hands deep into the pockets of his black nylon blouson and stared at her in amazement. 'Lady, you found the key. You ask them.'

'I'm very shy.'

'Then think of it as therapy.'

He walked on.

'I'll give you ten pounds,' she called out after him.

He pirouetted. 'So let me get this straight. I ring the doorbell of number nine and ask whether the key you found outside is theirs?'

'Yes, except I would prefer to stay out of it. You could say that you found it.'

He nodded. 'Sounds OK to me. And you'll give me ten pounds for my trouble, right?'

'Yes.' She took her keyring out of her handbag and detached her own garage key. She had a spare back at the house.

The youth took the key. 'Lady, aren't you forgetting something – it's not that I don't trust you or anything . . .?'

She handed him a ten-pound note. He slipped it inside his blouson. Then, without a word, he turned and sauntered down the mews until he reached number nine.

As soon as Imogen saw him press the bell, she started towards him. She was so nervous she nearly tripped on the cobbles.

She was about twenty yards from the house, and still no one had come to the door.

She walked on, nearly level now.

Suddenly the door sprang open and there was the woman, with a black pug at her feet. She was dressed in some kind of artist's smock. Short dark hair. Very pale skin. Huge hazel eyes. Very slight. The face was somehow familiar, but for the moment she could not place her.

She was not how Imogen had imagined her to be. Raymond liked blue-eyed blondes. He liked breasts. He liked girls with curves.

Imogen had heard that men often chose mistresses very similar to their wives; this woman was so different – did that make her more or less threatening? What did she have, apart from youth, that Imogen did not? Was it sex, pure and simple? As if sex could ever be pure and simple.

Imogen would have felt more comfortable if her rival had been more obviously voluptuous, more obviously a sex kitten. But there was intelligence in the woman's face, and a degree of self-possession which frightened her.

Then, as she turned and Imogen caught her side view, it came back to her. Katya Cornwale. The new girl at the convent who had lost both parents in a motorway accident.

In breaks, she remembered, Katya would run along the passage from the junior part of the school to the senior just so that she could see Imogen. She never used to say much: just stand close to her, eyes full of wonderment, watching every detail with a defensive, nervous smile on her lips.

Whenever Imogen was playing for the school, Katya would be cheering enthusiastically from the other side of the fence. When she was practising, Katya would be there too, clapping at every good shot.

As captain of the netball team, Imogen had had her fair share of admiration and crushes, but none of them had been like Katya's.

Halfway into the Easter term, Imogen could not help noticing the way Katya copied everything she did. She began wearing the same blue hairbands as her idol, cutting her hair to the same length and style, buying the same fine lawn handkerchiefs, even adopting the same mannerisms. But Imogen thought nothing of it, apart from being mildly flattered.

Then in the summer term things began disappearing from her locker – a hairband, a comb, a handkerchief, a pair of knickers.

They were all things of little value, and at first Imogen assumed she must have misplaced them, but as the disappearances continued, and just to rule out the possibility, she checked the first-year dormitory one afternoon when the junior school had a compulsory match.

At the back of the cupboard in Katya's cubicle she found a shoe box. The outside was undecorated. The inside, however, had been lined meticulously in padded blue satin, and nestling there, like the contents of a reliquary, were all the things Imogen had lost, along with her photograph cut from the school magazine.

Imogen was struck dumb. She knew that by rights she should report this to the Mother Superior, but she was sorry for Katya. The girl, after all, had lost her parents, was having to make her way in a new school, and what was the harm if she did have a crush on her? She would grow out of it. In time the captain of the netball team would be replaced, she was sure, by pop stars, horses, and finally boys.

Imogen reclaimed the things that had been stolen, replaced the box where she had found it, and did not mention it to anyone.

The next day, though, when Imogen wore the hairband at school line-up, Katya went crimson. Later, when Imogen went to her locker, she found all her shoes and boots lined up in a neat row, freshly cleaned, polished and buffed. From then on, the same thing happened every day: as soon as she finished with a pair of shoes or games boots, she would discover them, expertly cleaned, among her belongings.

That had been Imogen's last term at the convent, and she had not seen or heard from Katya since. Until now, that was.

A shudder passed down Imogen's spine. She forced herself to stop staring. Then she walked on, quickening her pace.

Twenty-Two

The Chelsea Sports Club had only been open a month but already membership was closed and there was a waiting list to join the waiting list.

It had its own modern building on the Thames, ten indoor tennis courts, six squash courts, an Olympic-sized swimming pool, a gym and a restaurant. The décor was brutal, with white walls interspersed with full-length mirrors lit by unforgiving spotlights. Wherever Imogen looked she could not escape being reminded of the contour of her hips; while the weight had dropped off her after the births of the two girls, after Archie it had remained stubbornly there, despite starvation diets and strenuous exercise.

She liked riding, tennis and skiing. She loathed gyms and weights and indoor swimming pools. Nevertheless, extraordinary circumstances demanded extreme countermeasures. So far this morning she had spent an hour contorting her body in an aerobics class and an hour in the gym amid shiny high-tech torture machines under the instruction of a woman with legs like car jacks.

The clientele might be well connected, beautiful and wealthy and the club brand new, but it still smelt of overripe stilton.

She only just had time to shower and change before meeting Pamela Ravenscroft for lunch in the club restaurant. They were seated at one of the best tables, between a view of the river and a potted plant.

Pamela was not dressed for sport. While Imogen wore a black tracksuit over a leotard, she was in a cream linen trouser suit with gold buttons. 'If you don't mind me asking,' she said casually as soon as she had studied the menu, 'are you subjecting your body to this appalling physical punishment with Raymond or someone else in mind?'

The question took Imogen by surprise. 'I'm doing it for myself,' she answered defensively. 'Myself and Raymond.'

'I only mention it because at that bridge game last week, absurdly I couldn't get out of my head the notion that you were asking advice not for a friend, but for someone closer to home. Wasn't that crazy of me?'

Imogen was about to deny the insinuation but the look of certainty on Pamela's face told her that it would be futile. 'If I'm that transparent, there's no point in me trying to pretend to Raymond I'm blissfully ignorant of the whole thing.'

'Not at all. He'll be worrying too much about his own performance to notice any deficiencies in yours.

'It's not much consolation, I know, but hundreds of thousands of other wives are wrestling with this same problem while we speak. What do you know about this woman?'

Before Imogen could answer, a waiter in a black T-shirt and tight black trousers came over to take their order.

Pamela glanced back at the menu. 'This is terribly difficult. Everything here is so extraordinarily healthy. I'll have the chicken, but would it be possible not to have the skin removed? And I suppose there wouldn't be any chance of roast potatoes?'

'Only salads, I'm afraid,' the man answered unapologetically.

'Then please make sure I have plenty of mayonnaise.'

As soon as the waiter had left, Imogen told Pamela what she had discovered. Pamela sipped at her vodka and nodded occasionally.

'You have been busy,' she announced when Imogen had finished. 'The key question, though, is whether this is a love match or just a passing flirtation which won't do serious harm to the marriage.'

'I wish I could be as coolly dispassionate as you,' Imogen answered. 'The trouble is, I have a really bad feeling about it, and I don't think I'm going to be able to control my anger much longer.

'It's not even the act itself which I find most distressing. It's the deceit. To think that all that time I trusted him. I listened to his lies and believed him.'

'I'm not trying to excuse his actions in any way but, honestly, would you be feeling any better now if he had asked your permission beforehand? How would you have answered?

'If, while we were married, Jack had ever asked me whether he could have an affair, I would have hit him. The very question implies that the marriage has already descended irredeemably into one of convenience. Mutual confidence is no substitute for mutual passion.'

Imogen was thoughtful for a moment. 'I would have said no, of course, but it would have given us an opportunity to talk things through.'

'He probably guessed that – another good reason for not asking you.'

Imogen noticed that the conversation at the next table had stopped. She leaned closer to Pamela. 'Do you think you could lower your voice a little, please? We don't want everyone to hear.'

'Certainly.' Pamela sipped at her vodka, then continued in exactly the same tones as before. 'So let's examine the options. You could, you know, do a lot worse than live with things as they are.

'If Raymond was a very ordinary man, he would be relatively easy to replace, but he is handsome, rich and talented. Exceptional gifts do allow those lucky enough to possess them greater latitude in behaviour than is tolerated in their plainer, poorer and less gifted cousins. It's infuriating for those on the receiving end, I know, but it's only human nature.'

The waiter laid a plate in front of Pamela. Contrary to her instructions, the skin had been stripped from the chicken and the salad was undressed. The corners of Lady Ravenscroft's mouth curled momentarily with displeasure, but she was too hungry to complain.

'Here in England for a man to have a mistress causes so much distress,' she continued, cutting a slice off the chicken, 'yet in France and Italy and all those Latin countries it is an accepted mode of behaviour after the first few years of marriage.

'Look, for instance, at my dear friend Louisa, married to Paulo Dringetti – you know, that handsome Italian who lives in that wonderful villa outside Milan. He's had a mistress for twenty years. She's charming apparently, comes from a good family and is devoted to Paulo. He takes her to Gstaad every year and parades her around the Palace Hotel dripping in expensive jewellery.

'Yet Louisa is a contented woman. She says it doesn't bother her provided Paulo keeps up appearances when in Italy, does not embarrass her and looks after the family. Despite everything, she tells me she is still in love with him and he is very amorous with her.'

'The Latins are different from us,' Imogen replied. 'The men are pampered from birth – first by their mothers then by their wives – and divorce is so difficult to obtain, they get away with murder. The wives are forced by circumstances to be tolerant. We're not. We have a choice. I think you've got to be brought up in a culture where it is accepted before you can accept it yourself.'

'What about Laura Knighton then?' Pamela asked. 'The whole of London knows Christopher has had a mistress for years, yet she's stayed put, ostensibly for the sake of the children.'

Imogen chewed slowly on her Scandinavian-style open sandwich of prawns, lettuce and reduced-calorie mayonnaise. 'I couldn't live like she does, in a state of emotional limbo. Apart from anything else, it would be so demeaning.'

'I think you judge people very harshly,' Pamela admonished her. 'Being married to a man with a mistress is not without its compensations. Guilt can make a husband generous to a fault. He is also in no position to complain should you decide to take a lover of your own. I don't think Laura has — she seems to find the garden a sufficient outlet for her creative energies. But for those less horticulturally inclined, it can be a great solace.

'Don't give me that old-fashioned look! I'm only trying to help you. Everyone aspires to a fairy-tale marriage, but in practice most of us have to muddle through. We're forced to choose whatever seems best from what is often a number of pretty uninviting alternatives. I wouldn't criticise anyone for falling short of the ideal.

'I don't want you to think I'm cynical, darling, but you can't ignore the facts. Biologically speaking the idea that a man and a woman should fall in love and stay in love with one another for the rest of their lives is absurd.

'The first rush of love is pure exhilaration. But what's happening? Your head is awash with hormones which are very strong natural drugs. No wonder you feel amazing. The tragedy, of course, is that it can't last. Your body can't go on releasing hormones at that manic rate and, as with most drugs, you become desensitised after a while. If you're lucky, you have two or three years of doped delirium. Then what are you going to do when the effects wear off?

'The truth of the matter is that marriage has had a surprisingly good run for a contract so contrary to nature.'

'That's the whole point of a developed society, isn't it?' Imogen countered. 'You create codes of behaviour for the mutual wellbeing of that society, and one of them is that marriage is meant to be monogamous and for life. I've kept my side of the bargain and I expected Raymond to keep his.'

'You're not going to walk out on him just because of this, are you?' Lady Ravenscroft asked urgently.

'I might.'

'I think you'd be a fool if you did. Although Laura cares deeply about her children, I don't think for a moment that they are the main reason why she has stayed with Christopher all these years. She's terrified of being alone and knows it's not a kind world waiting for her out there.

'Being single when you're nearly forty is not the same as at nineteen, my dear. Men, as we have both learnt only too painfully, are foolish enough to rate youth above experience. Don't be too hasty. You've got a marriage worth fighting for.'

'Of course I want to keep the marriage together if I possibly can,' Imogen answered, 'not only for myself but for the children. But I'd prefer not to have a marriage at all rather than one in name only. I couldn't live like Laura. You might think me a sentimental fool, but that's how I am.'

'So what are you going to do?'

'Start by getting back into shape.' She signalled to the waiter to bring her the bill. 'Would you like to join me once around the training circuit?'

'Imogen, have you gone quite mad?' Pamela asked, aghast. 'Why take exercise on machines when you can take it much more productively in shops?'

Twenty-Three

She drew into the kerb and looked through the archway down the mews. The dim light of the streetlamps sent a silver streak over the car outside number nine. She was sure it was his, though from where she was, she could tell neither its shape nor its colour.

She parked and climbed out, shutting the door silently behind her. She walked down the mews, quietly, confidently.

Why was she torturing herself like this? she wondered. She was unlikely to find out anything she didn't already know. Yet for some reason, she felt that she had to be here, that it would make her understand better, though how she was not sure.

She tried to recall all the times he had said he would be working late and she had believed him. Some weeks it had been virtually every evening when they did not have to attend some dinner together.

A Venetian blind was drawn over the downstairs window. Although the inside of the room was hidden, pencil lines of light still shone through, playing on the painted metal surfaces of the slats. Imogen stood in front of the window, staring in blindly, trying to imagine the scene inside.

She could not visualise the interior of the house. The idea of a mistress suggested to her red plush and *fin-de-*

siècle opulence; her glimpse of Katya, though, suggested spare modernity: these styles were too far apart to find a meeting point. So she imagined them side by side on a low Habitat sofa incongruously covered with red plush in a white-walled room in front of a gas log fire. Raymond had a glass of whisky within reach, she a cigarette.

A sound from inside the house startled her. It was a man's laughter. His laughter.

She had prepared herself mentally to cope with the sounds of lovemaking. But strangely she found the sound of laughter more disturbing still, stabbing her inside.

She tried to recall the last time she and Raymond had laughed either before or after they had made love. She was sure there must have been countless times, but she could not remember one right now. All she could recall were the more serious moments.

She had been brought up not to consider sex as something to be treated lightly – and quite rightly too, she thought – but she wondered whether she might not have brought too much of this seriousness with her into the act itself.

For her, deep down, sex had always been about babies and the meeting of two souls. Raymond, in contrast, seemed to treat it as some kind of recreational sport – something to do when there was nothing interesting on the television.

A mistress, she supposed, would provide sex on demand. She would never be too tired from looking after the children, have headaches or not be in the mood.

Imogen had not anticipated how much children changed a marriage. Given the chance again, she would have tried to ensure that she and Raymond had had a couple of years alone together before the worries of childcare had taken over their lives.

Some men, she knew, could get jealous of the love and attention lavished on their children which previously had been all theirs, but Raymond had tolerated the early-morning calls, the night feeds, and her moods and helpless exhaustion with good humour and a helping hand. So often then she had been too tired to make love. If he had resented this, he had always seemed understanding and never forced himself on her.

Yet, looking back, it could not have been easy for him. Raymond had always had a strong sex drive. Before the children had come along, the sex had been adventurous and passionate and loving.

On the occasions she refused him, he was understanding and did not press her. She thought that he genuinely understood how important it was that she too was in the mood and that it was the quality of the experience that mattered, not the frequency. Honesty, she had been brought up to believe, was all-important in a relationship.

Now she wondered whether she had been right to deny him, whether he would have taken a mistress if she had always been available to him regardless of headache or mood or condition.

A creak of floorboards. The voices were coming from inside again; this time they were nearer.

Imogen only had time to walk a few yards down the street before the door flew open, sending a wedge of light on to the road outside. She pressed herself against the wall of the nearby house and froze.

She wished now that she had not come. What would she say to Raymond if he saw her? To spot her, all he had to do was look in her direction. She had wanted to find out all that she could – nothing wrong with that – but there was something demeaning, she thought, about being caught outside the mistress's house.

He had stepped out of the door now into the beam of light. He was smoothing his hair into place with the palms of his hands. He turned and looked back to the house.

She tried to read the expression in his eyes. They were slightly misty – was that drink, confusion, post-coital stupor or love?

After sixteen years of marriage she ought to know. But she felt she could not trust her own judgement now. He had managed to put on a good enough performance to cheat on her without arousing her suspicions. Even if it did look like love, might it not be just another of his performances, this time for a different audience? After all, adoration would be expected of him.

Katya had come out too now. She was wearing some kind of long woollen cardigan, open at the front, over a loose-fitting brown dress. Her arms were wrapped about herself against the cool of the evening. Her head was turned towards him and away from Imogen, so she could not see her face, tilted ready to receive his kiss.

He touched her lips. 'Good night, darling,' he said. 'And thanks.'

'Take care,' she said, and shuffled back towards the house.

Raymond climbed into the car and drove off. Katya went back inside the house and shut the door. Moments later, Imogen heard music coming from inside. Blues.

She began walking. She would go to her car, return home and listen to Raymond's lies over dinner. She would try to block her ears, try not to let the lies get to her.

She had found the very ordinariness of the scene numbing. She had not known what to expect, but she had not anticipated seeing two people as comfortable with each other as Raymond and Katya seemed to be. A casual observer might even have mistaken them for a married couple.

Twenty-Four

Seducing your own husband should be as easy a job as a woman could ask for; yet the prospect filled Imogen with terror.

The following day, she tried to recall exactly when she and Raymond had last made love. Her broad recollection was that it had been fairly recently, but now that she came to plot out the weeks she realised that it must have been over four months ago.

For a number of years now she had felt a certain foreboding every evening as she took off her face and changed into her nightdress. When reading in bed, she was very aware of him beside her, always listening for the telltale signs that he was about to pounce – the rustle of the sheets, the creeping hand, the change in his breathing, the term of endearment. Then, without her even realising it, her body would stiffen, her mouth become dry and a feeling of dread suffuse her.

It was not as if she did not love him, because her feelings towards him were if anything stronger than they had been in the early days of their marriage. At the beginning they had just been two people in love: now they were a family, with children and responsibilities as well to bind them. It was not as if he were a poor lover either. Over the years, she had thrilled to him more times than she could remember.

It was the predictability of it all that she could not stand. The positions, the times of day and the locations might vary, but in the end it was the same body doing the same thing in one of the same ways it had for sixteen years.

When he did not murmur 'Darling . . .?' , the hand did not creep towards her or the contours of the bedclothes change, she felt like a schoolgirl given the afternoon off.

Recently, every day had been an afternoon off, but the feeling of relief had muffled the alarm bells which should have been set ringing.

Her mother had once told her that the wife who can provide good food and good sex will never have a problem. It should not be that difficult, Imogen thought, to rekindle the old flame provided she could swallow her pride and control and channel her anger. After all, it had been a love match at the beginning, and now they had a deeper understanding of one another and so much shared experience.

When Raymond returned at eight thirty, she was already waiting for him in a new figure-hugging black satin dress trimmed with lace. Her hair was fluffed out, her party face in place. Soft music played. Scented candles filled the air with musk. Since the Advisory Committee on Trade and Industry had met that evening, she knew he would not have had time to stop off at Craythorne Mews before coming home.

He entered the drawing room, took two paces forward, then stopped and stared at her in amazement. 'I didn't know we we were having a dinner party.'

'We're not,' she answered. She saw the confusion in his face as he tried to work out which anniversary he had forgotten. 'Archie's in bed and I've sent the girls off to the cinema. I thought it would be nice for us to have dinner by ourselves.'

He gave a quick, awkward smile. 'Yes. Good idea.'

They dined on caviare, pink roast beef decorated with heart-shaped slivers of foie gras, and summer pudding, washed down with champagne, Margaux, and Sauternes.

Even as she sat there across the table from him, she knew that it was not working. His eyes were dull. She was having to make conversation, rather than being swept along in its flow. Before, what they talked about had not even mattered – just being together would have been enough to make the evening sparkle.

She had bought a new nightdress of diaphanous black net which started on the breasts and ended abruptly just below the crotch. For the time being, it would stay in its box.

She sat in the waiting room, hiding behind a copy of *Tatler*. In the dim light, with her dark glasses on, she could hardly make out a word.

Every time the door opened, her heartbeat quickened. She prayed it was not someone she knew. She could always pretend that her dentist shared the Harley Street premises with the cosmetic surgeon, but would anyone believe her?

The door opened again, and this time the white-coated receptionist was looking at her. 'Mrs Punchard?'

Why on earth hadn't she given an assumed name? Why did the woman have to shout like that? People would hear. People would remember.

Imogen lowered *Tatler* a couple of inches and peeked over the top of the page. Her eyes swivelled this way and that. No one was staring at her. In fact, everyone had magazines raised like hers, except for one deeply tanned woman whose sunglasses were so huge that only her crimson mouth and blonde hair showed.

Imogen seized the opportunity. She darted for the door.

The surgeon was studying some X-rays on an illuminated screen when she entered his consulting room.

171

He smiled and shook her by the hand. He was dressed in a Savile Row blue suit, had a full head of grey hair, a broad face and, to Imogen's surprise, drooping folds of flesh under each eye. Even the bags had little bags of their own.

He offered her a seat. 'How can I help you?'

For a moment she was struck dumb. 'I've come to enquire about treatment,' she said finally. 'I was thinking about having the lines removed from around my eyes.'

He perched on the side of the desk close to her chair and studied the skin around her eyes under a bright light. 'They're only fine laughter lines. But if you want the skin tightened, it's a simple procedure.'

'Good. While you're about it, maybe the eyes could be enlarged a little to make them almond-shaped – although I don't want to risk looking permanently startled. And I'd also like a smaller nose and fuller lips.'

She stopped herself. Katya's eyes were almond-shaped, her nose was small, her lips full. Up until now she had not especially admired those looks and had found her own face quite serviceable for most occasions. Was she really now going to go under the knife to mimic a mistress, the girl who had modelled herself on Imogen at school?

'All these things are possible,' answered the surgeon. 'But we would have to discuss each of them in detail.'

'Please forgive me.' Imogen rose to her feet. 'I've made a mistake. I'm wasting your time.'

Twenty-Five

The following evening, the doorbell rang while the family were having dinner together.

Willa dropped her spoon into her plate of ice cream. 'I'll get it!'

'No, I'll get it!' Samantha answered, rising. 'It's hardly likely to be for you.'

'How do you know?'

''Cause it never is, that's why.'

'That's not true! What makes you think it's for you anyway? I bet it's only a courier with papers for Daddy.'

She was too late. Samantha had already gone, tripping into the hall, leaving the door open behind her.

When she returned, she was carrying a huge bouquet of lilies, roses and delphiniums, neatly wrapped in cellophane and tied with a huge blue bow. She smiled knowingly at Willa. 'Nice bike, pity about the rider.'

'Who sent you that?'

'Not telling.'

'You must tell. Your family have a right to know. Anyway we can read the card for ourselves.'

Springing up from her chair, Willa raced over to where Samantha stood, grabbed hold of the little envelope and ripped it off the cellophane. She danced away, holding it in the air out of range of her sister.

Suddenly she stopped. 'They're not for you. They're for Mummy!'

'I never said they were,' Samantha answered smugly. She gave an exaggerated formal curtsey full of self-mockery, and handed the bouquet to Imogen. 'For you, Mummy dearest.'

'Thank you, darling.'

Willa returned the envelope to her. 'Open it, Mummy. I want to know who sent them.'

Imogen tore open the envelope and took out the card. Apart from a printed border of roses, the card was blank on both sides. 'No message,' she said, affecting surprise. 'It's probably only a late thank-you from a dinner guest.' She pulled off the cellophane, releasing the smell of the lilies into the room.

'No,' Willa said thoughtfully. 'Someone thanking for dinner would have been sure to include their name.'

'An oversight at the shop,' Imogen answered with deliberate hesitation in her voice, all the time stealing glances at Raymond.

He had said nothing since the flowers had arrived. At first he had sat quietly eating his pudding and enjoying the rivalry between his daughters. Now he was slouched back in his chair, wine glass in his hand. He did not look as if it had even crossed his mind that the flowers might have come from a secret admirer. The bunch had cost her nearly a hundred pounds – where was the jealousy she had hoped it would arouse?

She slowly inhaled the scent one last time then, with apparent reluctance, handed the bouquet to Samantha. 'Could you ask Maria to snip the stems and put them in a vase on my bedside table, please?'

'Sure.'

She glanced again at Raymond. He must remember that she never liked flowers in her bedroom at night, let alone on her bedside table. If he did, he gave no sign.

The more she thought about it, the angrier she became. Jealousy in a husband could be claustrophobic and destructive if carried too far, but to show indifference when an expensive bouquet arrived unexpectedly was downright insulting.

She was determined to provoke some response from him. The following night, while changing to go out to dinner, she asked casually: 'Raymond, are you still going to the States at the end of next week?'

'Yes. What of it?'

'Would you mind if, while you were away, I went to the cinema with Benjy Mulford? I do get lonely at times.'

She hoped that the mention of such a notorious Lothario would make him jealous, angry, protective of her.

He hesitated for a moment. 'You'd like that, would you?'

'Yes.'

'Then go,' was all he said. Then he turned and went off to have his bath.

Was that really all she meant to him? she wondered. Did he really not mind, or was it that he no longer considered he had a right to object, in view of his own behaviour?

Then she thought back to his hesitation before answering and the resigned tone of the words themselves. It was not much, but it did give her some hope.

Pamela refused to have lunch at the Chelsea Sports Club on the grounds of the food. She said she had been so hungry after her last lunch there that she had had two cream cakes in the Patisserie Valerie, which had quite ruined her dinner.

So instead, muscles burning, Imogen left the club at twelve forty-five and joined her at a brasserie off the King's Road for what Pamela called 'a proper lunch'.

'So go to the cinema with Benjy,' advised Pamela after Imogen had explained the situation to her. 'I don't see why you are hesitating for a moment.'

'I only mentioned Benjy's name as I thought it might make Raymond jealous. It's not as if I have actually invited him or anything.'

'Well, you should,' Pamela insisted, while using a spoon to finish off the mushroom and cream sauce around the chicken. 'He's very attractive, available and has always been crazy about you.'

Imogen shook her head. 'It might sound very puritanical of me, but I don't want another man.'

'You need someone to boost your confidence and make you feel feminine again. If Raymond isn't doing his job, why not Benjy? Make Raymond jealous, have fun and get even at the same time – what more could a girl possibly ask for?'

Imogen had been surprised how often she had been propositioned during her married life, both by old suitors and by people she hardly knew. She had been flattered, if mildly shocked, by their attentions, and although at times she had been tempted, she had always declined. She had not wanted that kind of complication in her life and anyway, as she had told them, to their extreme annoyance, she loved her husband. Now the position was different, she was unsure what to do.

She made no attempt to contact Benjy Mulford, but strangely, on the day Raymond flew to New York, he rang her.

She recognised his relaxed drawl immediately. 'Imogen, where were you? I was hoping to see you at that party at the Staffords' last night.'

'We couldn't go because Raymond was off to the States early today.'

'So you're alone then?'

'Yes.'

'Then how about dinner?'

The timing was so perfect she was sure this must be

Pamela's doing. Her first response was anger; her second gratitude. 'Lunch,' she said.

'Tomorrow? I'll pick you up at one.'

Twenty-Six

Benjy Mulford was good-looking in a tortured way; his face was more lined than a contour map, his skin leathery, his eyes haunted, his hair dark and slicked back with long curling ends. Despite a huge appetite, he was slim to the point of anorexia.

Today, in deference to the weather, he had abandoned the shabby jacket of coarse Harris tweed and the corduroy trousers he habitually wore, and was dressed in an old cream linen jacket which Imogen suspected had come from a charity shop.

Uncharacteristically for someone so disorganised, he had booked a table in advance at an Italian restaurant along the Fulham Road. It was the best table – outside, jutting on to the pavement behind a box hedge.

She said that she would prefer to go indoors, despite the heat, citing petrol fumes but in fact more concerned about being seen lunching alone with such a well-known Lothario.

As soon as he sat down opposite her at the corner table at the back of the restaurant, she could tell that Benjy had lost none of his touch. He was popular with women because of his easy, relaxed manner and his charm, and because he genuinely adored female company.

'This is the first time since I was married that I've had lunch alone with a man who wasn't an interior decorator.'

'Then I'm flattered that it's with me,' he answered with his most winning smile. For a man so prematurely age-worn in other ways his dentistry was in excellent order. 'I only hope you won't make me wait another sixteen years before we repeat this.'

'That depends.'

Benjy lit a cigarette. Imogen had forgotten he smoked; very few of her friends did these days. 'To me it seems such a tragic waste that a beautiful, talented woman like you should languish away with a man who doesn't appreciate you.'

'I'm not languishing away,' she protested.

'You're too resourceful and independent to let it get to you. But it can't be a nice feeling being treated like that. You deserve better.'

Imogen had expected to spend time talking about old friends and the weather. She had not anticipated that Benjy would be so direct so soon. 'So you know, then.'

He refilled her glass. 'It's hardly a secret. It's something which was bound to come out sometime or other – all it takes is one slip. The more prominent you are, and the more careless, the sooner London will know.

'Raymond, I fear, is both prominent and careless. There have been many sightings of him and the woman in restaurants all over the place. It's only a matter of time before the press get hold of it.'

He drew again on his cigarette. 'You know, I've always resented Raymond.'

'Why?'

'Because I've always so admired you and he got to you first. He swept you off your feet before we even met. All along it should have been me.'

His continual flattery was making her lose her appetite; it was nectar to her failing confidence. She took only a very small mouthful of linguini, and even that nearly choked her. 'As far as I recall, you did recover from me fairly swiftly. Only two months later you were engaged to Cynthia Dallwood.'

'Yes,' he sighed. 'What a disaster that was. After the first year it became woefully apparent that all we had in common was a mutual antipathy to one another.

'Thank God you can learn from your mistakes. You can start again. You can have a second chance.'

After they'd shared a chocolate pudding, he asked, 'Why don't we have coffee in my flat?'

The question so reminded her of her courting days that it made her smile. 'Why not?'

His flat was not far from the restaurant. It was on the third floor of what had once been a grand London house overlooking a garden square.

A huge bookcase stacked with well-thumbed volumes filled one side of the drawing room. At the windows hung a pair of dark green damask curtains which did not quite fit. By the fireplace were two ancient sofas, covered in faded, dog-haired chintz; they had dips and gullies where the springs had long since given up any attempt to support the weight of the occupants. Imogen guessed the furnishings were cast-offs from Cynthia's country house.

Benjy had never remarried. There had been much talk a few years ago about his engagement to a rich and beautiful American divorcee but, for reasons which were never explained, nothing came of it.

The difference between Benjy and Raymond was stark. While Raymond had been one of the most successful men of his generation, Benjy had achieved next to nothing in his life. He had had a disastrous marriage to the beautiful Cynthia, who was totally self-absorbed and impossible to live with; had once acted as gardening correspondent to a national newspaper; had spent a period in a drying-out clinic successfully bucking alcohol; and now ran a landscape gardening service for pocket-sized Fulham gardens.

Imogen had expected that she might feel tense out on a date for the first time in sixteen years, yet despite being alone with Benjy in his flat, she felt remarkably at ease.

Raymond thrived on stress, she reflected. He never relaxed. She could understand that he wanted to prove himself, but he had done that long ago. Now it must be only the thrill of the marketplace and the desire to climb even higher that kept driving him.

She had known when she married him that he was a deeply competitive man; from the beginning, she had seen her role as a supportive one, leaving him free to concentrate on his business career. But eventually not even that had been enough for him. He had to compete on the sexual level, too. He had to prove to himself that at forty he was still attractive, still desirable to a woman like Katya – as if anybody could not have told him that money and power and success were greater aphrodisiacs for a certain type of woman than rugged good looks and bulging biceps ever were.

So what am I doing here? Imogen wondered. Did she have something to prove too – would she not accept that she was still an attractive, sexual creature until Benjy had demonstrated it to her by making love to her here in this flat? Would it be a kind of revenge?

He shuffled back from the kitchen, balancing a couple of mugs, a carton of milk and a cafetiere. He unloaded them on to the table in front of her, then sat down next to her on the sofa. He pushed down the plunger very slowly to stop the coffee spewing out around the mesh.

As Imogen watched him, she wondered whether she could have been happy with a man like Benjy – whether she would have been irked by his lack of financial drive and the sacrifices that would have entailed. All the energy which Raymond devoted to business, Benjy directed inwards. For him, success was keeping the inner demons at bay. Yet he had such a gentle smile, such a warm nature, and suffering had made him perceptive.

'Milk, sugar?'

'Milk, no sugar,' she answered.

'I won't forget.' He handed her a mug. 'A liqueur?'

'No thanks.'

They both sipped silently for a short while, yet strangely there was nothing awkward about the silence. Then she put down her mug; he put down his, and moved closer. 'You need someone to look after you,' he said quietly, then, touching her far cheek, he turned her face towards him, and brought his lips towards hers.

She let him kiss her once, then turned away. She was so confused. There seemed to be no moral certainties any more. She wanted this man but, even in the face of Raymond's deceit, it would still be a betrayal of all the values she stood for. What hope for her marriage then?

He put his hand under her chin and gently turned her head towards him for the second time.

'No, Benjy.'

'Why not?' he said. 'You're a free agent now. Raymond's deceit has liberated you to do what you will.'

She hesitated for a moment before replying. Despite her anger at Raymond, she was still not sure that she wanted to be free. 'You must allow me time,' she said.

She let him kiss her again, then gently pushed him away and rose to her feet. 'Thanks for lunch,' she said. 'Ring me.'

Twenty-Seven

Imogen climbed the stairs to Sotheby's Great Rooms, passed through the double doors and plucked a glass of orange juice off the waiter's silver tray. She took a deep breath and was about to head into the crowd when Pamela signalled, hurrying towards her.

'Before you take another step, I think you should know who I've just seen.'

'Who?'

'Her.'

'Her?'

'Don't be dense, darling – Miss Cornwale. I know it seems extraordinary that she might be invited to something like this, which is meant to be a social occasion as well as an auction preview, but there we are. Restoring paintings is, after all, one of her professions – although not, I am sure, as lucrative as restoring wilting male egos.'

'You're sure it's her?'

'Certain. I mean it's not on, is it? I'll have a quiet word with the chairman next time I see him. If she wants to view the paintings, she should go on one of the public days. She shouldn't mix socially. Mistresses are given nice flats so that they can stay in them.'

'The trouble is, nobody seems to keep the rules any more.'

Imogen glanced over Pamela's shoulder, searching for

Katya's slim outline among the crowd. Although the huge rooms imposed their own formality and muffled the sounds of laughter, groups were forming, separating and re-forming like busy cells.

Beyond the central group of men in blue and grey and women in sparkling black, a number of rather dusty, moth-like individuals hovered around the walls, catalogues in hand, actually studying the paintings on view. As trade, Imogen expected Katya to be among them rather than in the thick of the party, but she couldn't see her anywhere.

She sipped her orange juice, wishing she had chosen something stronger. 'Pamela, where did you see her?'

'In the next room. You'll be glad to know she is being ignored totally. I know of at least two people who have decided not to send her work out of consideration for you.'

Imogen blinked. 'It's already common knowledge then?'

'I wouldn't say common, but you can't stop people using their eyes.'

'Thanks for the warning. I'll ring you tomorrow.' She made to move off, but before she could do so, Pamela gripped her sleeve.

'Where are you going?'

'To join the party.'

'But she's there!'

'I'm not going to let her dictate what I can and cannot do,' Imogen answered grandly. She blew Pamela a kiss and walked on.

She dodged through the crowd, looking this way and that. She gazed blankly through Julia Stafford who was trying to catch her eye and ignored the Chandlers who had had her to dinner last week. She walked on blindly.

She wanted to find Katya Cornwale, if only to see how she looked in such surroundings, how she dressed, how she made up, what scent she wore.

In the next room, Imogen found her at last. She had

expected her to be studying the paintings or chatting up some man. Instead, Katya was standing alone by the far wall, staring through the crowd across at her.

Imogen shivered. Despite the distance, she felt those huge, savage eyes piercing through her. Even as a child, she remembered, Katya's eyes had had a chilling quality. Then she had attributed it to a resolve to overcome sadness: now they seemed to mock her with their defiance.

Imogen was determined not to show weakness by being the first to break the gaze and as Katya did not break it either, they kept staring at one another while the distance between them lessened with each step.

There was laughter around them, braying, the chink of glass, whispered asides, but all the sounds seemed to merge into one and grow distant as if coming from another place.

While Imogen was dressed in a black crêpe trouser suit, Katya wore a pink silk slip with a large crucifix around her neck. Her face had matured since those early days at school. The puppy fat had gone, to reveal good cheekbones, and the lips had grown fuller and more pronounced. The eyes, though, still dominated the face.

Even if she had wanted to, Imogen could not stop staring at those eyes. Her heart was beating so fast that for a moment she thought she was going to faint, but outwardly she remained very correct, very calm.

Closer still, she could smell Katya's scent. She recognised it immediately as the one which clung to Raymond when he came home late. Before the reorganisation of the bathroom cabinet, he had always come home smelling only of aftershave. Since, he had smelled like the perfume hall at Harrods, blissfully unaware of the sabotage.

'Hello, Katya,' she said at last. 'We haven't met since school.'

'No, we haven't, have we?'

'I am very impressed by the restoration work you've done for us.'

'Kind of you to say so.'

Imogen glanced down at her hands. 'If I were you and had such a talent, I'd try to make sure it wasn't wasted.'

Katya looked puzzled. 'I'm sorry. I don't follow.'

'Only that people can be so capricious. They could get it into their heads not to send you work for the silliest of reasons. Like stupid gossip, for instance.

'It always strikes me as grossly unfair how difficult it is to build a reputation, yet how easy it is to lose one.'

Imogen stared down from the three extra inches with which she had been blessed and which she had often resented. 'If I were you, I'd stay away from him.

'I've no intention of leaving Raymond, and he has no intention of leaving me. Tiresome though they are at the time, in my experience these little incidents never last long.

'Once they are over, people close ranks, and it's always those on the fringes who get hurt.'

'I wouldn't know about that,' Katya said blandly. 'I understand your anger. But it's not my fault if you don't make him happy any more.'

With that she turned and walked away.

Imogen felt sick. The orange juice was acid in her stomach and bile in her mouth.

She wished she could treat the liaison lightly, as so many of her friends would. She tried to tell herself that she still had his love, even if she shared his body with another woman, that she had the lion's share – she bore his name; she'd borne his children; she lived with him in their house.

But, for her, love, by its nature, had to be possessive. She wanted love, not companionship; she needed it, she craved it from the depths of her being.

Looking neither to the left nor to the right, she made

for the exit and the cool night air.

After ten paces Katya turned back and watched with satisfaction Imogen Punchard hurrying across the room towards the door.

She wondered what Imogen had hoped to achieve by accosting her in that fashion. If Imogen had genuinely believed that a few idle threats would deflect her from a relationship that had become the most important thing in her life, it showed her to be a poor judge of human nature. All she had achieved was the humiliation of making a desperate appeal without the slightest chance of success.

To Katya, the incident only confirmed how right she had been to make the affair known to her rival. All she had done was sow a seed of doubt. Pride and resentment had done the rest.

Feeling thoroughly elated, she picked a fresh glass of champagne off a passing tray and headed back into the midst of the party.

Twenty-Eight

Raymond's flight from America arrived at Heathrow at quarter to four in the afternoon.

Imogen's instinct was to do precisely nothing to mark his return, but on reflection, she changed her mind: jealousy was, after all, a great destroyer of relationships, and sulking had never been the way to a man's heart. So, as the children were still on holiday, she rounded them up, put them into the estate car and drove them to Heathrow to welcome him.

During the first year of their marriage, she had always gone to the airport to meet him, but after the children were born, for practical reasons, this little ritual, like so many others, had ceased to be part of their lives.

Archie was especially excited as he had never been to the airport before. She took the children up to the observation deck, fed them with ice cream sundaes and watched Archie's gawps of amazement at the huge planes hovering above the tarmac.

After they had watched Raymond's plane land, she collected the children, waited for them to finish their ice creams and led them to the escalators.

They glided down through the levels, past the shops for the desperate, last-minute duty presents, past the fast-food stalls, the newsagents and the departure halls. Halfway down the last of the escalators, they were carried

beneath a row of black metal girders and the arrivals hall
came into view.

It was then that she saw her. There, amid the bustling
crowd, stood Katya, in a cream linen jacket and black
leggings.

Imogen felt the acid return to her stomach. She might
not go to the airport to meet Raymond any more, but the
ritual still went on without her.

The moving staircase propelled her lower and ever
closer, at the same steady pace. At the bottom, she kept
her hand firmly around Archie's wriggling one and
stepped forward a few paces. Then, gathering the children
around her like a shield, she headed straight towards the
cordon by the customs hall without looking to left or right.

She crossed the concourse and joined the crush. Babies
in arms yelled their disapproval at the world. Chauffeurs
held placards inscribed with improbable names. Anxious
faces and nervous eyes flicked over the passengers as they
were released, drunk, dishevelled, dehydrated and
disorientated.

Although she did not look around, she still sensed
Katya's presence. She had expected her to have seen them
by now, slid back into the crowd and disappeared. Maybe
she had, but why then did her scent still seem to reach
Imogen over the garlic, curry, sweat and sickly sweet
perfumes of the crowd that pushed and jostled her?

Eventually he came. Unlike the other travellers, in his
blue suit and tie he was remarkably elegant and well
groomed. His eyes, though, darted about him, cutting
through the crowd. She felt a sinking inside, for, from
the pent-up anxiety and longing in them, she knew he
was not searching for his family.

Then Willa shouted, 'Daddy!'

His initial look of surprise changed into a broad smile,
a half-swallowed chuckle, and he scooped up each of the
children in turn.

Imogen felt Katya's presence lift, then. For that moment, at least, Raymond was theirs again.

Archie stayed up for dinner with them that evening. Although he refused to admit that he was tired, he only ate two mouthfuls of sorrel soup and none of the Dover sole.

Raymond ate sparingly too, blaming his lack of hunger on jet lag and being force-fed during the flight. He was anxious and on edge. He was, Imogen was sure, thinking of Katya.

As she sat there, smiling cheerfully and making light conversation, Imogen felt the black clouds of depression close around her. She wondered whether there was any real point in going on; she loathed this sham, these lies, these pretences of normality.

After dinner, she headed upstairs to put the children to bed. Raymond said he would follow in a moment. He never came. She checked that they had brushed their teeth, then tucked them up and kissed them good night.

Downstairs, outside on the landing, she could hear his voice. It sounded so animated, it had a singsong quality. Then it changed and she could hear the passion – 'Love you, miss you.'

He used to say that in just the same way to her. It had moved her then. It moved her still. This time, to sadness.

She opened the door of the drawing room and walked in. Raymond was standing on the far side, receiver in hand, facing the wall. Like a dog, she thought, when it has something to hide.

He did not turn at the sound, but his conversation changed. He was suddenly brisk and businesslike, talking options, futures and financial instruments. Only in his 'Goodbye, I'll ring you later' did his voice soften in a way it never would have talking to a stockbroker.

He turned. 'I'm sorry. I'll go up to the children now.'

'Too late. They're already in bed. You'll only unsettle them.'

Nodding, he walked over to the television and switched it on, then sat down on the sofa. She pulled up a chair and sat down next to him.

In their early years together, whatever he had said to her had seemed fascinating. He could cast a spell on even the simplest of words to give them a lustre they lacked from other mouths.

That phase had passed when they had their first child. The business of living and caring for a baby had squeezed out big ideas and abstract thought. There was always too much to do, with a fragile life to protect and nurture. Conversation lost its flirtatious edge then, and instead became only a tool for the exchange of information.

Now even the information came from the television.

Images of mean streets and derelict land flashed across the screen while a commentator droned on about urban decay. Raymond turned up the volume. She knew there was a film on Channel Four she particularly wanted to watch, but she kept quiet. Raymond did not like 'light comedies'.

Suddenly it all got to her – the incident at the airport, the telephone call, the lies, the deceit, and above all his silence. She could not go on living with this uncertainty, her spirit crushed.

She felt remarkably calm as she turned to him. 'Raymond. I know.'

He had a weak whisky and water in one hand, his head propped in the other. 'Know what?' he asked casually, automatically.

Then his body stiffened, his head swivelled towards her. From the look in his eyes, he already knew the answer to his question but was praying that he would be proved wrong.

She put her hands in her lap and crossed them. 'About her,' she said quietly, firmly.

'Her?'

'Don't insult me, Raymond. The picture restorer.'

'What about her?'

'You're not going to deny that you've been seeing her three or four evenings a week, are you? I've talked to her myself.'

He looked away. Then he got up and walked towards the window.

'And been lying to me every time? In a way, that's the worst part. Do you realise what it's like listening to those deliberate lies night after night from someone I love?'

'I'm sorry. I've been dreading this moment. I knew I couldn't keep it from you indefinitely.'

'That didn't seem to stop you, though.'

He turned and faced her across the room. His eyes showed sadness and discomfort rather than remorse. 'What can I say? I can't offer any excuses. All I can do is apologise.'

She waited for more but nothing came. 'It'll have to end, you know.'

His breathing suddenly became slow and clogged. 'I wish it were that simple.'

'What do you mean?'

He was silent for a moment. A couple of times she thought he was about to say something, but then he reined in the words. 'We are two grown adults. We should come to an arrangement.'

'By that I suppose you mean I should put up with her? No, Raymond. You might think it's very unsophisticated of me still to believe in monogamy, but you don't appreciate how painful this has been for me. I don't play second fiddle. I don't share my man. It's either her or me.'

Raymond turned from her. His fist was clenched, the veins on his neck swollen. He stood facing the window for a long while. 'I'm sorry,' he said finally. 'Please don't ask me to give her up. I can't do it.'

'Don't even think of coming near me again.' Imogen rose and left the room. She ran upstairs, slammed the bedroom door and turned the key in the lock.

Twenty-Nine

'Darling, wasn't that awfully risky?' asked Lady Ravenscroft over lunch the next day. 'I mean, giving him an ultimatum like that – it doesn't allow you much room for manoeuvre.

'Of course, being a woman, it is perfectly proper for you to change your mind, and if I were you I would do so at once.'

'I don't think you're following me,' Imogen said, trying to stab a recalcitrant lettuce leaf for the third time. 'I'm not playing games. If he won't give her up, I'm going to leave him.'

'You're not thinking straight. I understand how you must feel. I remember how hurt I was when I found out that Jack was unfaithful, despite the fact that by then I was totally indifferent to him physically. But once the initial shock is over, you have got to assess what makes most sense for you and the children.

'Is the fact that after so many years Raymond has taken a shine to another woman really something which should cause the break-up of a marriage? Is it really that significant? Did he say that he wanted to leave you for her?'

'No.'

'There we are then. It can't be that serious.'

'But he said he couldn't give her up.'

'That's men for you. Raymond is at a difficult age. He

197

feels he's getting old, is temporarily tired of home life, is worried that he's not as physically attractive as he once was, that his sexual powers are on the wane. He needed some kind of mid-life pick-me-up. It was just a great pity it happened to be her.

'If I were you, I'd just let him work through it. In all likelihood he'll get bored with her. Men usually do. They can't be glued together continually. In between they must talk, and I can't believe they have that much in common.'

Imogen shuddered and grimaced. 'So you think I should sit at home looking after the children and doing my charity work, then smile sweetly and gratefully at him when he finally climbs out of her bed of an evening and comes home? It's not me, Pamela.'

'It's not anybody, darling, but it is expedient.'

'But I've told him I know now, I can't go back. I couldn't go on pretending any longer; even thinking of her was giving me acid indigestion.'

'I did warn you. All you've done is play into the little minx's hands. If you'd wanted to make her a present of him, you couldn't have done more except have him gift-wrapped.'

The waiter came and removed Pamela's empty plate. He looked down at Imogen's, which she had hardly touched. 'Was the chicken not to your liking, madam?'

'It was perfect,' she answered. 'I'm just not hungry.'

'You should eat,' Pamela advised her, as the waiter removed Imogen's plate, too. 'You can't think clearly if you don't eat. And you're obviously not thinking clearly. There aren't many men like Raymond around. You'd be crazy to give him away. Better to grin and bear it than be out in the cold. If anything happens, ring me in Italy. Promise?'

That evening Imogen stayed in. She prayed that when he came home, Raymond would tell her it was all over between him and Katya.

Normally he or his secretary rang at about four and told her when to expect him back from the office. No message had been left when she returned home at five, and there was still no sign of him at nine. She knew he must be with her; that could be the only excuse for his silence.

At nine thirty, when he still had not come, she asked the cook to send the dinner through. The lamb was tough and dry, the vegetables overcooked: not that it mattered, as she had no appetite for food.

After dinner, all she felt like doing was going to bed, but she wanted to be up when he returned home. She sat down on the sofa in front of the television and waited. She tried to imagine the scene in the mews house. Would he break the news before or after making love? she wondered.

Before, she reckoned: Raymond was a gentleman. He would tell Katya that his wife had found out and that the affair must end. Katya would not accept it at first. There would be tears, pleading. She would make love to him using all her guile, in an attempt to hold him. But he would not weaken. He would dress quickly, wish her luck and leave.

Finally, past one o'clock, Imogen heard footsteps on the stairs. Her pulse quickened as he stepped into the drawing room. His glance was heavy with self-conscious embarrassment and contempt.

The last time she remembered him looking at her like that was after he came home drunk from a friend's stag party. This evening he was stone-cold sober. At first she thought the contempt was aimed at her, but on reflection, she realised it was directed inwards.

'You still up?' he asked.

'Yes,' she answered for something to say, as if it was not obvious.

'Oh.'

With that, he turned and left the room.

She was alone again. At that moment, as she gazed into the television with unfocused eyes, she saw a life of loneliness stretching before her. She turned up the volume to drown out her tears.

'Mummy, I don't understand why you are going away,' Willa said four days later.

Imogen and the three children were having tea in the nursery. She had thought it was a good moment to break the news to them, but the brown bread with home-made strawberry jam and the shortbread biscuits brought back such strong memories of the different stages of the children's lives that she had to force herself to keep smiling.

'Darling, you know that Daddy often goes away for several weeks at a time.'

Willa nodded.

'Well, now it's my turn.'

'When Daddy goes abroad, it's because he has to go to boring business meetings, but you don't run a business, so this must be holiday, and if it's holiday I don't see why we can't come too.'

'Because you are all going back to school in a few days, that's why.'

'Not until next week.'

'And I won't be going either until you're back at school. I don't know exactly how long I'll be away for, but I promise I'll be back for half-term.'

'Who's going to look after us?' asked Samantha.

'Janet will – in the same way as she helps out now when I can't be with you.'

'But *why* are you going?' Willa asked again. 'You don't normally go away without Daddy. Don't you love him any more?'

Imogen took a deep breath. 'Yes, well, I love him

200

because he's your father. But sometimes adults have disagreements about things. It makes it difficult for them to live together and it's better if they are apart for a while.'

Willa tilted her head and stared at her quizzically. 'Sabine's mother told her that she was going on holiday, too. A year later her mother and father got divorced.'

The word 'divorced' coming from the lips of her own daughter made something twist inside her.

'Yes, well, Daddy and I have had our differences, but hopefully we can sort them out.'

Both Samantha and Willa stared at her without speaking. She was not sure that Archie fully understood, but, copying the others, he stared at her too.

'I'm sorry.'

She could not think of anything else to say, so to make an excuse for her silence, she put a shortbread biscuit into her mouth.

The days until she was due to leave passed slowly. Raymond came back consistently late. Whenever he saw her, his manner became stilted and awkward. He spoke to her only when absolutely necessary.

Nothing in their sixteen years of marriage had prepared her for this. He was like a stranger. It was intolerable for her, but at least, she thought, the symptoms of guilt were preferable to the moral vacuum which a glib, easy manner might imply.

As the time approached for her to leave, she became suddenly scared that she was making a mistake in going away. She wondered whether it should not be Raymond leaving and she staying behind in the house with the children. But she needed time to think, away from the pressure of the children and the memories this house held for her.

Deep down, she had never believed he would actually let her walk out. Every day, she expected him to make some melodramatic gesture seeking forgiveness. Every day, she was disappointed.

When the new school term began, Imogen prepared for Raymond a long list of the children's likes and dislikes, and suggestions for the nanny's days off.

The following morning she flew to Pisa. From there, she would take a taxi to Lady Ravenscroft's villa high in the Tuscan hills.

PART III

Raymond

Thirty

Driving back from the office that evening, Raymond tried
to think of the best and most tactful way of introducing
Katya to the children. If he and Katya were going to spend
their lives together, the sooner the children got to know
and trust her the better.

He thought it would be insensitive to bring her to
Phillimore Gardens until the children had learnt to accept
her. He dismissed, too, the idea of organising a meeting
after school, as by then the children were often tired,
irritable and unpredictable.

He stabbed out her number on his mobile.

'Did she definitely go?' Katya asked. He could hear blues
playing in the background.

'Yes.'

'Thank God for that. It does no one any good to prolong
the agony. Are you coming over now?'

'Later,' he said. 'With Imogen away, I should spend
some time with the children. I don't want them to feel
that they've been abandoned. I'll have to have dinner with
the girls as usual, but as soon as they've gone to bed, I'll
slip away. Then we've got the whole night together.'

'Great.'

When he arrived home, he poured himself a drink, then
climbed the stairs to the children's floor.

The girls were busy at their homework with Janet, the

mother's help, looking on. Archie had finished his and was now slumped on his favourite beanbag in front of the television.

'Daddy!' Archie scrambled up first, then the girls came running towards him, almost knocking him over as they crowded round, Archie hugging his legs, the girls his waist.

He did not think he was a bad father, only a busy one, although, casting his mind back, he couldn't remember the last time he had been home before Archie had gone to bed – either he had been at the office or with Katya.

'You're home early, Daddy,' said Willa. 'You haven't been sacked, have you?'

He grinned. 'No. I just wanted to see how you all were. I didn't want to stop you doing your homework, though.'

'We've nearly finished anyway,' said Samantha.

The girls went back to the table, and Archie went to clean his teeth. Raymond accompanied him to make sure that he brushed properly, then went through to his bedroom and tucked him up.

'Would you like a story?'

'I'd like Mummy to read me a story.' Archie's eyes were huge and bright and quizzical.

'I'll read you a story. Mummy's gone to Italy.'

'Then I'll wait till she comes back.'

'She'll be a very long time.'

'Don't care. I want her to read it.'

'She can't read it from over there.'

Raymond looked through the books propped between bookends on the top of the chest of drawers, and plucked one out. It had a picture of a large orange cat on the front.

'How about this one?'

'Boring.'

He drew out *The Story of Babar*, which had been a favourite of his in his youth.

'No. Seen it on TV.'

'Which one would you like then?'

'The one Mummy was reading.'

'Which one was that?'

'Dunno.'

'What picture did it have on the cover?'

'Dunno.'

He went through to the nursery and asked Janet which book Imogen had been reading to Archie. When she did not know either, he returned to Archie's bedside, picked up the book he had first chosen and read it to him anyway.

It had been a long time since he had dined alone with the girls. They sat on either side of him in the candlelight, clearly excited at the prospect of having him to themselves.

He asked them about school and their projects for the new term.

On both subjects they gave monosyllabic replies, but on their plans for the weekend they were voluble. On the Saturday there was a gymkhana near Bradstoke to which Imogen had promised to drive them. Raymond quickly volunteered to take them instead.

'There might be someone staying for the weekend,' he told the girls, slipping the remark into the conversation.

'Who?' asked Samantha.

'Someone called Katya Cornwale,' he said casually. 'She's a very talented picture restorer. I do hope you will like her.'

The two girls exchanged glances.

They were eating crème caramel when Archie appeared in the doorway. He had bare feet beneath his striped pyjamas and he was clutching the one-eared rabbit which he had slept with since he was a baby.

'Archie, why aren't you wearing your slippers?' Willa called. 'We don't want your verrucas all over the house.'

'I'm sorry, I can't sleep,' he announced, rubbing his eyes. 'Mummy always kisses me good night.'

Raymond left the table. He lifted up his son and hugged him. 'I'm afraid Mummy can't kiss you tonight. I can kiss you, Willa, Samantha, Janet and Rabbit can kiss you, but not Mummy. You'll have to try to sleep without her because otherwise you're going to be a very tired boy in the morning.'

'I've tried, Daddy, and I can't.'

'Let's try again, shall we?'

He carried Archie up to the third floor, laid him back in his bed, tucked him up and kissed him, hoping he would settle this time. Then he returned downstairs.

Although they did not broach the subject directly, he could tell the girls were very upset by their mother's departure. Both of them seemed reluctant to go upstairs at the end of dinner, so he let them stay up later than usual and watch television with him.

When they finally went up to bed, he rang Katya to explain that as the children were still so unsettled he thought he ought to stay in Phillimore Gardens that night; at the same time he invited her to Bradstoke for the weekend. He then went to bed himself. He had found the evening with the children surprisingly tiring.

The house seemed strangely empty without Imogen. As he tramped up the stairs, he was undecided whether to sleep in the single bed in the dressing room or the double one in the master bedroom from which he had been banished a fortnight ago.

On reaching the landing, he went into the master bedroom and switched on the light. Imogen had finished her packing in a hurry. Cupboards and drawers were open. Coat hangers and discarded clothes lay on the bed. Her scent still hung in the air. Despite the chichi décor, the overelaborate pelmets and the chaos, this was still their room, and even if only because of its familiarity, he slept more soundly here than anywhere else.

He took her things off the bed, hung his suit in the

cupboard and slipped on his pyjamas.

Soon afterwards, Archie came in. He still couldn't sleep. He and the one-eared rabbit climbed into bed with Raymond.

When Raymond awoke the next morning, he was for a moment confused and uncertain as to who was sleeping beside him. Then, seeing his son there, face creased on the pillow, arms everywhere, mouth wide open, he laughed.

Thirty-One

As Imogen stepped off the plane at Pisa, heat cocooned her. Over the last few months she had hardly noticed the weather. Black clouds had been circling her which even the brightest sunlight could not penetrate. Even now, she took no pleasure in the change of climate; she merely registered the sensation of warmth upon her listless hands.

She had not been away on holiday without Raymond since before she was married. This should be an adventure. Walking across to the terminal building, she tried to conjure up foreign smells and tastes and a sense of freedom: all she felt was a sense of loss and of failure.

When she arrived in the Tuscan hills high above Siena some two hours later, she tried to derive pleasure from the undulating landscape against the brilliant blue sky, the stark reliefs of the cypresses on the horizon, the rows of neatly trimmed vines rising out of the red clay soil. They left her cold. She felt numb inside.

Lady Ravenscroft's house was set in a glade of olive trees at the end of a bumpy track. It was built around a central courtyard, and had white walls and pitched roofs of Roman tiles.

A maid answered the door and showed Imogen into the garden at the back of the house. Pamela was seated in the shade of a vine, wearing a beige T-shirt and white Bermuda shorts. A large straw hat was tied around her head with a scarf. 'Darling, did you have a dreadful journey?'

'No, not bad.'

'I did explain to you that it was only a farmhouse, didn't I? I hope you weren't expecting a *palazzo*.'

'Of course not. It couldn't be nicer here.'

'Thank goodness for that. It's just that you are looking so gloomy, I thought something must be wrong. No one would ever guess that you were on holiday.'

Imogen forced a smile. 'I'm sorry. With so much on my mind, it's difficult to get into a holiday mood.'

Pamela nodded. 'That's something I'm determined to change. Here you'll have time to think and relax. Would you like some tea, or perhaps something stronger?'

'Tea, please.' Imogen sat down in the chair next to her hostess. 'Love is such a strange emotion. Over the last few months, I've asked myself continually whether I still love Raymond – and this seems a ridiculous thing to say – but I don't know. At first I felt so angry and so humiliated I could have strangled him. Now I just don't feel anything any more. That side of me seems to have shut down entirely.'

Lady Ravenscroft flicked her wrist. Imogen could not be sure whether this gesture was directed at her or some insect. 'Don't worry, darling. It's all part of the healing process. Have you thought, though, about what you might do with your life should you decide to leave him?'

Imogen sighed. 'I don't know whether I'd feel like getting married again. I doubt it. My first responsibility, of course, would be to the children.

'If I look back at what I've achieved in my life so far, I'm really only proud of three things.

'First, I prevented Bradstoke Hall and its collection from being sold by being lucky enough to marry a man who could afford to maintain it.

'Secondly, I brought up three children largely by myself,

without relying on teams of nannies as my parents did with me.

'Thirdly, my charity work for the Crisis Call Trust. By that I don't mean raising money through balls and fashion shows, but the hands-on work where I've manned the telephones and dealt with potential suicides on the line. It makes you realise how very small your own problems are in comparison to those of others. In future I'll have much more time for that.'

'Very laudable, Imogen, but will that be enough for you? When Jack and I broke up, I vowed I would never have anything to do with men ever again. I kept that vow for precisely two weeks.

'Suddenly, I was free, available and, unlike in my blushing débutante days when my physical development far outstripped my mental progress, in a position to deal with any scrape I might get myself into. I was raring to go, eagerly waiting for the invitations to fall through my letterbox. Very few came.

'Even some people I had considered intimate friends dropped me. Presumably they saw me as a threat, a dangerous harpy stalking their husbands, which was quite unfair as, having just liberated myself from my own, I didn't want theirs. Not often, anyway.'

Pamela poured out the tea from the pot which the maid had put on the small wicker table by her side. 'So be warned! The attractive divorcee has to make her own way.'

Imogen smiled. 'I think you're painting an unnecessarily gloomy picture. You have more interesting friends than anyone else I know.'

'I get by. Being older, I'm not such a threat now. It's rather cruel, don't you think, the way that God gave us bodies that fall apart in no time, but minds that make us feel perpetually young?

'In those days I wanted a meaningful relationship. This might sound awful, but now it's my nightmare. I don't want someone sharing my bathroom. I don't want someone watching sport on TV while I want to watch a soap on another channel. I certainly don't want to cook anyone dinner night after night.

'These days I like a lover who's going to come and make me feel wonderful, then go away and let me carry on with all the other bits and pieces of my life. I've looked after so many people for so long I feel I've earned the right to wallow in some supremely selfish moments while I'm still young enough to enjoy them.

'You, though, are still young enough to start over again.'

'At thirty-eight, with three children in tow?'

'Certainly. But we've got plenty of time to talk about all these things later. I must show you your room.'

The wicker chair creaked as she rose. She led the way through the house and up the narrow tiled staircase to the first floor. She turned into the second doorway on the right.

The room had huge beams running across the ceiling and whitewashed walls. It was simply furnished, with a wooden-framed double bed by the window, a painted cupboard, a single wooden chair and an Indian durrie.

'I hope you'll like it,' Pamela said. 'The bed's comfortable and the bathroom's next door. I'm sorry there are no flowers. I did ask Nicola. She obviously forgot.'

'I love it. It's so kind of you to have me to stay.'

'Not at all. I'll make sure there are some flowers tomorrow.'

As soon as Pamela had left, Imogen heaved the first of her suitcases on to the bed and unzipped it. She had brought far too many clothes, but thought it prudent to err on the side of caution, especially somewhere as fashionable as Tuscany.

After she had finished her unpacking, she took a long bath in scented oils. Still she could not relax; she felt as if her life had gone on hold.

She knew that other women would be prepared to put up with their husband's philandering for the security, for the children, and for the memory of how it once had been. Other women would think that at her age she should be pragmatic rather than still an incurable romantic. Other women would think her foolish to play into Katya's hands like this.

But she had to be true to herself: she could not sit there like an actress, smiling while her world fell apart.

She tried to imagine what it would be like to be single again. She remembered the nervous excitement before a date, the cruelty and small-mindedness of many of the men, the anguish and heartbreak when things had not turned out as she had hoped: then Raymond had come along and she had found a love which she had felt sure would last a lifetime.

She had been so young then, so vulnerable and impressionable. This time round she would be moving among a small clutch of divorcees, confirmed bachelors and world-weary widowers.

She wanted to view the experience in a positive light as a period of self-growth, as a time for releasing her full potential. But she was qualified for nothing. She felt too young for religion, had too weak a liver for booze and was frightened of casual sex. The prospect made her shudder.

Voices below woke her from her thoughts. Worried in case she would be late for dinner, she applied her make-up, slipped into a loose-fitting printed silk dress and went downstairs.

She walked out on to the terrace. There was Pamela, now dressed in a kaftan, sitting at the head of a glass-topped table. On her left sat a tall, tanned man with dark curly hair, in a threadbare linen shirt.

As Imogen entered, he rose to his feet and turned. The lines in his face creased into smiles.

'I didn't know you were here,' she said, surprised.
'I'm staying in the next village,' Benjy Mulford replied.
Pamela grinned conspiratorially. 'Such a small world.'

Thirty-Two

On Friday evening, Raymond drove the children down to Bradstoke through the rush-hour traffic on the M4.

On Saturday morning, he helped them with their homework, dealt with estate business and read the briefs for the meetings on Monday morning; then he hitched the horsebox on to the Range Rover and took the children off to the gymkhana, where they stayed until four.

On the way back, Samantha was jubilant, having come second in her class in the dressage competition, Willa was furious, as her horse had refused at the third fence, and Archie was feeling sick and confused, having eaten far too much ice cream.

When they arrived home, the old Volvo estate which Katya used to cart paintings around was parked in front of the house.

'Whose car is that?' asked Willa immediately.

'That's Miss Cornwale's,' Raymond answered. 'Remember I told you she was coming to stay?'

'Oh, yes.' Willa nodded. 'The picture restorer. Doesn't she take weekends off?'

'She's not here to work. She's here as our guest, I'd like you all to be nice to her.'

While the children were taking off their boots, he went on ahead.

Briggs, the butler-cum-handyman, intercepted him. 'I

showed Miss Cornwale into the study, sir. I left her things in the hall as I did not know which bedroom she was in.'

'I'm sorry. The Chinese Bedroom.'

'The Chinese Bedroom,' the butler repeated. Raymond was perfectly aware that, although his expression did not change, Briggs was reassessing Miss Cornwale: the Chinese Bedroom was next to Raymond's own. 'Very well, sir. I'll take her luggage up immediately after I have brought in the tea.'

'Thank you.'

Raymond walked through the drawing room into the panelled study. She was sitting in the armchair by the stone fireplace, reading. The light from the window fell across her, catching the whiteness of her skin, the redness of her lips and the auburn of her hair.

Seeing her curled up in the same faded chintz armchair where Imogen always sat made him uncomfortable. She seemed somehow to be mocking and taunting Imogen with her sensuality. He wished she had chosen another chair.

'I'm so sorry,' he said, 'not to be here when you arrived . . .'

Her smile was so warm that it dispelled the awkwardness he felt. She uncurled herself, stretching her limbs with natural grace. She stood up, wrapped one arm around his neck and kissed him on the mouth.

'Where are the children?'

'They're coming.'

'Do you think they'll like me?'

'I'm sure they will. Just be natural.'

While the children filed in, he stood by Katya's side. 'This is Miss Cornwale,' he announced, and introduced the children one by one.

'You can call me Katya if you like,' she added breezily.

The two girls both looked up at her silently without smiling, across at their father, then down at the floor.

Only Archie tottered up, cheeks puffed from a broad smile, and said, 'Hello.'

Katya knelt down. 'Hello, young man. What's your favourite thing?'

'Poos,' he announced gleefully, then wandered off again, leaving Katya crouching in the middle of the Turkey rug.

'I've got some presents for you all to thank you for having me to stay,' she said. Returning to the armchair, she reached behind it and brought out three parcels wrapped in bright red paper.

Archie took his eagerly; he ripped off the paper and the cardboard box to find a toy robot.

The two girls, though, did not move. They sat on the sofa, eyes glaring at her, legs swinging and kicking against the cotton covers. Then curiosity got the better of them. Samantha came over first and took her present. Willa followed. Both girls muttered a reluctant thank-you.

'Give them time,' Raymond said when he and Katya were alone again. 'They've only just met you.'

After tea, Raymond took Katya on a tour of the grounds. They visited the rose garden, the stables, the ha-ha, the lake, the formal garden and the ilex walk.

Despite her love of art, architecture and the countryside, this mode of living had never been something to which Katya had aspired; neither had she hankered after possessions and grand houses. She had always seen herself as a free spirit.

Yet wandering with Raymond through the gardens, she felt their magic everywhere: in the light filtering through the trees; in the shadows on the lawns; in the amber glow on the old stonework; in the sound of the water trickling down the mossy bank; in the rose petals moving in the breeze; in the spring in the turf and the smell of freshly mown grass. The freedoms she held so dear seemed worth sacrificing for the joys of such a place.

She felt the same over dinner, sitting next to Raymond at the refectory table in the oak-panelled dining room. After Briggs had served artichoke soup, duck breasts and a chocolate pudding off the crested family china, the girls went off to watch television. She and Raymond stayed behind, lingering over coffee, chatting and, like teenagers, holding hands under the table.

When finally it was time for them to go to bed, in case one of the children was watching, she kissed him primly good night on the landing and went alone to the Chinese Bedroom. The room had a four-poster bed surrounded by a huge canopy of blue silk, and hand-painted wallpaper depicting exotic birds against a blue sky.

Katya undressed quickly. She climbed into bed, shivering at first at the coldness of the linen against her skin. She picked her book off the bedside table, propped herself on the soft down pillows and waited for him.

It was not long before she heard the soft falls of his slippered feet and the squeak of the hinges. There he was, standing in the doorway in his striped pyjamas and paisley silk dressing gown, hair neatly brushed, teeth cleaned, smelling of aftershave.

She thought it strange how the same man could summon from her such varying emotions. In London, there had been so much anger in the air it had often spilled over into their lovemaking as they had tried to assuage their frustrations in sexual oblivion. Here, though, the beauty of the house and its surroundings seemed to suck the angst from her.

Forget the flashy pyrotechnics, she hoped that this time Raymond would be gentle and slow, that the act of sex would be a true act of love expressing emotions deeper than he ever could in words.

He walked over to the side of the bed, slipped off his dressing gown and climbed in beside her. His body was warm after the cool sheets. She slipped her arm around his neck, kissed him twice, then unfastened the buttons of his pyjamas until he was naked beside her.

In London, they usually made love earlier in the evening. It was nearly midnight now. After the rich dinner, the wine and the busy day, Raymond's eyes were half closed and slightly bloodshot. He hugged her in his arms. He stroked her back, her sides. The movements of his hands became slower and slower. A few minutes later, they stopped entirely.

She glanced up. He was fast asleep.

When she awoke the following morning, she was alone. She was not sure what the arrangements for breakfast were. She hoped someone would bring her breakfast on a tray, but as none had appeared by ten o'clock, she climbed out of bed, dressed and went down to find what she could in the dining room.

Samantha and Willa were slurping coffee and reading the Sunday papers spread out on the refectory table.

She smiled at them both as she entered. 'Good morning, Samantha. Good morning, Willa.'

'Good morning, Miss Cornwale,' they both replied.

She poured herself coffee from the sideboard. 'You can call me Katya if you like.'

'Thank you, Miss Cornwale, but we don't like.'

Katya heard giggling behind her. One by one she raised the lids of the silver salvers on the hot plate and helped herself to a tomato, a sausage and scrambled eggs.

'Wouldn't it be more fun for everyone if we tried to get on?' she said as she sat down next to Samantha. 'I'd like to be friends.'

'Why?' asked Willa. 'Might you be coming back?'

'I might. If I'm asked.'

Samantha glanced up from the papers. 'Are you Daddy's girlfriend then?'

'Depends what you mean by girlfriend. We are friends, certainly.'

'I mean do you do *it*?'

Willa's eyes bulged. 'She means sex.'

'That's none of your business,' Katya answered.

'Oh yes it is,' Samantha said coldly. 'Especially when it takes our mother away from us.'

'As far as I understand, your mother went away of her own free will.'

'Only because you drove her away. I mean, even the *idea* of Daddy doing it at his age . . . it's seriously gross.'

Willa stared at Katya with eyes full of hate. 'Why don't you pick on someone who hasn't got a family? Leave him alone, you hear? He doesn't belong to you.'

With that, the two girls stood and walked out of the dining room, slamming the door behind them.

Thirty-Three

Benjy Mulford staying in the next village was too much of a coincidence. Imogen was convinced that, although she pretended otherwise, Pamela had engineered it. Initially she resented such blatant matchmaking: she was here to get away from her family so that she could plan the rest of her life; she did not want any decision muddled by a holiday romance.

Yet, as the days passed, she was increasingly grateful for his presence. Pamela had seen all the tourist sights many times and only a sense of politeness made her offer to go round them again. Benjy, on the other hand, was keen.

Every day he would come to the villa soon after breakfast in his hired Fiat Tipo and take Imogen off on an expedition. Together they marvelled at the *campo* in Siena, the *duomo* in Florence and the della Francescas in Arezzo. They also made three expeditions to the gardens of the Medici villas around Florence which Benjy said had inspired his designs for a hundred Fulham back yards.

It took time for her to get used to his incessant smoking, both in and out of the car. She hated the way it permeated her clothes and clung to her hair, but she did not ask him to stop as she knew he could not change now.

'One of the things I love about travelling,' said Benjy as they were on their way to visit the mountain village of

Pienza, 'is that you learn how totally contradictory the rules that govern social behaviour are.

'Consider that tribe who send their young men to be buggered for a year by elder warriors, or the African cultures where clitoridectomy is still practised.'

'Yes, but there you are referring to primitive cultures.'

'What about polygamy in the Arab world or the American habit of serial monogamy? What about arranged marriages in India or the Bedouins' belief that romantic love is shameful and that one should reserve deep love only for parents, siblings and children? No wonder sex causes as much pain as it ever does pleasure.'

'So what do you believe?'

He flicked cigarette ash out of the open window. 'Don't ask me to pronounce on what's right for mankind. All I know is that women have been responsible for the best moments in my life, and for that, I will happily put up with the rest. I must, though, have been temporarily insane ever to think my marriage to Cynthia stood a chance.'

'Why did you marry her then?'

His eyes twinkled. 'I was on the rebound from you, wasn't I?'

'You blame me!'

'Absolutely, categorically. You unhinged me. You made my life not worth living. I've been trying to put the pieces back together ever since.'

It was a pretty speech, if not entirely true. She had been too besotted with Raymond at the time to take much notice of other men, even Benjy; she certainly had done nothing to encourage him. Her ego, though, was so deflated, it could take all the massaging he could give it.

Playing along, she smiled at him coyly and rested her head on his shoulder as he drove. 'I'm sorry if I treated you badly.'

'Apology accepted,' he said, quickly throwing the

remains of his cigarette out of the window. 'Thank you for coming back into my life now.'

She stayed with her head on his shoulder for a while and found that his physical closeness made her feel comfortable and warm. It also made her very conscious of the lack of intimacy in her life. In his too, she suspected. Cynthia's neuroses had been camouflage for a steel core.

Soon after one, they were high in the hills near San Quirico. Parking the car on the grass verge, Benjy took the picnic basket out of the boot and led the way down a narrow track of dry, cracked earth. He walked on until they reached an olive grove.

While the leaves above them swayed in the breeze, dappling them with a confetti of light, they lunched off freshly baked bread, Parma ham, figs, salami, fruit and three different cheeses.

When she had eaten, Imogen sighed, lay back on the rug and stared at the panorama of hills stretching before her.

'Beautiful, isn't it?' Benjy remarked.

She nodded. 'I don't know why it is, but big landscapes make me melancholy. Sometimes I can't stop myself from crying.'

He leaned across and kissed her on the cheek. She brushed him away, but only gently. Moving closer, he kissed her on the lips.

There was something so deeply sensual about him that she was suddenly frightened. 'Stop it!' she said and pushed him away.

'You know how I've always adored you – from the very beginning,' he answered, his breath warm on her neck and her throat.

The last time she had tussled on a rug in the open air had been in the second year of her marriage. With the breeze on her skin, a man's hand on her thigh and his lips nuzzling her breasts, suddenly she felt young again.

'Stop it, Benjy. Someone might see us.'

'Only the sheep, and they don't get frightened half as easily as horses.'

'They will when I scream.'

'I like a woman who's noisy in bed.'

'No, Benjy. I mean it. I'll scream unless you stop.'

He raised his head from her breast. Her dress was halfway down to her waist now, and her erect nipples glistened with his saliva. He gazed down at her, his eyes full of desire, lust; maybe, she thought, even love. At that moment, though, most of all she wanted him not so much to love her as to desire her more intensely than he ever had a woman before.

As their lips met, she felt his hand sliding up her thigh. She had to swallow hard. It surprised her how thrilling she found it.

'No,' she said again, 'no.' But now her voice was hardly more than a whisper. His shirt was unbuttoned and his smooth chest lightly touching her breasts. She ran her hands over his back, down the nodules of his spine, along the dip where the back meets the buttocks, then she felt the muscles clench as he thrust forward and entered her.

She had to choke back the tears. Every part of her was so sensitive, she felt she was going to explode. She clung to his back, holding him to her as if afraid that he might depart.

For so long now, sex had had the predictability of the call of the cuckoo clock in the nursery. This felt so different. It was not only the smell, the touch and the way he moved that were different, but the rawness of his desire.

She felt the coarse grass against the soft white skin of her buttocks, the breeze on her limbs and her hair, the warmth from the sun on her body, then, as he pressed down on her again, the burning inside.

With every stroke, the fire intensified until it touched

every part of her, until the slightest movement made her gasp. Then, while he held her tight in his arms, her body shook and spasm after spasm passed through her, the tears rolled from her eyes into the grass and her cries sounded in the hillside.

Afterwards, they lay side by side in the grass while he smoked a cigarette. Neither of them spoke. Despite her tiredness, she felt exhilarated, her body glowing, alive.

'So what did you do today?' asked Pamela over dinner.

'We went to Pienza.'

'Such a charming place. Did you visit the cathedral?'

'I'm afraid we didn't have time.'

'I see.' Pamela spoke in such a knowing tone, Imogen blushed.

Thirty-Four

Since Imogen had left, their schedule had changed. Raymond no longer came to see Katya after work, but instead went home and spent time with the children. He usually came round to her at about nine thirty and took her out to dinner. Unless, of course, he rang her to cancel, as he frequently had to that week.

On Monday, he called to say that Archie had a tummy ache and was so upset that he could not leave him. On Tuesday, Archie's stomach was still bad. On Wednesday, Willa went down with the same symptoms.

Katya would have been more convinced that a highly contagious virus had taken a grip on the household if they all had not looked so exceedingly healthy the previous weekend.

When he rang to tell her that he could not come round on Wednesday, she said: 'Don't you think they might be putting it on just a little bit?'

'Probably, but if they are, it's because they're feeling insecure without their mother. I can't turn my back on them when they need me.'

'Why don't I come over to you then?' Katya suggested.

'Do you really think it would be such a good idea while the children are still missing Imogen? Later, my love, once things have settled down.'

'Of course. Miss you.'

'Miss you, too.'

At last, on Thursday, he came. No sooner had she got him a drink than he pulled one of Samantha's school books from his inside pocket. 'Could you help me out?' he asked. 'You were at school more recently than me. I've completely forgotten all the calculus I ever knew.'

She looked at him for a moment, speechless. This was their evening together. 'I'm sorry,' she said. 'I had nothing to forget.'

'Pity.'

'Where are we going to dinner?'

'Would you mind if it was somewhere quick?'

She smiled. 'Of course not.'

'Actually,' he said, 'on second thoughts, why don't we send out for something, or maybe you could rustle up an omelette? I don't like leaving the children alone for too long when they're like this.'

Katya checked the refrigerator. Apart from a half-drunk bottle of wine, all it contained was cottage cheese, milk and the remains of the salad she had eaten at lunchtime. She put on a coat and walked down to the all-night supermarket for some eggs and smoked salmon.

When she returned, Raymond was slumped on the sofa in front of the television. He woke up as she closed the door. 'I'm sorry,' he said. 'I've had terrible nights, with Archie being up all the time. Can I help you?'

'No,' she answered, 'everything is under control. You just relax.'

'Fine,' he said, flicking through the programmes until he found one on current affairs.

Meanwhile she set to work in the kitchen, heating the butter in the saucepan and mixing the eggs in a bowl.

The following weekend Raymond drove the children down to Bradstoke as usual. This time Katya came with them and brought Myrtle too.

She thought she was making headway with the girls, for in the car they answered her questions politely if rather formally. However, when unpacking her bag, she found her black crêpe de Chine trousers and her suede ankle boots running with pink shampoo, despite being certain that she had tightened the top of the bottle before she had left.

She had brought nothing else to wear in the evening, so she cleaned the trousers as best she could and ran an iron over them before going downstairs.

The two girls were already chatting with their father when she walked into the drawing room. Immediately, the conversation stopped. 'Katya, you look lovely,' Raymond said over the giggles of the girls, but she knew that he must have noticed the stain. 'Would you like some champagne?'

'Yes, please.'

'I'll get it for you, Daddy,' Samantha volunteered, jumping to her feet. 'You've been working hard all week.'

'Thank you, Samantha.' Raymond smiled at her, then gave Katya a knowing look, as if this was a sign that the girls were beginning to accept her.

Katya only wished it was true. She suspected, though, that it was another ghastly practical joke.

She watched Samantha carefully as the girl went over to the drinks tray, poured out the champagne and brought the glass over to her. Nothing seemed out of the ordinary, except that the colour of the liquid in her glass was darker than Raymond's. Whether this was due to laxative powder, sheep's urine or a sleeping draught she had no intention of finding out.

She smiled back at Samantha, thanked her for the drink, and left it on the table, untouched.

The two girls went to bed soon after dinner. When Raymond and Katya followed an hour or so later, she could still hear the rise and fall of their conversation coming from a room further along the passageway.

She changed out of her evening clothes and got ready for bed. In London she liked to go to bed nude even when sleeping alone: here, the bedroom was so cold and damp, she would have preferred something more practical, but did not want to disappoint Raymond.

When he finally arrived, she was almost asleep. 'I'm sorry,' he said. 'I just went to check the children were all right. I found Willa had gone to bed with wet hair. I made her dry it, especially with this chill going around.'

'You don't think she did that deliberately to keep you with her?' Katya asked.

'If she did, it's rather touching, don't you think?'

She felt a cold draught of air as he climbed into bed beside her. He cuddled up to her, his feet and hands icy cold after his tramp down the passage. He kissed her lazily once on the neck, then again on the lips, this time harder. She loved the way he kissed and his slightly salty, very masculine smell.

He caressed the soles of her feet with firm, regular strokes until she could feel a soothing warmth permeating through her. He kissed the nape of her neck and the pale skin around her armpits. He worked on her breasts until the nipples were hard.

When the longing in her belly was so intense she could not stand it a moment more, she made herself comfortable on the pillow, and took hold of him, ready to guide him into her.

'Daddy!' called a small voice.

Raymond turned, listened and went limp in her hand.

'Don't come in, Archie!' he shouted. 'I'm coming to you.'

'Sorry, darling,' he whispered to Katya, and throwing back the sheets, climbed out of bed. He reached for his dressing gown, opened the door and rushed out.

* * *

Archie stood in the corridor, shivering, eyes half closed from tiredness. 'Daddy,' he said, reaching for Raymond. 'I had a nightmare.'

Kneeling down, Raymond hugged his son's tiny figure. 'It's all right now. I'm with you.'

'What were you doing in Miss Cornwale's room?'

'She had a little nightmare, too, so I went to comfort her. Now come along to bed, Archie.'

'Could I have something to drink first?'

'Yes, of course.'

'Then will you read me a story?'

'It's very late.'

'A story will help to make the nightmare go away.'

'Very well then. A quick one.'

'Thank you, Daddy.'

Raymond could not refuse him; not after what had happened when he had been about Archie's age on that July afternoon in Tunis. The thought of it, even now, sent sweat trickling down his back.

He'd been living with his parents in the expatriate compound in a palm-lined suburb at the time. It was a Wednesday. He was meant to be out playing in a football match with the sons of the other oil executives. Instead, he had a fever and was lying in bed on a mattress damp with his sweat.

Mariette, a local native girl with fine, slender wrists, was looking after him. Although he liked her, he wanted and needed his mother. Each time he closed his eyes, his mind started reeling with strange images; he was too scared to close them again.

He had asked Mariette many times to fetch his mother. She had said that Mrs Punchard would come as soon as she could, but he had waited all afternoon for her and still she had not come: so when Mariette left the room to get him some fresh water, he got up and went in search of her himself.

He remembered how unsteady and light-headed he had felt when first he stood, and how cold he had been despite the heat. He thought for a second he was going to faint, but he managed to reach the door, opened it and, squinting against the intense glare of the sun, stepped out on to the stone terrace.

He followed the terrace halfway round the house until finally he reached his parents' bedroom. Their door was much the same as his; it was light blue with an aluminium handle and an air vent halfway up. 'Mummy!' he called.

No one heard. No one came. Turning the handle, he pushed the door open.

The room was large and bare. Apart from a wooden table, two chairs and a huge hanging cupboard, the only furniture was the double bed jutting from the left-hand wall.

The shutters were drawn against the heat and the light, but still he could see the outline of the figures on the bed.

His father was lying with his weight resting on his elbows, his broad back naked and glistening as if he too was sweating from a fever. Beneath was Mother, her head turned away, half hidden by the sheet and Father's forearm.

Although they both must have heard the squeak of the hinges, only his father twisted around towards him.

'Get out, Ray!' he yelled.

He did not want his father; he wanted his mother: she would understand. He stepped through the clothes scattered on the floor, closer to them, wondering why she had not already got out of bed and come to him.

'But I need Mummy!' he called. Still she did not answer.

The sinews on his father's neck swelled. His lips were pulled back, his teeth bared. 'Do what you're fucking well told, Ray – get the hell out of here!'

'Why didn't you lock the door?' asked the woman.

As soon as she spoke, he knew. It was not his mother's voice. It was the voice of the mother of a friend of his. The woman with wide lips and a tiny nose.

He turned and ran.

He was not sure exactly what was going on between his father and the woman, but he knew that in some way his father was betraying his mother, and in betraying his mother, he was betraying Raymond himself. At that moment he had stopped trusting his father and started despising him.

Now, as he walked along the cold passageway, he gripped the tiny hand tighter, and prayed that Archie would not do the same.

'When's Mummy coming back?' Willa asked at lunch the next day.

'I'm not sure,' answered Raymond, quickly swallowing a mouthful of roast lamb. 'Whenever she's finished her holiday.'

'And meanwhile will Miss Cornwale be coming here every weekend?' Willa looked directly at her father, ignoring Katya, who was across the table from her.

Raymond glanced at Katya and smiled reassuringly. 'Yes, if she wants to.'

'What if we don't want her to?' Samantha ventured.

'I'm sure you don't mean that. I know that in time you will grow as fond of her as I am.'

'Daddy,' Samantha sighed, 'I know it must be difficult sometimes for grown-ups to live together, but does that mean you've got to mess up our lives as well?'

'I want to do the best I can for you.'

'Then why are you destroying our family?'

Raymond paused for a second before replying. 'The best in the circumstances. That's all we can do.'

'I want to be your friend, honestly I do,' Katya told the children. 'I know we could have so much fun together –

riding, going on walks, playing games.'

'Prove it to us, then,' Samantha answered. 'Act like a true friend, and go away.'

Thirty-Five

Imogen and Benjy decided against sightseeing in the afternoons. On the occasions they had tried, they had tramped through the heat of the day only to find churches locked and galleries closed due to staff shortages and restoration in progress; instead, they stopped for a good lunch around one, then went back to Benjy's apartment for an afternoon siesta.

His bedroom was airy, with bleached floorboards, whitewashed walls and a small double bed. She loved to lie there under the quilt, resting against him, watching the patterns the shadows made on the ceiling as the muslin curtains swayed in the breeze. She loved the potpourri of smells: him, the bed, her own scent and the spices carried on the wind through the window.

It was a long time since she had lain in bed with a man in the afternoon. She had done so with Raymond when first they had married; their lovemaking had been hot, passionate and incessant, but after the children had come along, they had fallen out of the habit and had not made the time – which was silly, she thought, as it had been so important to them once.

Since that first time with Benjy, the sex between them had got better and better. He was a considerate lover who took his time, who joked and laughed and made her feel like she had not felt since those early days. Yet he did not require to be loved. All he expected was the companionship which he himself gave in abundance.

While Imogen had got ready for bed, he had made two cappuccinos and brought them up to the bedroom with a tub of ice cream, a bottle of chilled white wine and some fizzy mineral water. They had made love twice, and now they were lying there peaceful and content, flicking through the English newspapers.

'Will you come and live with me when we go back?' he said casually, still smoking his cigarette.

'Is that some kind of proposal?' Imogen asked, flattered.

'Of course.'

'If I may ask, what is the longest time you have ever lived with one woman?'

'Do you always answer a question with a question?'

'Only when I'm still working on the answer.'

He took a long draw on his cigarette. 'Twenty-three months and seventeen days with my dear divorced and unlamented first wife Cynthia. Not long enough for a gold watch, I'm afraid, but I would plead mitigating circumstances.'

'And the others?'

'The trouble is, I'm normally attracted to wonderfully charming but hopelessly unreliable people who, like me, find this world of ours something of a struggle.'

She grinned. 'Do I fall within that category?'

'Yes and no. You are sensitive and delicate and understanding, but at the same time you have the strength to cope. To me, that makes you the perfect woman. I knew it when you were a shy ingénue twenty-odd years ago, and it's as true today.'

She looked into his cool grey eyes with their boyish warmth, and almost believed him.

'Why are you saying this?' she asked lightly. 'You have already had your wicked way with me.'

'Yes,' he growled, leaning over and taking her nipple

into his mouth, 'but I want more, and I want you to live with me.'

She breathed in sharply. 'I do have three children.'

'No problem. We'll buy the flat upstairs and insulate the ceiling.'

'Could we stay in bed all day?'

'Of course, except when I have to get up to make the tea or open the door to take deliveries of smoked salmon and caviare.'

He burrowed under the quilt. She felt his breath on her as he gently parted her legs, then a sudden tremor of pleasure as his tongue set to work.

Whenever she thought of marriage, she thought of responsibility, duty and sacrifice, for she had always put the needs of others before her own. Now, though, she also thought of Raymond's overbearing ways and his indifference and selfishness in cheating on her.

While before, the prospect of the break-up of her marriage had made her brain go hazy and her temples throb, now she was beginning to think of it like the break-up of school on the last day of term. As the car had driven away and she'd seen the grey stone mass of the convent for the last time, she had felt a thrill at the prospect of exploring pastures new and relief that never again would she be subject to the petty discipline of the nuns.

Then, she had made herself into a perfect consort for Raymond: the beautiful bride in the Dior dress, hanging on the tycoon's bespoke sleeve. This time, she was older and wiser.

Thirty-Six

'Thank you very much for sparing the time to see me, Mr Punchard,' said the woman with the long white hair and the ashen face. She offered a surprisingly strong handshake.

'No trouble at all,' replied Raymond, who had just cancelled two meetings involving a total of sixteen people in order to get here.

'Do sit down.'

She indicated a chair opposite her desk. It was clear that none of the huge fees which the school charged each term had been spent recently on the decoration of the headmistress's study. The wallpaper was tobacco yellow through age rather than design, and small rugs were placed strategically about the floor to hide frays in the carpet. On the mantelpiece stood a collection of figurines in brass, wood and shell which Miss Withers had acquired on her travels in Africa and the Middle East.

'I wanted to see you about Samantha and Willa.' She positioned a cushion in the small of her back. 'So far this term the behaviour of both the girls has been deplorable. On two occasions Samantha has refused to eat lunch despite the food being carefully prepared and nutritious. She has been disruptive in class, and her work has not been up to standard. Willa's conduct, if anything, has been

worse. She was sent to me twice last week for rudeness
and bad behaviour.'

'I'm sorry.' School memories remained so fresh in his
mind that his sphincter contracted involuntarily. 'Is there
anything you want me to do about it?'

Miss Withers's fingers joined together to form an
arch. Her small, intense eyes stared at him. 'Experience
has shown us that sudden changes in children's behaviour
are often due to instability in their home life. Mr
Punchard, have there been any developments at home
which might account for their behaviour?'

Raymond felt an urge to uncross and recross his legs.
He resisted it. 'Our family is in something of a state of
flux at the moment. My wife is away in Italy visiting
friends.'

Her pen tapped on the desk. 'Mrs Punchard being away
in Italy is, I take it, a symptom rather than the cause of
this "state of flux"?'

He nodded.

'Of course we do have a considerable number of children
at the school with either divorced or separated parents.
Some of them cope remarkably well, but naturally all of
them are damaged to some degree. All that we can hope
is that we do whatever we can to minimise that damage.

'That's why I wanted to see you. I recognised the signs
immediately in the two girls, but it does help if we are
told, as then members of the staff know what to expect.'

She looked across at Raymond wearily. 'Were you the
child of divorced parents, Mr Punchard?'

He swallowed as he nodded. 'Yes.' Although long ago,
the pain he had felt at his parents' separation seemed
almost as acute now as when he was a boy.

'I suspected as much. Not because of any unusual
perspicacity on my part, but because it is so often the
case. The sins of the fathers are indeed visited on the
next generation: here in the form of an apparent inability

to form a lasting union. So sad, but there we are. In this job, you learn to be practical.'

A bell sounded outside. Miss Withers rose to her feet. 'Thank you so much for seeing me.' Her hand went out to him. 'I will warn my colleagues. Let me show you to the door.'

That evening, rather than going round to Katya, Raymond stayed with the children.

He recalled his own confusion and the numbing feeling of loss when his parents had divorced. Then, he had blamed himself entirely for what had happened. Now, as an adult, he knew that the break-up had been caused by his mother running out of patience with his father's womanising.

Yet the child in him still blamed himself, certain that there must have been something he could have done to keep his parents together.

Was he now going to replicate the past and behave in the same way to his children as his father had to him?

'So what are you going to do now?' Simon asked as they had a drink together at the club the following evening.

Raymond had been so busy with Katya that he had not played squash with Simon for over six months, but now that Imogen had left, he felt a need to talk things through with another man.

'I don't know,' he replied. 'The last thing I want to do is hurt Imogen or the children, yet the thought of giving Katya up makes me feel physically ill.'

Simon sipped his beer. 'You're going to have to make up your mind.'

'Would you ever leave Jane and marry Lucy?' Raymond asked.

'Not for as long as Jane is prepared to put up with me. First because it would be unfair on her and damaging to the children. Secondly because I'm enough of a realist to know that it would wreck my relationship with Lucy.'

Raymond was puzzled. 'I thought you and Lucy got on so well together?'

'We do. But marriage is something else entirely. At the moment, Lucy and I, like you and Katya, think ourselves lucky if we can snatch a few hours together, so we make sure that everything is special. It's like a fantasy world. A Disneyland for grown-ups. No one ever goes to the supermarket. There are no children to be ill or tired. Your only responsibility is to each other. All that matters is love and comfort and sex.

'If Lucy and I stay as we are, I reckon we could still be feeling as passionately about one another when we are both on zimmer frames. Expose that fantasy to the real world, to faulty plumbing, headaches, dirty dishes and demanding children, and see how long it lasts. There is no greater passion killer than everyday life.

'Say you marry Katya, what are you going to do when those first heady days are gone? Because, sure as night follows day, that overwhelming first rush of lust and love is not going to last forever. Marry someone else? Go through the process again and again until you are too knackered or broke to continue?

'Serial monogamy is awfully messy. It leaves a lot of unhappy, insecure children and angry ex-wives around, it's ruinously expensive and it's only likely to be a short-term fix.'

His hand dropped on to Raymond's shoulder. 'The passion might have let up a bit since the early days but Imogen is not only a great girl and a good wife, she is also the mother of vulnerable children – your children. Are you seriously going to put them through that sort of trauma?'

Raymond sighed and drained his glass. 'I wish it were that simple.'

Simon stared straight at him with a slow smile on his lips. 'You know what? It is. You've just got to have the courage and determination to make it so.'

Thirty-Seven

Raymond felt stiff, awkward and disorientated as he pressed the bell and waited on the doorstep. His head throbbed at the sound of the latch going back. Then the door opened inwards, and there she was by the jamb, smiling at him with those full, seductive blood-red lips of hers.

The sight of them made something twist inside him: the hours he had spent kissing those lips; the hours they had danced over his body, sending his pulse racing until he was beyond the limits of pleasure. He had to look away.

'Anything troubling you?' she asked as she took off his jacket.

He meant to say yes: he said no.

'I know you've been under a lot of pressure, but it's only until we can resolve this business,' she said as she loosened his tie and unfastened the top button of his shirt.

Already he felt some of the tension leaving him. Already what he had been sure of only a few moments before now seemed premature, misplaced, downright wrong.

He sat down on the sofa. For a moment Katya left his side, only to return with a whisky and water. He sipped at it and felt the fire in his mouth and the glow in his belly.

'How are the children?' she asked.

'Fine.' He assumed they were anyway; after his drink

with Simon, he had come straight here.

Looking at her now, he could not imagine how he could ever tire of her haunting beauty or stop thrilling to her caresses; or believe that she would ever cease to surprise him. As she sat down close to him, he could smell her scent, the sweetness of her body, the perfume of her skin. He swallowed hard.

'Hard day?' she asked, slipping her hand inside his shirt. He shuddered as if marble were against his skin. Her lips came then, with the taste of exotic fruits, and again he knew he could never leave her.

For the first time he was beginning to understand his father. He loved his children. He loved and respected Imogen. Yet with Katya wrapped around him, her scent on him, her hair brushing his neck, his limbs aching for her and her body opening to receive him amid sighs and gasps of ecstasy, he could not give her up, and he realised why his father could not give up the other women in his life either.

He loathed his father for it still, and even more, he loathed himself for his own weakness. But a man consumed cannot fight. Before Katya, he had only paid lip service to love and passion, uttering words like a schoolboy from a textbook. Now that he understood the sacrifices which had to be made, he knew that love made a mockery of the rest of life, and that, whatever the obstacles before them, whatever the wreckage they leave behind, lovers will find a way.

He hardly moved at all now. They were so in tune he could sense she was there with him, and any moment now she would wash him with her tears.

He wondered if one day his children would understand and learn to forgive him. He prayed that they would, as his body and Katya's shuddered and melted into one.

He lay next to her on the rug before the fire, naked, clutching her still, his body trembling as she gently stroked his back. He nuzzled into her, filling his nostrils once again with her scent, trying desperately to delay the moment when his head would clear and he would be drawn back to reality.

As he surfaced, the image of his father and the other woman in that bedroom in Tunis returned.

'I only wish this could last forever.'

'It can,' she answered drowsily, 'when we're living together.'

He shook his head. 'I'm afraid not.'

'Why ever not?'

He moved away from her and started to get dressed. 'I'm going to have to stop seeing you.'

She stared at him, shocked, vulnerable, hurt. 'Am I hearing right?'

'I'm sorry. Really sorry.'

'I thought you loved me.'

'I do,' he answered. 'It's the children. You've seen the way they react to you. I can't sit there watching the anguish in their faces.'

'It's early days still,' she said. 'Of course they are going to be upset and do everything they can to resist change – it's only to be expected. But at heart, all children are very adaptable. Once they've accepted what has happened, they will come to terms with it in the same way that all children whose parents separate must. I promise you I'll do everything I possibly can to make them feel secure.'

'I know how my father's behaviour affected me. I can't do it to them.'

She moved further away from him and sat on the carpet very still, back rigid. 'I can't believe that I'm hearing this after all we've been through. They will still have two loving parents. Apart, admittedly, but I would have thought that was better than having two who are bickering all the time. That's more than I had.

'As for the effect your father had on you, that was

probably the making of you – the source of your determination and business drive. I don't see what the problem is.'

'But they won't have a mother and father who are together,' he argued.

'Neither do one in four children in this country. Why are you making such a big issue out of all this?'

'This has nothing to do with my love for you. If I were free, I would marry you tomorrow.'

'But of course, as we both know, you are not.' She looked across at him with sudden hatred. 'People told me that married men behave like this. I didn't think this could be true of you. What we've got is so special and powerful – something most people will never experience in their whole lives and would give anything to feel – and you are talking about throwing it away.'

She rose to her feet. 'Ask yourself whether Imogen will ever make you feel like I make you feel. Ask yourself whether you are ready to return to a life of mind-numbing domesticity. Once you have experienced what we have, you can't go back. You will feel like a dead man. You will crave me every minute of every day for the rest of your life.'

The deep fear that what she said was true made him shudder. He knew that if he did not leave now he might never leave. He tried to imprint on his memory the image of her as she stood there in a kimono, cheeks flushed with anger, eyes coldly penetrating.

'I'm sorry,' he said. 'If you want this house, it's yours. Goodbye.' He turned towards the door.

'I don't want your house,' she called after him. 'If you walk out on me now, you had better be absolutely sure that you are making the right decision. Don't ever expect to be welcomed back.'

He swallowed hard, pulled back the latch and walked out.

* * *

She stood there for a moment staring at the closed door, perplexed, trying to work out what had happened. Only minutes earlier they had been making love; she still felt the warmth of him inside her. Would he really have made love to her with such passion if he planned to leave her?

She did not believe that this was the end. She and Raymond had gone too far for that. This display had been the last kick of conscience, cries to the wind from a man who already knew the force he was trying to fight was greater than he. She guessed that he would ring her tomorrow with an apology.

Tightening the kimono around her, she walked through to the kitchen. She threw Myrtle a biscuit and made herself a mug of tea to steady her nerves.

Thirty-Eight

'Could I speak to Imogen, please?'

'Who's calling?'

'Raymond.'

'I thought I recognised the voice. Pamela here. I'm afraid I haven't got the faintest idea where she is. She went off on an expedition two days ago to see some *palazzo* or other and I haven't seen her since.'

'When do you expect her back?'

'She didn't say. She did leave a contact number in case there was a problem with the children. Hang on and I'll get it.'

Raymond copied down the number, thanked Pamela and, after a brief exchange about the weather, cleared the line and dialled the number she had given him.

A man answered. With the hubbub in the background, Raymond had to strain to hear.

'Could I speak to Signora Punchard, please?'

'Do you know her room number?'

'No.'

'*Un momento.*' There was a muted conversation, the click of a pen. 'I'm afraid that we don't have anyone of that name staying here.'

'Could you look under Farleigh, please?' he asked, just in case she had registered under her maiden name.

'No, I'm afraid that we haven't got anyone of that name

either. I'm sorry. Maybe it was another hotel?'

Raymond swallowed. 'Thanks. If she does register, could you ask her to call her husband, please?'

That afternoon, Pat, his senior PA, came into the boardroom and whispered in his ear that his wife was on the line. He left the meeting and went to his office to take the call.

Her voice was cold and impersonal. 'Raymond, you called?'

'Yes. Are you enjoying your holiday?' he asked, although it was the last thing on his mind.

'Very much.'

'Good weather?'

'Excellent. Are the children OK?'

'They're missing you, their school work is suffering, and they seem to be plagued by a mystery virus. Otherwise they're fine.'

'Don't worry. I'll sort it all out when I return.'

'When is that going to be?'

'I don't know yet.'

'Are we talking weeks or months?'

'Raymond, please don't hassle me. As I said, I don't know yet.'

He took a deep breath. 'I'm missing you, too. I want you to know that it's over between me and Katya. I'm not seeing her any more.'

There was silence at the other end of the line. 'Over, you say – completely over?'

'Yes.'

'Good. I think you've made exactly the right decision. She was much too young for you. You need someone more mature – someone who could run a household and help you with the children when they come to stay.'

'I'm sorry,' he said, startled. 'I don't follow.'

'Obviously the children will live with me, but they will come and stay with you from time to time. When that happens, I would like to be sure they were properly looked after.'

'But, darling—'

'Don't you dare "darling" me!'

'Imogen, I don't think you understand. Maybe the line is poor your end. I said that I'd given up Katya. I want you back.'

'The line is quite clear, Raymond, and I understand perfectly. That is just the kind of patronising remark that I came to Italy to get away from.

'I've been thinking about my life. The truth is, I'm sick to death of playing the tycoon's wife and entertaining all those dreary people. I had planned to devote my life to you and the family, but, as you've demonstrated so well, maybe one should broaden one's horizons and live for oneself for a change. I think I've already done my bit for the British export drive.

'I've made a few preliminary calculations. I reckon that with what I'll be getting out of you by way of a divorce settlement, I'll have the freedom to do whatever I like for the rest of my life.'

Raymond's jaw set. Pat was waving at him urgently from between the doors. He signalled to her to go away. 'But Imogen, we want you back. The children need you. I need you.'

'Back for what?' she asked rhetorically. 'One of those loveless marriages where two people stay together for the sake of the children – you occasionally wandering off with some floozy or other, me staying at home looking after the dogs. No thanks. I would find it too depressing.'

He swallowed. 'But the children?'

'They'll be fine. After all, they'll be with me most of the time. They will only be visiting you for the occasional weekend, so you needn't worry yourself about their welfare. With my love and your money, they will hardly be deprived.'

'But they need a mother and a father who are together!'

'That's a bit rich coming from you, Raymond. If you do have any serious problems with the children, ring and leave a message with Pamela. I think it would be a good idea for them to come out here if I'm not back by half-term. We are part of the European Community so it would be good for the children to broaden their horizons, too. I'm afraid I've got to go now.'

'Imogen, I haven't finished yet!'

'I'm sorry. Something requires my urgent attention.'

The line went dead.

Raymond put down the receiver, bemused. He thought the stress must be getting to her. She was a family person, a homemaker, a devoted mother.

He was on his way back to the meeting when the telephone on his desk rang again. He thought it must be Imogen calling back, so he hurried to answer it.

'Raymond?' It was Katya.

'Yes.'

'We can't just stop it like that. We can't just pretend that all that happened between us didn't happen. We should meet and talk things through. You were upset, that's all. We can sort this out just as we have sorted out every other little difficulty that we've had. Who else is going to love you like I love you?'

He swallowed hard. Why did her voice still affect him so? 'I'm in a meeting. I've got to go.'

'You're always in some meeting or other. It hasn't stopped you talking to me before.'

'I'll ring you later, OK?'

'Don't forget.'

Thirty-Nine

The last flight to Pisa that evening was the seven forty-five via Milan. He booked the ticket over the telephone, picked up his passport and arrived at Heathrow just before the gate closed. He did not have time to park his car; he left it outside the terminal with a note of apology to the police.

He landed at Milan at nine fifty local time, fifty-five minutes before the connecting flight. He was dressed in his City suit and had no luggage. He had hoped to pick up a few essentials at the airport, but all the shops in the concourse were closed, except for the bar and the cafeteria; he was not hungry and had already had more than enough to drink.

He ordered a coffee and used the change to ring the number of the hotel Pamela had given him. He booked a room and took a note of the name, address and directions. There was a girl answering calls at the reception desk now, rather than the man he had spoken to earlier. She could find neither a record of the message he had left, nor the name Imogen Punchard in the hotel register.

It suddenly struck him how foolhardy this enterprise was: maybe Imogen had then changed her plans and never stayed at the hotel; maybe she had already left; maybe she had rung back only because Pamela had passed on the message.

With his last coin he rang Pamela's villa in case Imogen had already returned. There was no reply.

On the internal flight to Pisa, Raymond read through the paperwork for the meeting he was meant to be attending tomorrow afternoon in London. He could not concentrate. He kept thinking about Imogen and what she had said in their telephone conversation.

He ordered whisky from the bar, but it did not help his concentration, ease his headache, help him sleep or stop him thinking of her. He drank it anyway and ordered another.

As he had no luggage, he was the first out of the airport. It was midnight now and the air was cold; he would have put on a coat if he had had one. He was about to rent a car when he remembered that, in the rush to leave, he had forgotten his driving licence. Anyway, he was too tired and drunk to drive.

Instead, he walked along to the taxi rank and showed the driver the slip of paper with the hotel's address. The man looked it up on the map, turning the pages with painstaking slowness and tracing the route with a stubby finger crowned with a black nail. He consulted with a fellow driver, then asked for as much as, Raymond reckoned, he normally earned in a week. Raymond offered him half that amount and climbed in.

He must have slept for much of the journey because the last thing he remembered was driving through the suburbs of Pisa; when he woke, it was two in the morning, his clothes were damp from the airlessness in the car, he had a crick in his neck, a foul taste in his mouth and a dull ache in his head.

He wiped the mist of stale breath off the window and squinted out. He could just make out the line where the deep purple of the sky met the dark grey of the land and the occasional lone tree. He wound down the window and breathed in the cold, fresh air. It carried the aroma of fir

and scrub and smelt and tasted so good after London air.
He guessed that already they must be in the Tuscan hills,
and soon afterwards the road started undulating and
twisting back on itself as it made its way deeper into the
countryside.

About twenty minutes later, the sign for San Vito
showed up in the headlights; the driver signalled left and
drove up the narrow, winding road. After a few miles,
they stopped climbing. Raymond could not see much in
the darkness but he could make out the rough stone walls
of the houses beside the road, the silhouette of a church
against the night sky at the far end of a cobbled square
and the figure of a lone dog suddenly running away from
the car.

Then the driver turned left through a pair of gates.
Security lights came on automatically. The road surface
changed to closely packed gravel. They passed a row of
stone buildings lining a courtyard, with numbered doors
and window boxes full of brightly coloured bedding plants.
Then they reached the inn itself, a sixteenth-century
building of weathered yellow stone. Despite the lateness
of the hour, lights still blazed.

The driver drew the taxi to a halt in front of the main
door. Raymond paid him with English money and climbed
out. He shuddered at the sudden change in temperature
as he stood for a moment in the forecourt high in the
hills. He glanced up wistfully at the stars, then pushed
through the swing doors into the warmth of the hotel.

Laughter echoed down the passageway before him: a
woman's, followed by a man's. It set his pulse racing. He
was sure he recognised Imogen's tones.

He sped past the reception desk and along the passage,
past the line of tin sconces on the roughly plastered walls.
Ahead of him, through the archway, was the room from
where the sound was coming. It had green walls and soft,
seductive lighting. As he approached, the smell of cigars

and wood smoke grew stronger, the sound of laughter louder.

He passed through the doorway and there on the sofa were the laughing couple. The man had black greased hair and liver spots on his hands. The woman was auburn, elegant and young. Now he heard the woman's laugh again, he was amazed that he had thought it could be Imogen's. As he entered, the couple stopped laughing and looked up at him questioningly.

Even his own senses were playing tricks on him now. Feeling foolish, he retreated towards the door and back along the passageway to the reception desk. No one was there. He rang the bell on the desk and waited.

Eventually a woman arrived. He told her his name and she handed him a registration card to complete. She did not smile. The name Punchard might set heels clicking in New York, London and Tokyo; evidently not in San Vito.

'I'm meant to be meeting my wife, Imogen Punchard, here,' he said. 'Which room is she in?'

Sighing, the woman opened the register. Her finger ran down a pencilled column. 'There is no one of that name staying here.'

'Have I just missed her – how about last night?'

Turning back a page, the woman scanned another two columns. 'No. Nor the day before that.'

'What if she booked through a travel agent?' he queried.

The woman glanced up at Raymond with tired, bored eyes. 'It makes no difference. We list all the guests here. It is the regulations. I'm sorry. There is no Imogen Punchard staying in this hotel.'

He took the photograph of Imogen and the two girls out from where he always kept it in his wallet and showed it to the woman. He had taken the picture himself soon after Willa had been born.

She shook her head. 'I'm sorry. I can't help.' She

summoned the night porter, a twenty-year-old with a bull neck, and wished Raymond a pleasant stay.

Raymond showed the photograph to the porter, too. He glanced at it, said, 'Very nice,' and handed it back.

'Yes, but have you seen her?'

'Not tonight.' He picked Raymond's briefcase off the floor and began walking down the passage.

'But she has been here?'

'Yes. Last night. At least I think it's her. That is an old photograph, right?'

'Correct.'

The boy smiled. 'I thought so. She is here with her husband. They never eat in the restaurant. Always room service. Friends of yours?'

Raymond clenched his fist so tightly it hurt. He tried not to let his anger show. 'Yes,' he said. 'Great friends. They told me to let them know the moment I arrived. Which room are they in?'

'The honeymoon suite. Room Fourteen. In the courtyard.'

'Thank you. I wouldn't want to disappoint them.'

Raymond only stayed in his room long enough to tip the boy and slip a miniature of whisky from the mini-bar into his pocket, then he headed back down the corridor, through the swing doors and into the night air.

His eyes took a moment to become accustomed to the light from the carriage lamps which punctuated the darkness. He could make out the gravel path leading from the main entrance of the hotel, the strip of worn grass on dry, cracked soil, and the green-painted doors of the rooms facing on to the courtyard.

Raymond stalked along the path without looking where he was going, his eyes staring only at the numbers on the doors. When he reached Number 14, he stopped. He peered underneath the shutters and at the gap beneath the door. The room was in darkness.

His heart was beating a tattoo; he needed to calm it. He reached in his pocket, unscrewed the top of the miniature bottle and tipped the whisky down his throat.

He looked around to check that no one was watching, then put his ear to the window and listened. Beneath the chirping of the cicadas and the bark of a dog, he was sure he heard rhythmic breathing. The bark came again, then he heard, or at least he thought he heard, the rustling of the bedclothes and a slow, sleepy sigh.

A sharp pain stabbed at his heart.

He walked over to the door and rapped on it twice. When no reply came, he knocked again.

'Hello?' he called.

A rustling inside. 'It can't be breakfast already,' he heard. Then, 'Who is it?' called a voice. Imogen.

'Raymond.'

He heard whispering, more rustling of the bedclothes. The light went on, spilling out under the bottom of the door. 'What on earth are you doing here?'

'I've come to see you. Open the door!'

'No, Raymond. It's late and I'm tired.'

'Is there someone in there with you?'

'That's none of your business.'

'I'm your husband. I have a right to know.'

'Any rights you might have had you forfeited long ago. Now don't be a bore. Go away and let me get some sleep.'

'Let me in or I'll break the door down!'

'Raymond, did I go around and make a spectacle of myself when you spent evening after evening with your little picture restorer? Please go away!'

'I won't.'

'If you don't, I'll call the management and have you removed.'

'But I've given up Katya. I want us to make a fresh start.'

'Raymond, please!' she called, her voice cold and crisp.

'If you respect me even a little, please go away. If we absolutely must, I'll talk to you in the morning. Good night.'

Raymond shuddered. The thought of some man in there sleeping with his wife made his gut tighten. He paced to the end of the courtyard and back, trying to work out what to do.

Just then he heard rapid, purposeful footsteps. He turned. A maid in a pink and white uniform was striding down the gravel path towards the main building with a tray in her hands.

He intercepted her. 'Could you help me, please?' he pleaded, beaming his best smile at her. 'I've locked myself out of my room.'

She was a dark-haired girl with a leathery skin. She looked at him, bemused, and pointed to the reception.

'No, I left my key in my room. I need you to let me in.' He pointed to her, then twisted his wrist, acting out the movement of a key being turned in a lock.

A flash of comprehension suddenly crossed her face. Putting down the tray, she rattled the keys on her belt. *'La chiave?'*

'Yes!'

. He pointed further along the courtyard, then put his finger to his mouth. 'Room Fourteen. But we must be quiet. My wife is asleep.'

'Sua moglie dorme?'

'Si, si!' he answered enthusiastically.

He retraced his steps to the door of Room 14. The maid fumbled with her keys, searching for the right one. He felt a quickening of his pulse as she inserted it in the lock. As she turned the key, he twisted the handle and pushed on the door. It opened a few inches then suddenly stopped as the security chain inside became taut.

A scream came from the bed. The maid looked across at Raymond, shocked and wide-eyed. He smiled at her reassuringly as he tried to dislodge the chain with his left hand. When he realised he could not unfasten it, he stepped back a few paces, ran forward and threw his full weight against the door.

The second time he tried, there was a splintering sound, the chain gave way and Raymond found himself propelled into the room.

Only a dim light followed him through the doorway. Raymond squinted, struggling to discern what was before him. He could make out the white sheet of the bed, the white of the pillows, the splash of Imogen's fair skin and blonde hair, then, on the other pillow, a man's head and, beneath it, his bare chest. He could smell the man's aftershave, Imogen's scent and the odour of the bed. He felt a deep and sudden revulsion at all he saw.

'Get out!' he yelled.

'Steady on, old chap,' answered a male voice.

'Can't you hear me? Get out!'

'I want him to stay,' put in Imogen calmly, defiantly.

Raymond was not sure what happened then. He felt the bile rising in his mouth, the muscles tightening around his neck. He lunged forward and jumped, propelling himself on to the bed. He reached out, flailing, trying to grab hold of the man by the shoulders.

A white fist came towards him out of the darkness. He tried to duck, but too late. The blow landed on his jaw, sending a dull pain reverberating through his skull.

For a second, the man's frightened eyes caught the light from the doorway. Raymond tightened his fist, flexed his arm and returned the blow. He heard his jacket rip as his fist landed on the man's jaw. He knew it must have hurt because his hand was vibrating with pain, too.

Meanwhile the man in the bed had managed to grab Raymond around the middle in some kind of bear hug. He was crushing his rib cage and squeezing the air out of him. Raymond suddenly felt his whole body spinning around, rolling, his head buzzing. One moment he was above the man, the next hard against the bed.

Then the bed was to his side and they were both falling through the air. He landed, crashing his hip bone on the hard floor. The man was on top of him, naked, sweating, gasping.

'For God's sake, stop it!' Imogen called.

The bedside lamp suddenly went on, shining straight into Raymond's eyes. He could see the creased face, pale grey eyes and black hair of the man above him now. Tightening his fist, he directed it once more at the man's moving jaw. He missed. Then Imogen, breasts flapping out of the sheet she had wrapped around her, was pulling them apart.

'Raymond, stop it!' she called. 'Benjy, go and take a walk while I talk to Raymond.'

'OK,' said Benjy, 'if you feel safe with him and that's what you want.' Watching Raymond carefully, he climbed to his feet.

Raymond got up too. 'How dare you touch my wife!' he yelled.

'You weren't much of a husband to her,' Benjy shouted back.

At that, Raymond went for him again. Before, in an argument words had always been enough: now, only the infliction of physical pain was a sufficient palliative.

Benjy saw the punch coming. He moved quickly, raising his arms to protect his face, so Raymond changed direction in mid-flight and dug his fist into the soft muscle tissue of the solar plexus. Benjy grunted as the air went out of him; his body jackknifed. Grinning, Raymond jabbed his fist upwards as the head descended and caught Benjy again on the jaw.

Then a blow hard on the cheek curled from nowhere, sending Raymond reeling backwards and propelling him back on to the bed.

'Pax!' Benjy called, grabbing his underpants from the floor beside the bed and slipping them up over his thin legs. 'I'm getting dressed now so that you and Imogen can have a talk – OK?'

Raymond nodded, pulling himself up until he was sitting on the bed. His lip was hurting, and when he dabbed it, he found his handkerchief smeared with blood. 'OK.' The sight of the naked man turned his stomach. 'Just get out of here.'

The manager of the hotel came in then, a man of thick build with sealskin hair, followed by the maid who had let Raymond in, now in tears. He glanced at the damage to the fittings on the door. 'Is this how you behave at home?' he asked angrily. 'You must leave. Now.'

'I'm sorry. There has been a misunderstanding,' Raymond soothed, pushing them out and closing the door. 'I'll pay for any damage. Please give me and my wife a few minutes to get ready.'

'You shouldn't have come,' said Imogen as soon as the others had left.

'Get dressed,' he ordered. 'I'll help you with your packing.'

She was sitting on the edge of the bed in her nightdress and dressing gown. The side of her face closest to him was in shadow. 'No, Raymond.'

'What do you mean, no?'

'What do you think I mean, for heaven's sake? I'm not budging.'

'I've come to take you back to London, back home, where you belong.'

She stared for a moment at the shuttered window. 'I'm not sure where I belong now. I'm not certain it's Phillimore Gardens any longer.'

'But it's not here, with that clown, surely?' he answered angrily.

'Don't be rude about Benjy. If you are, I won't continue

this conversation. I happen to be extremely fond of him.'

Raymond turned away. He could not bear to look at her any longer. The tenderness with which she spoke of this outsider pained him more than physical injury ever could.

'It might or might not be with Benjy,' she continued. 'After all, it's still early days in our relationship – although already I feel I've learnt more in a couple of weeks than I did in years in Phillimore Gardens.

'There are other Imogen Farleighs, you know – ones you don't know about. Some, I confess, I was barely aware of myself until now. Others, I feel sure are there, but even I haven't met them yet. These last few weeks have set me thinking – the role of Imogen Punchard, the tycoon's wife, the socialite with a polished line in small talk, has had a very good run, but like an actor after years in the same play, I wouldn't mind playing someone different now. Preferably someone a bit more like me.'

He spun around and stared at her, astounded. 'What do you mean, "someone a bit more like me"? That's crazy talk.'

'Maybe to you it is, but to me it makes perfect sense. The truth is, you went off with your little bit of fluff because our marriage was getting stale. I understand that better now. I've come to terms with it and am almost ready to forgive you. I was not prepared to face it at first, partly, I imagine, because as a woman I have inbuilt a much stronger nesting instinct and desire to keep the family together, especially while Archie is so young. I got there in the end.

'Marriage is a very restrictive institution and the business of childcare, even with the help I have, is so time-consuming that parts of me were never allowed to develop. I don't say I resent this, because nothing means more to me than my children, and you and I have had some wonderful times together, but I think the moment has come to give these other parts the time and space they need.'

'What other parts?' Raymond asked. 'Explain what you mean.'

Imogen adjusted her position on the edge of the bed. 'My creative side for one, my caring side for another. Somewhere along the line I lost touch with the real me. I drifted along, spending too much time on what I now see as the silly, unimportant things of life – the surface things. I feel there is so much I can do for other people that I'm not doing. Being here with Benjy has made me see that.

'This is a crazy world. Every time we walk down the street we are stepping over casualties. Before, I just looked away. I don't think I can do that any longer. I don't just want to raise money for charities as I have been doing in the past. I want to actually be there, working on the ground with the homeless, the drug abusers and the mentally disturbed so that I can better understand their problems and what can be done to help.'

'A sort of Mother Teresa in Chanel?'

'Mock if you like, but it's exactly those kind of remarks which made me realise we have drifted apart.'

Raymond took two paces across the room towards her. 'I'm sorry. Look, I understand. If you want to spend more time on charity work, on art – whatever – it's fine by me.'

'But it's more,' she replied. 'I refuse to exist in an emotional vacuum. I can't live as I have done over the last eighteen months, watching the slow death of a marriage beneath a façade of politeness and civilised behaviour. You have no idea how wonderful it feels now to have stepped out of that stifling atmosphere.

'Go home, Raymond. Send my love to the children.'

'I want you to come back with me.'

'And I don't want to go. This is the first time in years I've felt that I'm living. Please close what you've left of the door on the way out.'

'But I've completely finished with Katya,' he pleaded. 'I love you and I want you back.'

She sighed slowly. 'I just wish I could believe you, Raymond. Why is it that I just don't any more?'

Forty

No sooner had Raymond cleared customs at Heathrow than he saw her standing on the other side of the barrier. A bored and anxious crowd jostled around her, but the area immediately surrounding her remained somehow inviolate, serene. Her smile seemed to radiate out, filling the space between them, the sensuality so raw he could barely keep on looking at her.

'I didn't expect you to be here.'

'It was meant to be a surprise.'

'How did you know which flight I was on?'

She leant forward, nearly on tiptoe, and kissed him. 'From Pat at the office. She has also rescheduled all your appointments for the afternoon as she understood the plane has been delayed for three hours due to a mechanical failure. We're free to do what we like.'

'Where did she get that idea from?'

She grinned. 'Where do you think? Have you any luggage apart from your briefcase?'

'No.'

'OK, my car's in the short-stay car park.'

She threaded her arm through his. As they moved off together, he felt the wool of her skirt against his leg, touching, caressing him all the way to the car park. Her hand was in his, her fingers squeezing gently and her small palm pressing against his. In the darkness of the

271

car park, between a concrete support and a row of trolleys, she wrapped her body around him and kissed him. When she sat down in the driver's seat of the car, the already short skirt rode up, revealing a large expanse of fit and shapely white thigh. She made no attempt to hide it. With the skirt so skimpy, it wouldn't have made much difference anyway.

She leaned over to kiss him again, lips waxed, shining and inviting, the fragrance of sex all about her, then ran her hand lightly over his crotch. 'Let's go home.' She put the car into gear and reversed out of the parking space.

'I told you it was over,' Raymond said.

'We all say silly things once in a while.'

'I meant it.'

'You've just been out to Italy to see Imogen and bring her back, haven't you? She didn't come, did she?'

'No.'

'So it was her choice. No one can say that you didn't try. Conscience is satisfied. We are now free to do exactly what we want.'

'I'm sorry. I can't give up that easily.'

'But it's mutual now. She must feel there's no future for the marriage, otherwise she would have been on that plane.

'I might remind you that when I first came on the scene, your marriage had about as much life in it as a pair of kippers on a marble slab, which is the only reason we got started. It would be somewhat ironic if I were now to get the credit for giving it the kiss of life.

'What about me, Raymond? What about my love for you?'

'It's for the children mainly, Katya.'

She sighed. 'What would we do without the little darlings, when they are such a mine of plausible excuses?'

'I can't do what my father did to me. You must

272

understand that. If I did, I would end up hating myself and probably hating you as well.'

'You can't mollycoddle them all their lives. They are going to learn sooner or later that the world out there is a far from reliable place.'

'I know. But they need their dreams for a while longer.' Raymond was silent for a time as they drove towards the motorway.

'I wouldn't want what we've had to die,' he said finally, 'and inevitably in marriage things would change. Neither of us is good at compromise, and you would be desperately bored doing the things you would have to do as a businessman's wife. I'm going to miss you, though, every day of my life.'

After crawling down the Cromwell Road, she turned into Craythorne Mews.

'Do you want to come in?' she asked as she drew the car to a halt in front of number nine.

He shook his head. 'Will you be all right?'

She nodded, staring ahead of her. 'Don't worry about me. I'm a survivor. I'll get over it. Next time you see me, I'll probably have someone else on my arm. I don't know who or what he'll look like, but I do know one thing – he won't be married. I don't need this kind of relationship any more.'

'Take care,' he said. He climbed out of the car and began walking down the street towards the stone archway at the end. He looked neither to the left nor to the right. He did not trust himself to turn around. There were too many memories, too much happiness, too much pain. When finally he reached the arch, it felt like one of the longest walks of his life.

He did not want to go to the office or back to an empty house. He just kept walking along the crowded streets of South Kensington. He needed time to think. Somehow he had to find a way of persuading Imogen to come back to him.

As he passed a confectioner's, he remembered that she liked the violet creams made by a particular shop in the King's Road. He stopped at the next telephone kiosk, rang the shop, ordered the biggest box they had and told them to expect a courier who would be taking the box to Italy.

Ten paces on, he remembered that when they had last been in the South of France, she had been amused by the small aircraft which flew along the beach trailing banners with advertisements. Walking back to the telephone kiosk, he rang an advertising company and asked them to arrange for an aircraft to circle the hotel in San Vito and the Ravenscroft villa with a banner proclaiming, 'IMOGEN FORGIVE ME I LOVE YOU RAYMOND'.

Then he stopped at the florist's and, once they had confirmed they could deliver to Italy, ordered a huge arrangement. He looked in the window of every shop he passed to see if there was anything he could buy which might make her nostalgic for the good times they had shared.

He walked on until he reached Hyde Park. There, he sat down on a bench and stared out blindly at the stagnant green sludge of the Serpentine. He watched the ducks as they waddled up the bank after the stale bread an old woman threw to them.

In the early days of their marriage, he and Imogen had enjoyed such simple pleasures, but since the huge success of the Group, he had never had time.

A tramp crouched down on the grass before him. He had huge staring eyes and purple patches on his weathered skin. 'Got a problem?' he asked.

Before, Raymond would have sent the man away, but he suddenly felt the need for companionship. He nodded back.

'That's something we've got in common, mate, 'cause

I've got a problem, too. Mine is an acute deficiency of alcoholic beverage. What's yours?'

'My wife's left me.'

The man sucked in air through the side of his mouth. 'Some, so I'm told, would see that as their lucky day. Can't help you there, I'm afraid, seeing that so far I have escaped the marital state.

'My problem, though, is easily solved. Wave upon it one crisp five-pound note and it will disappear.' He took the battered trilby off his head and bared a set of rotting teeth.

Raymond reached for his wallet and held out a note.

'Much obliged,' said the man, 'my blessings to you,' and went on his way.

It was nearly seven when Raymond reached home. He had not told anybody he would be coming back today. All the lights were out in the main body of the house, although they blazed upstairs.

As he went into the hall, he could hear the children's voices coming down the stairwell. They sounded so immature, so defenceless, so trusting of adults.

They would have learnt last night that he had gone to Italy and would assume that he would be returning with Imogen. As he climbed the first stairs, he dreaded seeing the excitement in their faces turn to disappointment when they realised he was alone. He knew how desperately important children's fantasies were, and of those none was more important than the permanence and immutability of love, which children assumed but adults found so hard to achieve.

Suddenly Archie's head appeared through the banisters. He called out, 'Daddy's back!' and he and the two girls started racing down the stairs towards their father.

Raymond noticed the way the girls looked beyond him,

searching the space with wide, eager eyes. Then the sparkle went out of them, and the eyes they turned on him were cold and hurt and full of disappointment. 'Where's Mummy?' asked Samantha. 'I thought you went to get her?'

'I did. She didn't want to come.'

'What do you mean, "didn't want to come"?'

'Parents have their own lives to lead, too. At the moment Mummy is going through a very busy phase.'

Archie hung on to Raymond's trouser leg and looked up at him with wide, pleading eyes. 'What about us?'

'Although she is not here at the moment, she still loves you all very much.'

'We need her, Daddy!' Archie exclaimed.

Raymond nodded. 'I know. We all do.'

He led the children back upstairs and read them a story to keep their minds occupied. No one was concentrating. The small sound of the lock turning downstairs was enough to send Archie scurrying back on to the landing, and when he called out, they all followed.

Imogen stood in the hallway, tanned and fit, gazing up at them, a large carrier bag in her hand. 'Hello, everyone,' she called. 'I've brought you some presents from Italy.'

The children hurried down the stairs and crowded around her eagerly. She looked up at Raymond. 'Could you help with the luggage, please?' Her tone was brisk and businesslike.

'Yes, of course.' He went to collect her suitcases while Imogen reached deep into her carrier bag and pulled out a cylindrical parcel wrapped in hand-printed paper.

'Now, let me get this right. This is for you, Willa.'

Willa tore off the paper to reveal a doll in a pageboy outfit, and a box of chocolates.

'It's from Siena,' Imogen explained as she delved in the bag for Archie's present. 'They stage a horse race there where everyone dresses up in medieval costumes.'

'Mummy, did you enjoy your holiday?' Samantha asked while she opened her present.

'Yes, darling. I had a wonderful time. Very relaxing. Very rejuvenating.'

'Mummy?' Willa looked up with a mixture of affection and nervousness.

'Yes, darling.'

'You're not going away again, are you?'

Imogen's eyes caught Raymond's. 'That rather depends.'

All three children stayed up for supper that evening. As neither Raymond nor Imogen had been expected back, there was virtually no food in the house; they dined off baked beans and scrambled eggs, washed down with the very best champagne. Raymond could not help noticing that the children were laughing and giggling and grinning in a way that they had not for months.

The pleasure he derived from watching the happiness and relief in their faces was so different from that which he had found in Katya's arms, but just then, he would have sacrificed anything for it.

Archie was the first to fall asleep. He was already in his dressing gown when he came down to dinner, and soon after the ice cream and Italian chocolates, his head lolled on to his shoulder and his eyes closed.

Raymond carried him upstairs, made him brush his teeth, then tucked him up in bed. When he kissed him good night, for the first time for weeks there was not the slightest sign of anxiety in his face or tension in his small body. Archie whispered, 'Please ask Mummy to come and kiss me good night too,' but before she had come he was already sound asleep.

Imogen and the girls went to bed at about midnight. Raymond blew out the candles, put the security chain on the front door, turned out the lights and followed.

When he reached the landing, the door of the master bedroom was closed and bathwater was running.

He was just about to go into the dressing room when Imogen stepped out into the passage in her dressing gown. 'The cupboards are full of your clothes and your wash things are all over the bathroom.'

'I'm sorry,' he answered. 'I'll move them.'

He walked into the bathroom and started collecting his things. Steam was rising from the bath, and with it, the scent of the bath oils Imogen always used. Smelling them again now was like stepping back in time; he inhaled slowly and deeply.

When he returned to the bedroom, Imogen was lying on the bed flicking through a magazine. On the floor in front of her were her two suitcases, half unpacked.

'Your bath's ready,' he said.

'Thanks. I'll go through in a moment.'

'I want to thank you for coming back.'

She looked at him and sighed. 'If you want to know, the thought of that woman acting as mother to my children during their visits to you sent a chill down my spine. It's the main reason I'm here. I've spent so much time trying to make sure the children had the kind of emotional security I never knew as a girl, I didn't want to give that up while there was still a chance that we could make a go of it. It is difficult to find happiness when you see pain in your children's eyes.

'It's up to you now, Raymond. What has happened has happened. But, regardless of the children, I won't hang around a second time.'

He opened the cupboard and removed the suit he would wear tomorrow. 'I'm sorry if it's only a sense of duty which brings you back. Was Benjy Mulford so exceptional a lover?'

She flicked over a page. 'If you are talking about lovemaking as a branch of gymnastics, probably not. But he did know how to make a woman feel wanted, loved. For me, that's the most powerful aphrodisiac of all.

'If you really want to know, it reminded me of what we were like in the early days. Made me nostalgic for them. Made me realise how much we once had and how far we have let it slip.'

'I suppose Katya, too, reminded me of the excitement of those early days,' he answered. 'Anyway, it's good to have you back.'

He kissed her good night, then piling up the suits in his arms, he shuffled back to the dressing room.

Katya kept her mobile telephone by her side wherever she was, waiting for his call. She reckoned it would only be a week before he came back to her, a month at the outside.

During that first week, every day she woke up in her lone bed, she woke up happy, sure that this was the day. She felt the break from him so fiercely that she was convinced he must feel the same way, too.

After a month of waiting, however, that optimism turned to despair.

Even then, she did not regret making Raymond choose between her and Imogen. Her love for Raymond was becoming a destructive force. She was losing control of her emotions and her self-respect, and was destined to the lonely life of the long-term mistress.

She had to pluck up courage, take control, accept his answer whatever it might be. Love, to her, had always been about giving and sharing, and it needed light and openness in which to grow. If this was not to be, it was better for her to know.

After six weeks a letter arrived from Raymond. She did not realise it was from him at first for it came in a large typed manila envelope.

The letter said simply, 'I know you are fond of the mews

279

house, so I enclose a little present. Miss you always, Raymond.' Inside the envelope was a letter from his solicitors and copies of the draft documents to transfer the freehold of the mews house into her name.

This was Raymond's way of saying how much she meant to him, and she had to admit the generosity of the gift had a certain eloquence. She knew, though, that it was the act of a man tying up loose ends, and that thought made her break down in tears.

Even in her sadness, she tried to look to the future rather than the past. At least now that she knew for certain that it was over, she argued, she could begin to rebuild her life.

Extraordinary though her time with Raymond had been, and on occasions the intensity of the emotion they had both shared had shocked her, she would never seek to repeat the experience. Over the last two years, she had discovered much about herself and of what she was capable. She had changed, too. In future she would avoid men who had to compromise between love and duty, or had to hide their love in shadows. She had too much love to give for compromise.

Next time she became involved with a man, he would not be frightened of being seen with her in public, she knew that for sure.

It was at about the same time that Imogen allowed Raymond back into the marital bed.

Their lovemaking that first evening was not like it had been in the early days. It was better. Then, the intensity had come from the blind imaginings of youth. Now, it came from bitterly won self-knowledge. They were still raw and hurting from the pain each had caused the other and the realisation that they could so easily have drifted apart. This gave a tenderness and sensitivity to each movement and made them so attuned to one another that the actions of their bodies were one as never before.

When it was over, all they could do was hug one another and cry for joy. This was the first time Imogen had ever seen Raymond cry. As they kissed again, their tears intermingled so that it was impossible to tell from whose eyes they came, and the falling tears ran down their faces and hair to their already glistening bodies.

They both knew that the wounds of the last two years would take a long time to heal, but they were both confident now that the process had begun.

A selection of bestsellers from Headline